SWING WITH THE WING

A lighthearted look at Aviation Marines during the Vietnam War

by James E. Bulman

Master Sergeant
United States Marine Corps (Retired)

Copyright © James E. Bulman 2018

They say there is only one thing tougher than a Marine. That's a Marine wife. This novel is dedicated to my wife, Linda Maxine Dilger Bulman, for being the perfect Marine wife and for believing in me for the past 47 years.

A special thank you to my niece, Gayle King Warhola, for reviewing the manuscript and providing much needed guidance and encouragement.

PREFACE

Not all Marines fit the stereotype. We are not all six-foot-four, lean, mean, fighting machines as the recruiting posters would want potential enlistees to believe. Many of us (and I might be so bold as to say, most of us) are of average height and build with no burning desire to start a brawl in the local honky-tonk every payday night.

In addition, regardless of what our sister services may believe, we are not all dumb as dirt.

Yes, during the Vietnam Era, we had our fair share of high school dropouts and court-recommended "volunteers," but with the inception of the lottery draft, we had more recruits with some college behind them than our Air Force, Army, and Navy brethren might be willing to admit.

So, we were not all ground-pounding, knuckle-dragging, mouth-breathing grunts whose most earnest desire was to disconnect the ears from recently terminated enemy soldiers and display the rather grotesque souvenir like a string of fish.

Undeniably, on payday nights, we enjoy a beer or two (okay, maybe three or four). Yes, I'll grant you that we tend to frequent establishments of less-than-admirable repute, and we may on occasion (How shall I put this?) "date" women of low character.

Yet, for the most part, when our enlistments are up, we return to our hometowns. We are no longer unfocused teenagers. We are now more disciplined, mature individuals ready to straighten out the civilian world.

We may even marry our high school sweethearts, get jobs at the local factory, father two-and-a-half children, join the American Legion or the Veterans of Foreign Wars, and retire at age 65, having lead a life worth living.

But, even on our deathbed, we will still lie about our exploits during the Vietnam War.

With that said, I must concede when asked, "What did you do in the war?" we rarely tell the truth. We might avoid the question with a cryptic reply like, "I'd rather not talk about the war." or "You're too young to understand."

Yes, some Marines will slightly exaggerate their role in history. Few of us will fess up to the real reason we don't talk about the war.... we were in the rear with the gear.

Our war was spent in supporting roles picking combat equipment from warehouse shelves, repairing jeeps in the motor pool, calculating the pay for a company of "real" combat Marines, or cooking "mid-rats" (midnight rations to you civilians out there) for the night maintenance crew of an F-4 Phantom jet squadron.

I recently learned that the "tooth-to-tail" ratio for the III Marine Amphibious Force (MAF) operating in the northern most area of the Republic of Vietnam (I Corps) in 1967 was 6.5 support personnel for every one combat Marine.

A large portion of that support provided to the Marine infantryman (then and now) is supplied by the Marine Corps' aviation element. The Air Wing or simply "the Wing", as it is affectionately called, provides assault support, anti-aircraft fire, offensive air support, electronic countermeasures, control of aircraft and missiles, and aerial reconnaissance.

While there is camaraderie between all Marines, there is an inherently friendly (okay, maybe not so friendly) internal rivalry between infantry Marines (grunts) and aviation Marines (air wingers).

But for all the whining, crying, pissing and moaning, when it comes time to re-enlist, air-wing-hating grunts usually opt for an aviation billet. They want to *"Swing with the Wing!"*

During the universally unpopular war in Vietnam most air wingers were quite happy plying their trade in a support role. We knew a good thing when we saw it. We figured the grunts were just upset that they weren't quite bright enough to qualify for aviation in the first place.

When it came to combat action during the Vietnam War, the Marine Corps was responsible for coordinating all military activities in the five northernmost provinces of the country, referred to as I Corps Tactical Zone or simply "I Corps" (pronounced "eye core.") Nearly all of the Marine Corps' fixed-wing aircraft were flown out of the Da Nang Air Base, while most of the Corps' helicopters (also referred to as rotary-wing aircraft) were positioned just south of Da Nang at the relatively secure Marble Mountain Air Facility. That's where I was assigned.

Keeping hundreds of helicopters of every type and model operational in a war zone takes a lot of spare parts, long hours of hard work, and brains.

Yes, brains.

I know that doesn't fit the stereotype of the Vietnam Era Marines I mentioned earlier, but Marine aviation personnel or "wingers" are smart, innovative and dedicated to keeping their helicopters flying safely.

Engine mechanics, metalsmiths, hydraulic specialists, ordnance men, and electricians work together to return malfunctioning or combat-damaged helicopters back to "full-mission-capable" status.

That's what I did.

You see, although all Marines are trained as basic riflemen, the grunts do the dirty work. They slog through ankle-deep mud. They are fed decades-old C-rations whose mysterious contents are revealed only by using a tiny, inch-long can opener, nicknamed a "John Wayne." Those hapless ground-pounders are, to quote one battle-seasoned Marine, "Shot at and missed. Shit on and hit."

It's no wonder they are jealous of us. You see, our infantry brothers believe all air wingers work in climate-controlled buildings, sleep on Sealy Posturepedic mattresses in air-conditioned barracks, eat three hot meals a day and party at the Enlisted Club every night.

I would love to dispel those rumors right here and now.

I would love to... but I can't.

While we did not sleep on foot-thick mattresses in air-conditioned barracks, some of us were "forced" to work in climate-controlled buildings necessary to maintain the optimal operating temperatures and humidity required for the sensitive electronic equipment.

The rest of the rumors, I must confess, are true. It was three squares (sometimes four) and the E-club nearly every night.

Sure, there are plenty of air wingers who would like to take the reverse route and get into the mix of things with their gung-ho brothers.

Although we may not have been trudging through rice paddies daily, in our defense, to quote four-star General Leonard F. Chapman, Commandant of the Marine Corps (1968-1972), "When a Marine in Vietnam is wounded, surrounded, hungry, low on ammunition or water, he looks to the sky. He knows the choppers are coming."

This is the story of a small group of the mechanics and technicians who kept the choppers flying to support their sometimes less-than-grateful Marine Corps brothers on the ground.

But the stories are true...well, mostly true...okay, they are based on truth.

Oh, Hell! Everyone knows that all war stories told by Marines are a pack of lies. That is, unless the story begins with the phrase, "This is no shit!"

CHAPTER ONE

Assault on Marble Mountain Air Facility - July 1970

This is no shit, he decided.

The explosion from the satchel charge threw him backwards into the opening of one of the corrugated steel revetments that arched over each parked helicopter.

On his back, staring at the underside of the Quonset hut-like structure, Lance Corporal Daniel J. Keegan was dazed and confused. The young Marine had always thought he would have time to duck or to shout a warning.

Not even close.

Hell, he thought, *I don't even know which squadron's choppers are being targeted.*

His ears were ringing. His head was pounding. His heart was racing. He was sure he had been unconscious. He could swear he heard Eric Burden singing, "We gotta get out of the place" but he knew that was impossible.

He slowly rolled onto his stomach and raised himself on his elbows to figure out what, the Hell, was going on.

Like watching a slow-motion silent movie, he could see Marines running every which way for cover. There was confusion everywhere. That was understandable since they were supposed to be behind the lines.

Was there such a place in this God forsaken country?

He could see senior Non-Commissioned Officers (NCOs) were rapidly gaining control of the situation. Orders were being shouted; arms were pointing towards the direction of the runway.

by James E. Bulman

Dan quickly zeroed in on one tee-shirted Marine who calmly bent down onto one knee, raised his M-16A1 rifle to his shoulder and fired a handful of rounds in the direction of the squadrons south of their position.

Dan was aghast.

Is he nuts? Does he think he's at marksmanship training on the rifle range at Camp Lejeune?

"Get your ass down!" he imagined himself screaming but no words emerged.

A second explosion gave the tee-shirted Marine pause. Deciding he agreed with Shakespeare that "discretion is the better part of valor," he looked left, then right, and ran with alacrity for cover behind some metal Conex shipping containers used to transport aircraft engines and transmissions.

Although Dan couldn't figure out exactly what was happening, he knew he was going to die. There was no doubt in his New England mind.

No heroics. No Medal of Honor. No Navy Cross. He hadn't even been in the Marine Corps long enough to earn his Good Conduct Medal. Just KIA... Killed in Action.

The line from the song by Country Joe and the Fish, "*Be the first one on your block to have your son sent home in a box,*" was a fleeting thought but Dan pushed it out of his mind as fast as he had thought of it.

Slowly the "Fog of War" began to lift. Dan started to think more clearly. He was on Revetment Watch guarding his squadron's choppers.

"That's it. I'm on guard duty," he whispered to himself.

As he began to grasp that thought, a sudden realization hit him. He had no rifle!

Where is my rifle?

Great! I'm in my first real firefight and in less than two minutes I've already lost my rifle.

His mind raced.

They court-martial you if you lose your rifle! Damn!

Can they court-martial you if you're dead? Shit!

What a great way for a Marine to go. Confused, unarmed, court-martialed and dead. Fuck!

Crawling out of the revetment, he scrambled for protection behind the large rear wheels of an old Schramm tractor used for towing aircraft.

He was still having a difficult time focusing but he had to find his rifle.

In frustration, he bellowed to nobody in particular, "What, the hell, is happening?"

"Sappers," was the abbreviated reply from Private First Class "Ski" Baratoski. Dan spun around and saw nobody near him.

"Great, now I'm hearing voices!"

Bit by bit, the wailing of a siren was becoming louder and louder. The popping of rifle shots pierced the sound of the alarm.

Another explosion forced Dan and his invisible friend earthward.

"They hit 168's revetments," the mysterious voice continued, "It looks like a bonfire down there."

He was referring to the Marine Medium Helicopter Squadron (HMM)–168 which was immediately next door to Dan's unit. He could see several of the squadron's Boeing-Vertol tandem-rotor CH-46 Sea Knight cargo helicopters completely engulfed in flames.

"Their Revetment Watch must have been asleep… or something…," Baratoski's voice trailed off, not wanting to verbalize his fears.

Dan's eyes searched the immediate vicinity for the source of the commentary only to discover Baratoski concealed under the tractor. His steady voice had a calming effect on the lance corporal.

"Ski? I sure am glad to see you."

"I'm glad to be seen," he grinned, adding, "… given the circumstances."

Then he added, "Hey, Dan?"

"What?" Dan responded.

"What ever happened to being 'in the rear with the gear?'"

The last time Dan had heard those words was when they were departing the United States Marines Corps Recruiting Office in their home town. Each had a smile on his face. They had beaten the system. They would not be drafted. They were not going to be 'grunts.' They would be in the rear with the gear.

At least that's what they thought back then.

by James E. Bulman

CHAPTER TWO

Recruitment - 1968

Back then, like thousands of other young men of his age, the draft loomed largely over Dan's head. Dan could hardly be blamed for the situation he was in. It was completely out of his control.

In 1968, the lottery for the military draft had not yet begun. (The draft lottery based on birthdates began late in 1969.)

Here's how it worked before the Selective Service System lottery.

Soon after your eighteenth birthday, the Selective Service System would send you a letter requesting your presence at the nearest Armed Forces Examining and Entrance Station (AFEES) for aptitude testing and a physical. Passing the written exams combined with a successful medical evaluation meant the potential draftee had about thirty days to decide what to do with the rest of his life.

To demonstrate how lopsided the system was, all it takes is a quick glance at the opportunities for a draft deferment.

In 1968, the Selective Service System had close to two dozen draft classifications. A classification of 1-A meant you were classified as "Available" for military service. A classification of 4-F identified the registrant as "not qualified for military service." Classifications 1-C and 1-D meant you were currently on active or reserve duty in one of the branches of the armed forces. The remaining classifications were deferments.

So, if you were an overage, sole surviving son who was an ordained minister and a true conscientious objector with eight children whom you supported by working in a defense plant while moonlighting as a farmer who was trying to better himself by taking a full load of courses at the local community college with a major in military studies and was a member of the ROTC... you probably qualified for one or more of the nearly twenty deferments.

On the other hand, if you were an unmarried, 18-year-old high school graduate with average grades, working for minimum wage (back then $1.40 an hour!) and had no financial means to continue your education, you, young man, were about to be drafted into the United States Army or the United States Marine Corps.

As a draftee, none of the services were going to invest too much time and trouble training you. You were soon to be a basic infantryman, a grunt, a ground-pounder, cannon fodder.

You had choices, but they were few.

Choice One: Accept the inevitable and await your draft notice. Dan never thought the title "draftee" had much "zing" to it.

Choice Two: Appeal the evaluation by concocting some wild medical story. Dan gave it some thought, but he was confident he would end up in jail for making false official statements.

Choice Three: Claim you were a homosexual. There was a downside to that ploy. The rumor was, if you claimed you were gay, they would lock you in a room with a real homosexual who would have his way with you. During an era when homophobia was the norm, that option was rapidly eliminated.

Choice Four: Make a run for the northern border to Canada. The moniker of "Draft Dodger" never really appealed to Dan.

Choice Five: Try to enlist in one of the other branches of the armed services before your draft notice arrived. By offering the Navy or Air Force a four-year contract, Dan hoped he might receive training for a "real" occupation and maybe, just maybe, even avoid getting killed in combat.

That seemed like the best option.

A few days after receiving the letter from the Selective Service System advising Dan he was classified 1-A, Dan reluctantly headed for the local federal building in his hometown that housed the main post office and the recruiters from each branch of service.

Staring down the vast art deco corridor, Dan decided that the Navy recruiter was the safest bet. He had not heard of any U.S. naval vessels sinking since World War II.

As he entered the Navy recruiter's office, he was surprised to be greeted by a Marine Corps staff sergeant in dress blue trousers and short-sleeve khaki shirt.

"Can I help you?" the staff sergeant asked politely.

Dan replied with a terse "No," then quickly added, "I'd like to talk to him," pointing to the Navy chief petty officer sitting at his desk towards the rear of the office.

"Have you had you draft physical?" the sailor shouted from across the room.

"Yes, Sir," Dan threw in the "sir" to impress the seaman, "Passed it with flying colors," he admitted proudly.

"Sorry, son. I have a six-month waiting list. I'm not even allowed to talk to you."

Stunned, Dan did a slow about-face and was again greeted by the Marine.

"I had a scheduled appointment with another young man. He seems to be running late. Have a seat. Let's talk." The friendly staff sergeant cordially pushed a green guest chair towards Dan.

"I don't think so." Dan responded, scurrying from the room.

Reentering the corridor, Dan made a bee line for the Air Force recruiter. *They were the smartest service, anyway.* Dan rationalized. *They send the officers into combat and the enlisted folks stay behind in the rear.*

"Have you had your draft physical?" the airman asked without looking up from his New York Times crossword puzzle.

Anticipating the airman's response, Dan answered with "I have a feeling I know what you're going to say but… yes, I've had my physical."

"Sorry. I have a nine-month waiting list. I'm not even allowed to talk to you."

Crap!

Dan glanced up and down the grand hallway and decided the Army wasn't so bad after all.

Reaching the Army recruiter required Dan to walk past the U.S. Navy/Marine Corps Recruiting Office and past that staff sergeant who was now standing at its entrance.

As Dan whistled past the graveyard, the Marine informed Dan, "I'll see you in a few minutes."

I don't think so! Dan's inside voice silently countered as he sped along.

The Army recruiter asked the same introductory question.

Nearly sobbing, Dan replied with the usual answer.

"Well, let's look at your scores."

Wow, now we're getting somewhere.

Dan handed the soldier the letter from the Selective Service containing his test scores.

"You have very good scores," the sergeant seemed truly impressed.

"Have you ever thought about electronics?"

"Sounds great!" Dan blurted a bit too eagerly.

"Communications it is then." The recruiter said with finality as he rolled a new contract into his Remington Quiet-Riter typewriter.

Dan may have been born in the night, but it wasn't last night.

"Communications?"

"Yeah, electronics, y'know?"

"Do you mean radios?"

"Well, yeah."

The normally docile Dan became quite animated. Dan made a large "L – 7" with his fingers representing about a 12-inch by 12-inch square.

"Radios about this big?"

He continued, "Fits on your back?"

Then pointing over his shoulder, "With a big antenna?"

Stretching his arm straight up then waving his hand, "With a sign on it that says, 'Shoot me first'?"

"That's not necessarily the case," the soldier stammered.

Knowing that radio operators were easy targets, Dan offered a speedy, "No thanks!"

Rushing to his last option, Dan ran into the Navy/Marine Corps recruiters' office as if he was being chased by the local constabulary.

The staff sergeant was obviously pleased with himself. Yet, he never said the "I told you so" he desperately wanted to verbalize.

Looking at Dan's scores, the leatherneck was also impressed.

"Ground or aviation?" was his first offer.

"What in aviation?"

"Ground or aviation?" was his second offer.

"What in aviation?" Dan insisted.

"Don't know. They'll figure it out later. Ground or aviation?" was his third and final offer.

Exhausted, Dan relented.

"I guess it's aviation."

As Dan sat and began filling out the required enlistment forms, "Ski" Baratoski skidded to a stop in front of the recruiter's desk. Late for his appointment, Ski was panting as if he had just finished running a marathon.

Dan was surprised to see his high school buddy in the same predicament as he, but not surprised Ski was late. Ski was always late. He was never on time. The adage, "Fifteen minutes early is on time" always produced the same response.

"Why be early? It's just a waste of time."

After quick greetings, Dan told Ski, "I'll save you a lot of time… it's aviation."

Less than a week later a Marine gunnery sergeant addressed the new draftees who sat frozen with fear in the Armed Forces Examining and Entrance Station (AFEES) in New Haven, Connecticut.

by James E. Bulman

"The Marine Corps has fallen short of its monthly recruiting quota. I need three volunteers to be inducted into the Marine Corps," he informed the group, "It's still a two-year hitch for draftees."

Dan Keegan chuckled to himself. He could afford to see the levity since he had already signed up for a four-year hitch in the Marine Corps. He was not one of the draftees being coerced to switch from the Army to the Marines. He was not a draftee, he thought disdainfully. Quite full of himself, Dan had enlisted in the United States Marine Corps.

Dan watched as several of the inductees squirmed in their chairs. Two or three tried to hide behind the person in the seat directly in front of them hoping the lack of eye contact with the gunnery sergeant might prevent a fate worse than being drafted into the Army ... being drafted into the Marines!

"If I don't have any volunteers, I will select three names at random."

The room was quieter than a gathering of Gallaudet University alumni.

"Okay," the gunny began, quickly rattling off three names he had obviously pre-selected. "Bassett, Grogan, and Withers. You are now proud recruits in the United States Marine Corps."

One of the lucky three refused to accept the reality of the situation.

"Whoa!" a long-haired draftee interrupted, "No, no, no... NO!" the draftee insisted.

"Yes, yes, yes... YES!" the Marine mocked to everyone's amusement. "I'm afraid it's true."

The active duty soldiers and Marines behind the gunny all chuckled.

"NO!"

"YES!" the gunny insisted one last time as the gunny's smile turned to a frown. He was no longer amused. "Now, get your whiney ass into the passageway where the Marine recruits are eagerly awaiting your arrival."

The three reluctantly obeyed.

Dan could hear the long-haired recruit asking another, "Can they do this? Is it legal?"

Already tired of the whiner, one of the three advised the recalcitrant draftee, "So write to your congressman."

"That's it. I'll write my congressman." After some thought he asked, "Hey! Who is my congressman, anyway?"

The pool of Marines-to-be chuckled.

Another gunnery sergeant began to voir dire the band of inductees concerning their education level and suitability for leadership. The six-foot-four individual with a year and a half of college was selected as the group's leader. All the team's military documents were entrusted to this "college man."

The college was none other than Yale University. The "college man" was Jerry McCoy originally from West Virginia and claimed to be descended from the real McCoy's of the infamous Hatfield and McCoy feud. He was a country doctor's son who had reluctantly applied to his father's alma mater, Yale. He was as surprised as anyone when he was accepted. Unfortunately, he hated every minute of it. It was obvious he and Daddy didn't see eye to eye. Determined to control his own destiny, Jerry decided to enlist as a private in the United States Marine Corps.

The remaining members were instructed to obey every order voiced by the newly sworn in Private McCoy as if it emanated from the burning bush on Mount Sinai or face the wrath of God.

They were each provided a packet containing railway tickets from New Haven, Connecticut to Yemassee, South Carolina with a change of trains at Grand Central Station in New York City, a layover-over in Washington, D.C., and a bus ride from Yemassee to Beaufort, S.C. They were also given a bag lunch.

A staff sergeant accompanied the group on their seven-minute charter bus ride from the AFEES building on Chapel Street to New Haven's rundown Union Station.

A quick glance at the train schedule on the overhead mechanical split-flip display informed Private Dan that their timing was near perfect. It was a little after three o'clock in the afternoon.

Oops! Reminding himself that he was officially on active duty, Dan decided he had better start thinking in military time. Since it was after twelve o'clock noon, his newly-focused Marine Corps brain added twelve hours to three and calculated that it was currently 1500. (Verbalized as "fifteen hundred hours")

They would be departing in only a few minutes. Once they boarded the New York, New Haven and Hartford Railroad railcar, they would be on their own. The staff sergeant reminded them to obey the "college man's" instructions... or "There will be hell to pay!" He waited on the platform for the train to begin moving before he departed in a huff.

The new privates began the process of introducing themselves to one another. They had much in common. Most were from working class families. Most had family members who were serving or had served in the armed forces. The young men exchanged tales. They had yet to master the fine Marine Corps art of the "sea story." They would later learn that the trick is to embellish a yarn so that it balances on the cusp between believability and bullshit. Their stories helped to pass the time during the hour-and-a-half-hour trip to the Big Apple.

Upon arrival, they left their coach and entered the immense chasm of Grand Central Terminal in the Borough of Manhattan, New York City, New York. a.k.a. Grand Central Station.

Jerry gathered his small ragtag group in a circle and quickly made his first leadership mistake. He trusted people he did not truly know.

by James E. Bulman

After reminding them of the current time (It was a little before five o'clock.), the four-hour layover and their departure time (approximately nine o'clock in the evening.), he ended with "We're all adults. I'm trusting you not to drink and to be back here on time. See you back here at nine o'clock."

The group scattered to the four winds.

To understand the college man's error requires an understanding of the differences between the alcohol consumption laws of Connecticut and those of New York State. In 1968, the drinking age in Connecticut was twenty-one. In New York, it was eighteen.

Many of these young men had never consumed a legal drop of liquor. As for that matter, some had never consumed any liquor at all but fifteen minutes after their arrival in New York City, it was no longer an issue.

Four hours later, in groups of twos and threes, the gang staggered from points unknown to their muster area in the great terminus. Most were giddy. A couple were crying drunks. And one... was missing.

And this time, Dan sighed to himself, *it was not Ski.*

The college man was beside himself.

"What will they do to me if he is AWOL?" He fretted aloud.

The tipsy ones attempted to soothe his worries but one of the crying drunks made matters worse. Thick-tongued, he informed the college man, "You're going to da brig."

The others hushed him.

"I'm telling ya'. You're going to da brig, man!" the crying drunk insisted.

"I seriously doubt that," a booming voice chimed in.

All heads turned to see an older gentleman strong-arming the tardy private.

Looking at the college man, the gentleman asked, "Does this piece of shit belong to you?"

The crying private was first to respond. "Yep, thass our piece of shit, alright. Thass him," he slurred matter-of-factly.

The group nodded in unison, affirming the response.

Flashing his retired military I.D. card, the gentleman announced his presence.

"I'm retired Marine Master Sergeant Santiago. I tend bar over there," pointing to one of the nearby adult establishments. "This young stud was bragging about going over the hill. I thought I had better return him to you before he had a chance to act."

Jerry thanked the retiree profusely who wished them well. As the "Top" departed, he paused then turned back to the group and offered the boot-camp-bound recruits a bit of advice.

"Do you want to get through basic training as easily as possible?"

They all shouted in the affirmative. In an instant, all ears were tuned to Master Sergeant Santiago's frequency. The retiree raised his voice a few decibels.

"Never volunteer." (Pause for effect.)

"Stay in the middle of the group." (Pause two.)

"And do what everyone else does."

Quite pleased with himself, he grinned and wished them well as they boarded their ride to their next stop, Union Station, Washington, D.C.

Jerry and several of the less intoxicated young men agreed on a rotating schedule to keep an eye on their wayward compatriot. The remainder dispersed and went about locating their sleeper compartments.

Each private found his very-compact sleeping compartment and organized his meager belongings. Once they settled down, in their solitude, each was alone with his own thoughts. A few had never been away from family and were already a bit homesick. Some were aching for a chance to show their stuff and prove the naysayers back home wrong. Most were just hoping to return home alive.

The surprisingly quiet railcar accompanied by its imperceptible swaying, soon rocked them to sleep in their pull-out sofa bed.

Three-and-a-half hours later they arrived at Union Station in Washington, D.C. They were instructed by the conductor that they were not allowed to leave the train during the overnight delay. And, if they attempted to do so, the military police patrolling the terminal would place them under arrest and the violators would face courts-martial.

Already exhausted, our weary travelers slept quietly through the night.

Unbeknownst to our Marines-to-be, throughout the night additional railcars from every state east of the Mississippi River entered Union Station and were carefully added to those already destined for the little town of Yemassee, South Carolina. When dawn came, there were over two hundred Marines recruits berthed within the long line of sleeper cars. And, they were informed, more cars were being added as they waited.

The "Marine Express" departed Washington around nine o'clock that morning stopping at every train station in Virginia, North and South Carolina. When they arrived in Yemassee nearly ten hours later, the young men were instructed to gathered up their belongings and disembark. As they left the train they were directed to board one of a caravan of chartered busses idling nearby. Climbing aboard the bus, each recruit provided his name to the bus driver who checked them off his list.

It was now about seven o'clock in the evening. In an hour or so they would arrive at the Marine Corps Recruit Depot, Parris Island, South Carolina.

CHAPTER THREE

Assault on the Marble Mountain Air Facility - July 1970

From under the Schramm tractor Ski grinned, "You still with me, Dan? You're awful quiet."

"Yeah, I'm here," Dan replied, "Just thinking."

"Well, don't think too hard," Ski joked, "The last time I saw you thinking that hard you joined the Marine Corps!"

Dan's mind raced to refocus on the predicament at hand.

Although assigned to different squadrons, Dan and Ski kept in touch via occasional, okay, nightly visits to the enlisted club.

Ski was assigned to HMH-154, the Sikorsky CH-53 heavy cargo helicopter squadron while Dan was attached to the Headquarters & Maintenance Squadron–16 (H&MS-16 or more familiarly, simply "HAMS") providing more in-depth support to the entire fleet of helicopters assigned to the various squadrons at the Marble Mountain Air Facility.

"I can't find my rifle," Dan said despondently.

"Over there... somewhere." Ski pointed vaguely toward what seemed to be the center of the flight line.

Envisioning his M-16 lying in those wide-open spaces made Dan's heart sink.

Seeing the look on his face, Ski smiled and added, "Man, you should have seen it. It was a helluva sight."

He gave the lance corporal an unsolicited play-by-play as if he was Dandy Don Meredith recounting one of his college football games for Howard Cosell on an ABC's *Monday Night Football* broadcast.

"That satchel charge exploded. You went one way and your rifle went another."

He grinned and repeated, "It was a helluva sight."

With a sheepish grin, Dan reluctantly concurred.

"What do we do now?" he asked the slightly junior Marine.

Ski looked at Dan as if he was speaking a foreign language. The private first class' steady response made perfect sense to Dan.

"I don't know about your young Marine Corps ass, but this PFC is staying right under this here tractor 'til the 'All Clear' sounds."

With another sheepish grin, Dan concurred, all the time trying to figure out how he was going to get his gear.

CHAPTER FOUR

Boot Camp - 1968

By design, the bus carrying the new recruits arrived at the Marine Corps Recruit Depot, Parris Island, South Carolina in the evening.

Tired and disoriented, the gawking young passengers strained to see anything that might forewarn them of what lie ahead. All they could see was the Marine military policeman as he motioned the bus through the main gate with crisp hand signals that left no doubt as to their meaning.

The bus rolled to a stop in front of a two-story wooden H-shaped building displaying its singular purpose in life... "Recruit Receiving."

Awaiting their arrival were three Marines standing at parade rest. (Dan didn't know "parade rest" from a hole in the ground but he would soon learn.)

Each Marine was wearing sharply-creased khaki trousers, a short-sleeve khaki shirt with military creases, a web cartridge belt with a shiny brass buckle emblazoned with the Marine Corps Eagle, Globe and Anchor. All topped off with, of course, the unmistakable Smokey-the-Bear hat (officially titled "campaign cover").

The instant the bus driver opened the door, the three Marines snapped to attention. The Marine with the most stripes strode with purpose into the vehicle.

Stopping in front of the white line on the bus floor, the Marine drill instructor loudly announced his presence, "I am Senior Drill Instructor Gunnery Sergeant Raymond!"

He proceeded to ejaculate a stream of profanities that would make George Carlin blush.

"If you have a cigarette...put it out! If you are chewing gum...swallow it! On my order, you will quickly gather up your belongings and smartly exit this bus. You will place your feet on the little yellow footprints you will see on the road. You will leave nothing on this vehicle. Do you understand?"

by James E. Bulman

There was a mixture of mumbled "Yeses," "Yes, Sirs," "Uh-huhs," and "Yeps."

"Do you understand!!?"

The mumbles became one voice, "Yes, Sir!"

Still dumbfounded over his induction into the Marine Corps, the stunned long-haired passenger voiced a shell-shocked, "Whoa!"

In a microsecond, the Marine sprang from the front of the bus to the long-haired recruit's location. The drill instructor leaned so close to the recruit that the brim of his Smokey-the-Bear hat hit the young man on the forehead.

In a loud booming voice, the gunnery sergeant demanded, "Whoa? WHOA? Did I fucking hear you correctly, shit-for-brains? You don't fucking 'whoa' me. You fucking do what the fuck you are told to fucking do. Do you fucking understand me, ass-wipe?"

With the Marine's spittle landing on the recruit's face, he attempted a meek "Yes, Sir," but was immediately interrupted with an even louder, "DO YOU UNDERSTAND ME?" The drill instructor was nearly foaming at the mouth.

In unison, the entire bus erupted in a "YES, SIR!" that extricated the recruit from his predicament.

They scampered off the bus only to be welcomed by a cacophony of insults as the remaining two drill instructors pounced on the shell-shocked recruits like vultures on carrion.

"What, the hell, is taking you so long, sweetheart?"

"Hurry the fuck up!"

Any dropped item or misstep was greeted by two or more screaming drill instructors.

"Do you think I'm going to pick up your shit?"

"Get your Goddamn gear!" And as soon as any recruit turned to retrieve his gear he heard a volley of expletives.

"Where, the hell, do you think you're going?"

"Get your pansy ass on those yellow footprints!"

"Where's your fucking gear?"

The recruits raced to position their trembling feet upon the legendary "little yellow footprints."

Wincing at every bark, every shouted word, every hand gesture, the recruits eventually formed a rag-tag platoon of sorts.

Any head movement by a recruit was greeted with a near-insane drill instructor demanding answers to questions that had no right answers.

Dan made the mistake of turning towards the recruit next to him as the drill instructor berated the young man.

The drill instructor's attention immediately shifted to Dan.

"And what, the hell, are you looking at, maggot?"

"Nothing, Sir."

Acting stunned, the drill instructor "Nothing. Nothing! You were looking at me. Weren't you, maggot?"

"No, Sir!"

"Are you calling me a liar?"

"No, Sir! I was looking at the recruit next to you."

"Oh. You just like looking at other men? You think he's prettier than me, faggot?"

Not knowing how to answer, Dan decided to keep his mouth shut and prayed another recruit would screw up and take this drill instructor's focus away from Dan.

And his prayer was answered.

The senior drill instructor called the platoon to attention and marched the raw recruits single-file into the receiving barracks. The room contained a series of tables arranged in a horseshoe pattern. The newbies were positioned with their backs against the wall, so they faced the tables. They were told to empty all their belongings onto the tables. The three drill instructors inspected every item, every pocket, every wallet and every seam.

Pictures of girlfriends, wives and sisters were confiscated only after shared viewings accompanied by lewd comments by the trio of non-coms. Several of the new-comers had the condoms in their wallets confiscated with the inevitable, "Who you hoping to screw here?"

Several pocket knives, two straight razors and one .22 caliber pocket pistol were also removed.

The recruits were provided a pencil, a sheet of paper, and one stamped envelope. They were told exactly what to write.

"Dear Mom, Dad,
I have arrived safely at Parris Island. They are treating me well. I will write to you soon.
Love, Your Name"

Several of the recruits wrote the letter exactly as instructed including "Love, Your Name." The drill instructors had a field day with those Marines-to-be.

The recruits were marched (Well, kinda-sorta. Let's say they moved in a group.) to the barber shop where their locks were reduced to stubble. Most of the recruits had enough sense to obtain decent haircuts prior to their arrival at Parris Island but not the long-haired "Whoa" recruit. The drill instructors could not miss the opportunity to have their fun.

The senior drill instructor stood close to "Long-hair" as the recruit mounted the barber's chair. The recruit could feel the drill instructor's breath on his ear as the drill instructor's voice hissed through his teeth, "How, the hell, did you get into my Marine Corps?"

"You see, Sir, there's been a mistake."

He was immediately interrupted by the senior drill instructor.

"You! Ewe! Do I look like a female sheep?"

The long-haired draftee stammered a "No, Sir."

Hoping to plead his case one more time, he attempted to explain.

"It's just that I was supposed to go into the Army but the sergeant in New Haven mistakenly..."

"Private, let me explain something to you. Marine Corps sergeants don't make mistakes, and I don't give a rat's ass about your life story. Shut the fuck up so the barber can make you look just like your fellow recruits."

The recruit answered with a tired, "Yes, Sir!"

"The Army sent you here just to fuck with me, didn't they?"

"No, Sir!"

"Am I going to have trouble with you, son?

"No, Sir!"

The drill instructor stepped back, looked the young man over then added, "Damn, son. You got more blonde hair than Trigger."

"Yes, Sir!" the recruit agreed without truly comprehending the comparison to Roy Rogers' golden palomino.

With a wink and a nod from the barber, a path was shorn from the center of the recruit's forehead to the nape of his neck. Kind of a reverse Mohawk.

The stunned recruit was ordered out of the chair and back onto the little yellow footprints with the rest of the freshly barbered jarheads. Dan could hear him mumbling, "They can't do this stuff to us. They gotta have some sort of rules or something."

A nearby recruit whispered a gritty, "Shut up or you'll get us all in trouble" then added, "He doesn't have the sense God gave a goose."

That comment came from Ben Haroldson.

Dan would soon learn Ben "Catfish" Haroldson was the true southerner of this small collection of leathernecks-to-be. He had more stories than any other human being below or above the Mason-Dixon Line. Everything seemed to remind him of something said by his momma, his pa, his high school football coach, his elementary school math teacher, or his uncle Spurgeon (yep, Spurgeon). Nicknamed "Catfish" (a tribute to future baseball Hall-of-Famer and fellow North Carolinian "Catfish" Hunter), he had the best sense of humor, the broadest smile this side of Mayberry, and more southern witticisms than Minnie Pearl and Jerry Clower put together.

Realizing he had no defenders, the semi-long-haired recruit stopped complaining. As the last recruit exited the barber's chair the partially-shorn recruit was ordered back into the barber shop to have the remainder of his locks were cut to regulation length.

Marine Corps recruit training in 1968 was an abbreviated version from what was provided to those who had come only a few years before. It made perfect sense in military thinking. You increase the training time during peace and reduce training time during war. What's so hard to understand about that?

In May of 1968, just a few months after the infamous Tet Offensive in Vietnam, recruit training was only eight weeks long... exactly 56 days of the most rigorist physical and mental exertion Dan had ever experienced. Additional infantry training would immediately follow at the Infantry Training Regiment (ITR) at Camp Geiger in North Carolina. However, they had to make it through boot camp first.

On the first day of recruit training (during a week-long period referred to as Forming) recruits were apprised of the rules. The senior Drill Instructor assured the newly-formed platoon that they would all be treated equally, regardless of race, creed, color, religion or national origin.

"There is only one color here. That color is Marine Corps green. I don't care if you are white, brown, black, red or yellow. You will all be treated equally."

He added a warning aimed at a select group.

"And for you 'aviation guarantee' recruits, you'll be treated just the same as those assigned to ground units. Don't think you're gonna get special treatment!"

He continued, "Upon graduation, you will all be part of the big green fighting machine, the United States Marine Corps. Until that time, you will be called recruit, private or by your last name. You are not Marines until you successfully complete recruit training."

The recruits were also informed of their rights to *Request Mast*, that is, to go up the chain of command to speak to the officer in charge. In addition, if your issue is not resolved, you may continue up the chain of command to speak to the Regimental Commander.

Upon hearing this bit of information, there was but one thought crossing everyone's sarcastic mind. *"Yeah, right. Like that's going to improve my chances of surviving the ordeal!"*

They were advised that any period of inactivity would be punished.

"There will be no goofing off in my platoon."

To avoid those periods of inactivity, the recruit must have his "Little Red Book" opened and held at eye level to be read, studied, re-read, and memorized while standing at the position of attention.

by James E. Bulman

The little red book had all the information a soon-to-be Marine would need to know. Marine Corps organizational and rank structure, a listing of Military Occupational Specialties (MOS), hand-held and crew-served weapons information, small unit tactics and hand signals, artillery data, topographical map reading, amphibious assault plans, nuclear-biological-chemical defense procedures, landmine countermeasures, the eleven General Orders, the Prisoner of War Code of Conduct, and how to raise, lower and fold the national flag. It was all in there.

The drill instructor added a note to his lecture.

Dan's senior drill instructor ended the data dump with a thoughtful silence. Then, as if a thought had just come to mind, in a booming voice and a smirk on his face, he declared, "Marines do three things!" (*Pause for effect.*)

"We march real straight." (*Pause.*)

"We shoot really good." (*Then completing the triplet in a softer tone.*)

"And," (*Add a shit-eating grin to the mix.*) "We look real pretty."

The drill instructor was true to his words.

Recruit training was as difficult as Dan could imagine.

Dan was a one-hundred-twenty-eight-pound kid who had never excelled in any of the physical sports while in high school. He certainly was no athlete. His biggest fear was getting "set back." A severe injury or illness, a serious disciplinary infraction, failure to pass a critical written exam, or inability to meet the demanding physical requirements could result in your expulsion from your platoon and subsequent insertion into one of the newly arrived groups of recruits, typically adding two or more weeks to your training. Dan was determined to graduate with the platoon to which he was initially assigned. During the next eight weeks, he would push himself to the limit... and farther.

Dan deduced that the drill instructors (NEVER use the term "D.I.") each took on a different role.

There was Senior Drill Instructor Gunnery Sergeant Raymond who was the father-figure, of sorts.

The nice guy was played by Drill Instructor Staff Sergeant Washington.

Drill Instructor Staff Sergeant Carpenter was the out-of-control, insane Marine.

All three played their parts well... especially Drill Instructor Staff Sergeant Carpenter.

Early on, during a "school circle" (a hasty gathering of the platoon around the drill instructor so he can quickly pass on important information), the platoon was informed by Staff Sergeant Washington that Staff Sergeant Carpenter had just rotated back from his third tour of duty in Vietnam where, only a few months earlier, he survived the battle to retake the Citadel in Hue City from the invading North Vietnamese Army (NVA). Staff Sergeant Washington inferred that Staff Sergeant Carpenter was "not quite right in the head" after seeing 142 fellow Marines killed, not to mention 74 soldiers from the Army's 1st Calvary and 382 ARVN (Army of the Republic of (South) Vietnam – commonly referred to as "Arvin") soldiers killed. The North Vietnamese Army suffered over 5000 killed.

Dan made a mental note to keep a watchful eye on Staff Sergeant Carpenter. He soon determined the staff sergeant wasn't acting.

On the second day of recruit training the drill instructors made several selections.

The recruit with the highest scores on the aptitude tests and typically a year or two of college under his belt, became the Platoon Scribe. The Platoon Scribe maintained the unit's training records for the drill instructors. That assignment was given to Brian Walker, the recruit with the off-the-wall I.Q. Unfortunately, that assignment only lasted two days. Brian, in an effort to increase efficiency, Xeroxed all the first day's training records, lined out the date and penciled-in the next 55 days over the senior drill instructor's signature.

Like magic, eight weeks of daily training documentation was completed in 48 hours! It didn't seem to register with Brian that every day had the exact same training scheduled, but it did register with the senior drill instructor.

What Brian had in I.Q. he lacked in common sense. He was fired on day three.

by James E. Bulman

The smallest recruit became the "House Mouse", running errands for the drill instructors as directed. That position fell to Lou Archer. Former Golden Gloves champ in his weight class in Ohio, Lou Archer was one of those "little" guys they tell you to watch out for. Officially he was five-foot-four. The truth be told, he was quite a bit shorter... with a fuse to match. The scoop on Archer was "He's a great guy but don't ever piss him off!"

Unfortunately, he had a penchant for flirting with the young ladies. Upon his return from running his first errand on Parris Island he became a bit disoriented. He flagged down a car to ask the female driver for directions to his barracks. One thing led to another and he asked the lass her name. As soon as she uttered the two words "Rachael Raymond", Lou knew he was toast. She was the senior drill instructor's daughter. She pointed Lou in the right direction.

After Senior Drill Instructor Gunnery Sergeant Raymond spoke to his daughter over dinner that evening and was informed of Lou's interaction with the young lady, Lou was fired as House Mouse first thing the next morning.

The three most athletic-looking recruits were dubbed Squad Leaders, each leading a squad of thirteen trainees. A fourth choice for Squad Leader shocked everybody.

None of the original four squad leaders would graduate with the platoon. One by one, they fell from grace.

The initial few weeks were filled with classroom instruction on Marine Corps history, the rank structure, and the organization of the Corps. There was great emphasis on physical exercise especially running. The first mile-and-a-half run had quite a few stragglers who could not keep up with the platoon as well as a handful of recruits who simply quit. That, of course, incurred the wrath of the drill instructors.

Equal emphasis was placed on close order drill (marching practice). Each movement was thoroughly explained and practiced... over... and over... and over...

The first squad leader to be relieved couldn't march worth a lick. The steady cadence of "Left...Right...Left" became a faltering "La-left... Ra-right... (pause) La-right-la-right..." Get the picture? Scratch one squad leader.

Next came water survival training. After all, Marines are expected to serve on board ship.

Two squad leaders lost their leadership positions during "drown proofing." Marine Corps water survival training required recruits to swim one length of the Olympic-sized pool, swim one width of the pool with hands tied and a rifle slung around the neck, jump from the twenty-foot high platform into the pool and stay afloat in the water, without touching the bottom or sides for 30 minutes.

After a demonstration by the swimming instructors on the various methods of staying afloat for an extended period, the testing began.

A few recruits struggled with basic swimming. The swimming instructors (not the drill instructors) patiently guided them through the activities.

To advance to the final exercise of treading water for half an hour, each recruit had to jump from the twenty-foot high platform into the deep end of the pool. The recruits were advised that the ladder was unique among all ladders. It had a steadfast rule. The ladder to the platform was a special one-way ladder. Once you climbed up to the platform, you could not return via the same route. You had to jump off.

This proved one squad leader's downfall. Afraid of heights, the squad leader barely made it up to the platform. Once he reached the edge, he refused to jump and clung to one of the support beams like a child being torn from its loving mother's arms.

The swimming instructor's attempts at peeling the recruit's arms from around the stanchion proved useless.

The drill instructor's orders and threats shouted from the bottom of the ladder proved fruitless.

Finally, in a fit of rage, Drill Instructor Staff Sergeant Carpenter, snatched off his Smokey-the-Bear hat, threw it to the ground to wide-eyed gasps from the entire assemblage, and proceeded up the ladder where the duo of the swimming instructor and drill instructor wrenched the squad leader from the support beam and threw him bodily into the pool to a resounding round of catcalls, insults and raspberries from the poolside recruits. Deep six squad leader number two.

But the best was yet to come.

As the drill instructor turned to descend the ladder, the congregation of recruits erupted in hisses, boos, and more cat-calls. Even the other drill instructors joined in.

Realizing he was stuck on the wrong end of a one-way ladder, the drill instructor hesitated but relented without a fight. He removed his dress shoes and wallet and tossed them to one of the swimming instructors. The staff sergeant paused at the edge of the platform. With a bull-doggish "Ooh – Rah," he jumped, fully dressed, into the pool to the cheers of all.

The third squad leader to be dethroned simply couldn't swim. To be honest, he couldn't even float. As soon as he jumped into the pool, he sank to the bottom. And there he sat seemingly without complaint until the swimming instructor realized that the recruit would prefer to drown than incur the ire of his drill instructors.

He was rescued and stripped of his title.

The fourth squad leader was a shocking selection made by the senior drill instructor. And surprisingly, it took a little longer for squad leader number four to meet his fate.

The senior drill instructor used a tactic of putting a problem child in a position of responsibility. Often the selectee turns a new leaf and becomes a responsible Marine. Disregarding the input from the two junior drill instructors, the senior drill instructor selected the "Whoa!" recruit to be Squad Leader number four!

The new squad leader amazed the non-commissioned officers by excelling in his new position. That is, until about three weeks into the eight-week regimen.

The platoon was being punished for crimes committed or imagined. It didn't matter.

Drill Instructor Staff Sergeant Carpenter instructed the group to stand at the ends of their bunks and to face away from the center of the open squad bay. They instantly complied. Then in a commanding voice, he ordered, "Side straddle hops… forever! Ready… Begin!"

Now, side straddle hops (jumping jacks to you civilians) was the easiest of exercises the drill instructor could have selected but throwing in the "… forever!" added a new twist. You see, this far along in boot camp, the recruits believed him. They believed every word that came from his mouth. They truly thought they would be performing jumping jacks for the remainder of their lives.

As they began flailing their arms and legs about, they counted aloud in unison the number of jumping jacks performed.

"One, two, three, ONE."

"One, two, three, TWO."

"One, two, three, THREE."

Facing away from the center of the squad bay was another new twist. This allowed the drill instructor to move about the barracks without the recruits' knowledge.

As Dan counted the repetitions along with his fellow Marines-to-be, he spotted the drill instructor stepping from top bunk to top bunk. The D.I. (Oops!), the drill instructor was in search of anyone attempting to cheat by hiding between the bunks.

Slowly he crept. Bunk by bunk.

Then, in a moment of discovery, the drill instructor stopped on the bunk of the fourth squad leader. The "Whoa!" recruit was hiding between the racks to avoid the lengthy exercise commanded by the staff sergeant. The recruit was stealing glances towards the center of the barracks in a feeble attempt to determine the location of the missing drill instructor.

Dan wanted to forewarn the cheating squad leader but decided that he had better keep his mouth shut.

Drill Instructor Staff Sergeant Carpenter silently reached for what the Marine Corps would call "a weapon of opportunity". In this case, a silver-painted, fiberglass helmet liner (a.k.a. chrome dome) set upon the muzzle of the miscreant's rifle hanging from the end of the bunk.

The drill instructor raised the helmet liner then, with all his strength, brought it down on the squad leader's cranium.

The soon-to-be-former squad leader dropped as if pole-axed and lay unconscious on the wooden floor.

Realizing what he may have done, the drill instructor shouted, "Fuck! I killed him!!"

Quickly regaining his composure, he ordered, "Stop. Stop! Someone get me some water."

Several recruits grabbed their metal buckets and rushed to the head. When the water-boys returned with the requested liquid, drill instructor demanded, "Throw it on him!"

One by one, buckets of water were poured over the comatose recruit who became more and more alert as the near-water-boarding almost drown him.

The semi-comatose fourth squad leader, the "Whoa!" recruit, was transported to the sick bay. The disappointed senior drill instructor used the old standby when explaining to the Navy doctor the injury to the recruit.

"He fell down the stairs."

Surprisingly, the feeble excuse was repeated by the injured (now-former) squad leader. It appears that the "Whoa!" recruit recognized a path out of the Marine Corps due to dizziness, blurred vision, and migraine headaches... real or imagined.

The four replacements squad leaders learned from the mistakes of their predecessors and fared much better.

by James E. Bulman

After several days of close order drill without weapons, the members of the platoon were finally issued their M14 rifles, officially titled "United States Rifle, 7.62mm, M-14." The M-16A1 had not yet been introduced into recruit training.

As the recruits exited the armory housing the weapons, they handed the rifle they were issued to Senior Drill Instructor Gunnery Sergeant Raymond. One by one, he gave each of the newly-issued M-14's a thorough visual inspection to ensure the issued firearm had been properly taken care of by its previous owner. External stock, hand guard, butt plate, trigger mechanism (a.k.a. trigger housing group), barrel and flash suppressor. Internal inspection included, barrel, opening the butt plate, inventorying the cleaning gear inside, and removing the trigger housing group. A handful of rifles were immediately returned to the armor for seemingly minor discrepancies and new rifles issued. This gave the recruits a sense that the drill instructors were looking out for their best interests.

They were admonished to memorize the serial number of their weapon and to keep the rifle spotlessly clean. Each evening they were given time to tear down their weapon to its smallest pieces, clean and oil each item and reassemble it.

The next day, the recruits were instructed in a few rifle drill movements. "Order Arms" was the logical first movement and "Inspection Arms" the second. The latter is a bit tricky.

During "Inspection Arms", the inspector (the drill instructor) takes the rifle from the recruit in a move that requires the recruit to release his rifle a split second before the inspector grabs it.

Release too soon, the rifle falls to the ground. A mortal sin.

Release it too late and the inspector must pull it from the recruit. Not quite a mortal sin... but close.

Upon obtaining the recruit's rifle the inspector gives the weapon a complete once-over then returns it to its owner.

Since it takes quite a bit of time to inspect 60-plus rifles, the inspections were not conducted each day. Instead, they were held randomly. Therefore, the recruits never knew if or when a rifle inspection would be conducted.

Failure to clean your rifle would bring the wrath of the drill instructors upon the individual.

Thinking he could sneak by one evening without properly cleaning his rifle, Dan gave the barrel a quick in-and-out with the cleaning rod.

Of course, the very next morning the senior drill instructor decided to inspect rifles.

Dan knew he was in for it. His mind raced. He had to figure out a way to, at least, wipe the exterior of his rifle barrel. Eye-balling the position of the drill instructor as he moved about the formation of recruits, Dan found a moment when he was out of sight of the roving inspector.

Dan squatted slightly. He untucked his white tee-shirt and wiped the muzzle of his weapon then slowly returned to the position of "Order Arms."

The moment of truth arrived. Now standing ready, he raised his M-14 with his right hand and brought the barrel across his chest grasping the upper hand guard with his left hand and in one smooth motion slid his right hand along the rifle opening the breach and locking the bolt to the rear. One quick peek into the chamber to ensure it is empty and Dan was ready to release his rifle the instant the senior drill instructor grabbed it.

The drill instructor paused in front of Dan...

Wait ...

Wait ...

Wait ... then raised his right arm to grab Dan's rifle. Dan released the weapon the instant the drill instructor's hand grasped the upper hand guard.

Then Dan's heart stopped beating. How many discrepancies would the inspector find?

A few seconds later, the drill instructor returned the inspected rifle with the unheard-of comment, "Looks good."

Dan nearly fainted. He had gotten away with it. He actually started to grin until the drill instructor paused as he was stepping away, "Your tee-shirt is dirty. What did you do? Wipe you ass with it? Drop down and give me fifty!"

Damn! Dan thought, *you can't get away with anything.*

To engender a sense of purpose and provide a peek into the life of a "real Marine," the recruits were assigned interior guard duty. That is, guard duty within the confines of the military base, as opposed to perimeter guard duty.

After repeated instruction in the eleven General Orders, posting and relieving procedures, and the manning structure of the guard organization, the recruits were assigned Fire Watch. The Fire Watch's areas of responsibility included the platoon's squad bay and the adjoining shower room and head, as well as the passageway and stairwell connecting Dan's platoon to the three other platoons housed in the barracks.

The watch began each evening at taps and ended each morning at reveille. The watches were broken into two-hour shifts. The recruit assigned the watch was given a duty belt (a web cartridge belt signifying his authority as a member of the guard) and a flashlight.

In addition, any Marine wearing a duty belt is considered "under arms" meaning "armed" but with raw recruits that was never the case. "Under arms" also required the sentry to wear a cover (hat) of some sort. In boot camp, the only "cover" worn was the silver "chrome dome." Also, being under arms requires the Marine "to salute all officers and all colors and standards not cased."

For the first few nights, one of the drill instructors was in attendance each time a new Fire Watch began his shift. The drill instructor ensured proper posting and relieving procedures were followed. He also provided guidance concerning any special orders that were to be passed on to the on-coming watch.

Dan's turn as Fire Watch came one morning at 0400 (Civilian or not, there's no adding or subtracting so that is an easy one. It's four in the morning.) during which time he was informed that the drill instructor's alarm clock was out of order. The Fire Watch (Dan) was to awaken the drill instructor at 0545 (C'mon. That's not that much harder... 5:45 AM) by pounding three times on door jamb of the drill instructor's duty room. The drill instructor reminded Dan to use his "Marine Corps voice" to loudly and clearly announce himself.

The drill instructor continued his special orders, "If I don't answer, you are to wait exactly five minutes. You are to enter the duty room and, without turning on the light, bang on the metal wall locker three times. Understood?"

Dan answered by repeating the special orders in a strong, confident manner but deep inside he was scared to death about entering the inner sanctum of the drill instructor's darkened duty room.

But, orders are orders, he sighed to himself.

The two-hours passed excruciatingly slow, with Dan walking up and down the open squad bay, hushing the occasional whisperer, and giving permission to recruits needing to go to the head... one at a time.

As 0545 approached, Dan's heart began beating faster and faster in anticipation but like any good Marine, he would follow his orders to the letter. Dan watched the analog Seth Thomas clock on the squad bay wall as the minute hand and the second hand ticked their way to H-hour (Dan had learned from his little red book that D-Day is the day on which a military operation is to take place. H-Hour is the time on D-Day at which the operation will commence.) Dan took a deep breath and positioned himself in the passageway standing perpendicular to the duty room door. Then with the flat of his right hand...

Bang!
Bang!
Bang!

And in as loud a voice as he could conger up, "Sir, the Fire Watch was instructed to awaken the drill instructor at 0545, Sir! The time on deck is now 0545, Sir!"

There was a long pause but there was no answer.

To Dan the next five minutes seemed to take hours.

When precisely 0550 arrived (That would be five minutes later.), Dan was sure his teeth were chattering as he slowly turned the door knob to the drill instructor's private space. With only the light from the open door to guide him, Dan inched forward until he could see the gray metal wall locker. With much trepidation, he positioned himself perpendicular to the wall locker. Then with the flat of his right hand...

Bang!
Bang!
Bang!

"Sir, the Fire Watch was instructed to..."

Suddenly the wall locker door burst open causing the startled Dan to stumble backwards onto the passageway floor in fright. As Dan struggled to regain his composure, to his amazement, drill instructor stepped out of the wall locker... fully dressed. Khaki shirt, khaki trousers, spit-shined shoes and, to top it off, wearing his Smokey-the Bear hat. The drill instructor stretched his arms wide and exhaled a deep yawn.

Dan's mouth was agape. Poor Dan's Marine Corps brain was whirring with the idea of the drill instructor sleeping in the wall locker, fully dressed in order to maintain his uniform in its immaculate manner.

The drill instructor greeted Dan with a matter-of-fact "Good morning, recruit. Consider yourself properly relieved from duty."

Dan sat on his rear end in stunned silence.

"You are relieved, Private!" the drill instructor repeated.

Dan stood and snapped to attention and acknowledge the greeting, "Yes, Sir. Good morning, Sir," as he promptly retreated to the squad bay.

Of course, his story spread like wildfire throughout the platoon with half of the recruits believing every word Dan said. Of course, the other half raising the bullshit flag while walking away shaking their heads.

Little did he know, this was the first of many sea stories Dan would accumulate over the years.

by James E. Bulman

Punishment by means of physical exercise was a daily affair during recruit training. For the first two or three weeks: they marched; they screwed up; they were punished. They marched; they screwed up; they were punished. They marched...well, you get the picture.

Typically, the type of physical exercise selected indicated the degree of displeasure they had caused the drill instructor. A minor misstep during close order drill warranted side-straddle-hops (as previously explained).

A dirty, dropped, or mishandled rifle was punishable with push-ups. Not those "girlie" civilian push-ups but Marine push-ups. Starting in the prone position, toes touching the ground, palms flat against the ground, elbows unbent, back straight. Knees cannot touch the ground. A fellow recruit would place his fist directly under the solar plexus of the errant recruit. The recruit was required to lower his body until his chest touched the fist and then re-straighten his elbows.

Any breach of military order or any action that embarrassed the drill instructor brought on "Mountain climbers" or "bends and Thrusts."

Mountain climbers begin from the push-up position. The recruit would bring his right knee to his chest (ONE!) then back to the starting position. As the right leg was moving rearward, the step was repeated with the left leg (TWO!). Right-leg up and back (THREE!); left leg up and back (FOUR!). This would be repeated twice for each leg to count as one repetition. From a distance, the recruit appeared to be simulating scrabbling up the side of a hill. Hence, the nickname "mountain climbers."

Bends and thrusts (a.k.a. "bends and mother F......) begin at the position of attention. The recruit would drop down onto the palms of his hands (ONE!) then thrust both of his feet to the rear (TWO!) then bring his feet forward to the starting position (THREE!) then stand at attention (FOUR). Of course, being the first repetition of the exercise, the count would go like this: One, Two, Three, ONE!... One, Two, Three, TWO! etc.

There were times when it seemed the drill instructor just felt like toying with the platoon.

SWING WITH THE WING

As graduation day neared, the recruits became more and more sure of themselves. They began to feel that they could handle anything the drill instructors could throw at them. They began to feel like... well, like Marines.

This self-assurance did not sit well with the drill instructors. After all, these recruits were not yet Marines.

While cleaning the squad bay, a misstep by one private brought out the drill instructor's warped sense of humor.

After calling the platoon to attention, the drill instructor ordered "Bends and thrusts, one hundred of them. Ready. BEGIN!"

After completing the bends and thrusts with little effort, the recruits exchanged smiles over their shared success.

Without hesitation, he followed up with, "Pushups. Fifty of them. Ready. BEGIN!"

The sweat was pouring off the recruits, but they were up to the challenge.

Seeing this, the drill instructor berated the recruits for being "too cocky."

"On your bellies, you maggots!"

The recruits dropped to the floor.

Then the drill instructor barked, "On your backs!"

The recruits rolled over.

Then without a pause, he blurted out a rapid-fire series of orders knowing the recruits could not keep up.

"Stand up; on your bellies; on your backs; on you bellies; on your backs; stand up; about face; on your backs; on your bellies."

The commands continued faster and faster. The recruits weren't all that cocky now. The sweat soaked through their t-shirts, poured off the exhausted privates, and puddled on the barracks floor. Now the recruits were completely confused. Some standing. Some on their backs. Some on their bellies. All wallowing in their sweat.

Enjoying his success, the drill instructor couldn't help but smile.

Unfortunately, Dan saw the humor in it, too.

Looking up and down the squad bay at his fellow recruits, all moving in different directions, on their bellies and on their backs, flopping around in puddles of sweat, Dan was reminded of fish stranded out of water.

Like perch on a pier. He mumbled to himself.

Dan smiled and scanned the room only to make direct eye contact with the drill instructor... who had stopped smiling.

Oh, oh! Dan thought.

The drill instructor shouted, "Platoon...Atten- Shun!"

The platoon ceased the exercise and snapped to the position of "Attention."

"Private Keegan seems to think this is funny. Don't you, Private Keegan?"

"No, Sir!"

"Are you calling me a liar?"

Caught in the trap, Dan knew he was going to lose regardless of what he said so he tried to outwit the senior Marine.

"Sir, the private regrets any misunderstanding he may have caused but the private does not think this is funny, Sir!"

Undeterred by the intelligent retort, the drill instructor played his trump card.

The drill instructor announced, "Private Keegan seems to think this is funny," then added, "Does anybody else think this is funny?"

There was a resounding, "No, Sir!"

"Y'know, Private Keegan, everybody likes a little ass... but nobody likes a wise ass."

Then, rubbing his chin as he pondered Keegan's fate, the drill instructor made his decision.

"I think the platoon should decide your punishment."

The drill instructor stepped in front of the nearest recruit, "How many bends-and-thrusts should Private Keegan do?"

The poor recruit was torn by his friendship with Dan and the knowledge that he, himself, would be punished if he were too lenient.

"Fifty, Sir."

"Fifty." the drill instructor repeated as if agreeing. He side-stepped to the next recruit, "What do you think, Private?"

Taking the lead from the first recruit's answer, he quickly responded, "Fifty. Sir!"

This went on from recruit to recruit until the drill instructor had surveyed the entire platoon.

Upon conclusion of the survey the drill instructor announced, "It seems we have a unanimous decision. Fifty bends-and-thrusts."

Finally stepping in front of Dan, the drill instructor seemed to take pity, "Fifty. I would have been a little easier on a fellow member of this platoon. I would have said one hundred."

Confusion reigned.

Dan's face scrunched up. *Since when is one hundred less than fifty?*

The drill instructor continued, rubbing his chin, "Let me see, there are 51 other recruits. They each said fifty. That would be fifty times fifty-one which would equal 2550 bends-and-thrusts ..." Then with a wry smile, "... assuming my math is correct."

"That should wipe that wise-ass grin off your face, Private."

"Ready! Begin."

The bends and thrusts went on until meal time then continued upon return from the mess hall. This went on intermittently for several days. Dan would do one hundred or so, break for some training activity, then continue his punishment. Dan lost track at one point. When asked by the senior drill instructor where he was on the count, Dan purposely gave a lower number than what he thought he had done.

That proved to be a blessing in disguise. Unbeknownst to Dan, the three drill instructors had been closely monitoring and keeping each other informed as to Dan's progress. When Dan gave a lower number, the senior drill instructor queried Dan.

"Are you sure that's how many you have done?"

"Yes, Sir!"

A bit confused, Senior Drill Instructor Gunnery Sergeant Raymond asked again.

"Private, I want your honest answer. Is the number you gave me correct?"

Knowing there would be some trick behind the question, Dan decided to tell the truth.

"Sir, the private lost track so he gave a lower number to be sure he would complete the 2550 without any doubt."

The senior drill instructor seemed puzzled then with a broad smile announced to the entire platoon, "Here, recruits, is the makings of a true Marine."

He then turned to Dan and informed the private, "By my count you have reached 2550. Your physical activity is complete. If either of the drill instructors question my count, you will instruct them to ask me."

"Yes, Sir!" Dan wanted to smile but he clamped his jaw closed so tightly that his face hurt. Private Keegan had learned his lesson.

Another of Dan's smiling moments occurred in an outdoor classroom to learn about nuclear, biological, and chemical (NBC) warfare.

As the instructor explained ways to survive an atomic bomb attack, Dan smiled (to himself!) as he thought, *In the event of an atomic bomb attack, place your head between your knees and kiss your ass goodbye!*

Biological warfare was just plain scary.

Chemical warfare involved the use of the M-17A1 Chemical and Biological Field Mask. They were instructed on the different chemicals the enemy might deploy and the gas mask filters that could be used to protect the individual Marine against the various threats.

Dan was issued a mask and, along with his fellow recruits, shown how to don and clear it of any residual chemicals or biological agents. They were instructed when the order "GAS!" was given, they were to immediately stop whatever they were doing (including breathing) and don the mask. Once the mask was on his face, the recruit was told to cover the exhalation valve with his hand and exhale as hard as he could to blow any remaining contaminants out of the mask. Dan found it easy to adjust the straps to ensure a tight seal. Others had some difficulty.

It was the procedure for determining when to remove the mask that got Dan giggling. There are two axioms that apply. One: Rank has its privileges. Two: Shit rolls downhill.

Picture yourself in a combat situation where your unit has just survived a chemical attack. You are not sure if the air is clear or not. The procedure for unmasking begins with the most junior Marine breaking the seal of his mask. If he lives, everyone can unmask. If he dies, everyone remains masked.

Needless to say, explaining this procedure to a classroom full of privates created more than one set of doubters. One private in the classroom interrupted the instructor with a shocked, "You gotta be shitting us."

The instructor assured the class he was quite serious. The instructor added a motivational comment at the end of his presentation.

"That should make you run a little faster during the quarterly Physical Readiness Test (PRT), study a little longer for the annual General Military Subjects Test (GMST), work a bit harder to improve your proficiency marks and keep your nose clean to maintain high conduct marks so you can get your ass promoted before the next guy."

The stunned class sat in silence until Dan tossed in the comment, "When do we get our SGLI (Serviceman's Group Life Insurance) lesson?"

Even the drill instructors laughed.

As usual, classroom training was followed up with some sort of hands-on activity.

You guessed it. Up next... the tear gas chamber!

Dan along with a dozen other masked recruits were paraded into the tear gas chamber. The doors were closed behind them.

Like most of the recruits, Dan had seen dozens of old Jimmy Cagney and Edward G. Robinson movies where the "feds" toss tear gas into the hoodlum's hideout. The glass shatters, the tear gas canister rolls across the floor, snaps open and begins hissing the choking agent into the room. The small room soon fills with a dense fog so thick the bad guys can't see one another. Eventually the bad guys cough a couple times (not too many... got to get the dialog in). The gang leader yells out, "Come and get me you dirty coppers." Finally, the two-bit hood opens the door to the outside begins shooting wildly and is gunned down by the good guys.

This small chamber was nothing like that.

As Dan's squad entered the dimly lit shack, they saw an instructor monitoring the small, Sterno-fueled fire. A wafer about the size of an Alka-Seltzer tablet sat atop the tiny six inch-by-six inch wire-frame stove. There was a slight mist in the air.

Piece of cake, Dan decided as he snugged the straps of his M-17A1 mask a bit tighter just to be safe.

The instructor ordered them to march in a circle while singing the Marine Corps Hymn. This ensured the masks were properly sealed. Poorly sealed masks would be identified quite noticeably. The next step was to remove the masks.

Upon hearing the command, "Un... MASK!" the recruits removed their protective face gear. After an extended period of holding their breath until they could hold it no longer, the coughing and choking commenced with enthusiasm. (Now, I don't mean a couple of "ahem, ahem" coughs. I mean choking, gagging, eyes burning, snot running out of the nose, puking coughs. So much for Cagney and Robinson!)

Upon inhaling his first breath of tear gas, Dan thought an elephant had sat on his chest. He simply couldn't breathe. Gasping for air only aggravated the lung irritation.

Dan and his fellow recruits were most grateful when the order finally came to "Don and clear!" their masks. After ensuring each recruit had cleared the gas from their mask, the drill instructor called the recruits, one at a time, "Front and Center!" The young leathernecks-to-be stood in front of the drill instructor one at a time and was required to remove his mask, state his name, rank, and service number. After inhaling a deep gulp of air, removing the mask and successfully bellowing the required personal data as quickly as he could, he was allowed to exit the chamber.

When the door opened, some recruits stumbled just far enough away to be clear of the gas cloud surrounding the chamber. Most of the gagging, vomiting recruits fled as if chased by wild animals.

Running helter-skelter with their burning eyes closed could only lead to disaster.

One "blind" private ran full-force into a tree.

As the Navy medical corpsman rushed to care for the unconscious jarhead, the Senior Drill Instructor Gunnery Sergeant Raymond commented, matter-of-factly, "Damn, that's the third time someone's run into that tree. I'll have to notify base facilities to remove it," then he added with a wry smile, "If I don't forget."

by James E. Bulman

Successfully completing recruit training was a matter of determination.

At first unsure of himself, eventually, Dan decided that he could do this. He could finish Marine Corps boot camp and he might even like the idea of being a Marine.

Success built upon success.

The Marine Corps had, after all, been building Marines for nearly two centuries. They knew what they were doing.

As the days progressed, challenges like climbing a knotted rope using every muscle in his arms and legs soon only required his upper body strength to ascend a straight, unknotted rope.

One-mile marches turned into three-mile runs which eventually became twenty-mile forced marches. Dan never dropped out.

Initially staring with trepidation at the thirteen-obstacle Confidence Course, Dan soon began viewing it with a sense of accomplishment and exhilaration.

The Confidence Course began by stepping onto a two-foot high stump followed by a leap onto and over the unnamed eight-foot-high horizontal telephone pole. "You'll give it a name all your own," the recruits were informed. Dan dubbed it "ball-buster."

Constructed mainly of telephone-pole-sized logs, the course reached its apogee on the 40-foot-high log A-frame that culminated with the declining rope over a muddy four-foot-deep pond. This monstrosity was referred to as the Slide-for-Life. Most remembered of all the obstacles, completing the Slide-for-Life took quite a bit of physical strength and balance.

To successfully accomplish this final task, the recruit had to straddle the rope, lay face-down, hook one foot onto the rope behind them, and slowly pull himself down the declining rope. The free leg dangled below to lower his center of gravity. Halfway down the slide the recruit was required to perform a changeover by hooking his legs together and roll so the recruit hung facing skyward under the rope with his feet laced together on the rope with his hands free to pull himself downward. That's where the troubles began.

While Dan waited atop the forty-foot high platform for one of his fellow recruits to complete his own slide down the rope, the recruit slipped during the changeover and found himself dangling by two hands over the murky pond below. His feeble attempts at swinging his legs over the rope to regain the proper position only worsened his already tenuous grip.

The orders from the drill instructor proved useless. The recruit was not letting go.

The drill instructor finally barked an order to Dan.

"Keegan. Get that silly son-of-a-bitch off my Marine Corps rope!"

Dan hesitated.

"... NOW!" the drill instructor demanded.

Dan positioned himself properly on the rope and carefully slid to the halfway point. As he approached the dangling recruit he felt sympathy for this fellow platoon member, but orders were orders. Dan began to unpeel the other recruit's fingers from the rope.

The recruit did not speak a word.

While he said nothing, his eyes told the story. *Please don't. Please!*

As Dan pried the last set of fingers from the rope, he added a whispered, "Sorry, Mac."

The recruit dropped into the pond without injury but as Newton stated in his Third Law: For every action, there is an equal and opposite reaction.

The loss of the recruit's weight caused to rope to spring violently upwards resulting in Dan losing his balance. Now Dan dangled from the rope.

The drill instructor didn't miss the opportunity.

"Private Keegan,"

"Yes, Sir."

"Atten...HUT!"

Dan immediately let go of the rope, slapped his fists to his sides, thumbs pressed against the leg seams of his trousers, snapped his heels together and dropped like an arrow into the pond.

As the water-soaked Dan climbed out of the muddy pool, the drill instructor stopped him in his place.

"And where do you think you're going?"

"To the finish line, Sir." Dan responded with hesitancy.

"Bullshit! You haven't successfully completed the Slide-for-Life, Private. Get your ass back up there."

Dan knew not to plead his case. He simply replied with an exhausted, "Yes, Sir."

Soaked to the bone, Dan repeated his climb up... and down the obstacle.

by James E. Bulman

Four or five weeks into recruit training Dan overheard one of the drill instructors from a nearby platoon refer to Senior Drill Instructor Gunnery Sergeant Raymond by his first name. Dan kept this tidbit of information to himself as if it were marked "Top Secret: White House Access Only!"

But Dan could only keep this highly-classified information for so long. He waited like a hunter in a tree stand patiently knowing the appropriate time would come.

Several nights later, as the senior drill instructor was about to turn off the squad bay lights, he made his usual evening comment, "Good night, recruits."

The required response was voiced by the entire platoon. "Good night Drill Instructor Gunnery Sergeant Raymond," adding, "And good night Chesty Puller, wherever you are."

With homage paid to the most decorated member of the Marine Corps, the senior drill instructor turned off the lights only to hear a singular, "Good night, Sidney."

The squad bay immediately brightened as "Sidney" turned the lights back on. The senior Marine marched directly to the Seth Thomas clock, took it off the wall, reset the time back thirty minutes.

Without asking who had made the wise comment, the drill instructor ordered, "Bends and thrusts. One hundred of them. Ready. Begin!"

The next thirty minutes were filled with a variety of exercises designed, on the spot by the drill instructor, as a lesson in group punishment. One Marine screws up and all feel the repercussions.

Despite the lesson in group dynamics, Dan was just grateful the drill instructor never asked who the culprit was.

About mid-training, Dan's platoon was assigned to two weeks of mess duty. The individual assignments varied from server on the line, assistant cook, vegetable locker, spud locker, scullery, cleaning tables, etc. The choice assignment was server in the Staff Non-Commissioned Officer (Staff NCO) section of the mess hall.

Senior Marines (mostly drill instructors) did not have to side-step along the food line holding a metal tray for their meals. Instead, they ordered from a menu. Their food was retrieved by the server who delivered the meals on real plates to their "customer's" table.

It was menial work, but if the recruit did an outstanding job, he just might have a chance at private first class when he graduated.

Several of the drill instructors felt this assignment bordered on personal servitude and made it known to their superiors. They quickly learned that tradition is tradition, good or bad. It was not easy to buck a system that has been in place for decades.

But you can have some fun with it.

When he was informed that he was required to assign one recruit to the Staff NCO mess, Senior Drill Instructor Gunnery Sergeant Raymond chose one of his Spanish speaking privates for the task.

At first blush, this sounded like a smart move. A bilingual server could interact with some of the Hispanic drill instructors thereby increasing his chances for promotion. The trick was the private spoke Spanish fluently... but spoke or understood little English!

The day the bilingual private was assigned, Dan could hear the mass confusion in the Staff NCO dining area.

The first drill instructor placed his order, "Three eggs over medium, two sausage links, hash browns smothered with sausage gravy, a cup of black coffee with two sugars."

The server was overwhelmed. Understanding less than ten percent of what the drill instructor had ordered, the private did his best to get the order correct. Back in the kitchen, the private relayed the order to the cook, "Two egg sausages, over brown coffee, medium brown gravy, and two smothered sugars."

The cook turned the private around and pointed him back toward the table of the "customer."

The second go-'round wasn't much better as the irritated senior NCO recited his order a second time but much slower and louder. "Three eggs over medium, two sausage links, hash browns smothered with sausage gravy, a cup of black coffee with two sugars."

The private's eyeballs widened with every item added to the list.

In the kitchen for the second time, the private tried again.

"Three sausages over brown, eggs with hash, cup of sausage gravy with two sugars."

Turned around once again, the private was nearly in tears. When the Staff NCO "customer" began berating the young man for his incompetence, Senior Drill Instructor Gunnery Sergeant Raymond stepped in to protect his trooper. The "customer" soon realized he was on the receiving end of a prank and eventually laughed along with the rest of the NCOs.

The young server was reassigned.

by James E. Bulman

Dan's rag-tag band of "hippity-hop-mob-stop" civilians stumbling from the receiving barracks evolved into a platoon of Marines parading before the base commander as the winner of the regimental marching competition. While that took weeks of practice, qualifying with the M-14 rifle was a bit trickier. The lighter M-16 had not yet been introduced to Marine Corps recruit training.

Although there are three degrees of shooting competency (Marksman, Sharpshooter, and Expert) all Marines strive to be an expert rifleman. It becomes obvious to the most casual listener what Marines think of the three accompanying badges.

The marksman badge is a simple square with a bull's eye (a.k.a. "the toilet seat").

Sharpshooters earn a badge that closely resembles a German Iron Cross.

Experts wear "crossed-rifles" amidst a laurel wreath. Much classier.

Near the end of recruit training the platoon packed its bags and moved lock-stock-and-barrel to the rifle range for two weeks of intensive marksmanship training.

One week of "snapping in." That is, learning the care and cleaning of the weapon, practicing its disassembly and assembly, followed by disassembling and assembling the rifle while blindfolded. They were instructed to repeat the mantra "sight-alignment-sight-picture," a method of aligning the front and rear sights to ensure accurate fire. Late in the first week they began dry-firing the unloaded rifle from the prone position while a fellow recruit simulates its recoil by kicking the empty rifle into the "shooter's" shoulder each time he pulls the trigger of the weapon.

During the second week of marksmanship training, the mornings and afternoons are spent in actual live fire. Every day of that second week, the first rounds go down-range as soon as the sun breaks the horizon.

Recruits fire ten rounds in each of five positions from three different distances from the target. At 200 yards, recruits fire ten rounds in the standing ("off-hand") position and ten rounds in the kneeling position. Moving back to the 300-yard line, recruits continue by firing ten rounds in the sitting position and ten more in the prone position. Finally, at 500 yards (Yes, over one-quarter of a mile) the final ten rounds are fired in the prone position.

A total of fifty rounds are fired. Five points are scored for each bull's eye with decreasing points awarded for hitting the outer rings of the target. A score of 250 is the maximum one can achieve.

A score of 190 to 209 qualifies as a Marksman.

Shooting 210 to 219 receives the Sharpshooter badge.

Anything above 219 earns the coveted Expert badge.

Dan struggled a bit on the first day of live fire. Having missed the target completely, Dan raised his hand for guidance. A Primary Marksmanship Instructor (PMI), not one of Dan's drill instructors, advised the young recruit that he was jerking the trigger.

In a moment of extreme stupidity Dan replied, "No, Sir! I am not."

The PMI's temperature rose several degrees.

"Oh, you're not, are you?"

Dan realized his mistake but couldn't undo his error.

"Give me your finger!" the PMI demanded.

"Excuse me, Sir?"

"Give me your Goddamned finger!"

Slowly, Dan took his right hand from his rifle and gave it to the pith-helmeted instructor who proceeded to place Dan's trigger finger in his mouth and bite down on the Dan's nail. Dan winced in pain. He was sure the PMI would penetrate the nail and draw blood.

Releasing Dan's appendage, the PMI loaded a single round in the M-14's chamber and ordered the shooter to fire one round at the target.

Dan took a deep breath. His trembling trigger finger hurt so badly he could hardly hold the rifle. He knew he could not screw this up. He repeated the mantra to himself... *sight-alignment-sight-picture*. His finger ached as he gently squeezed the trigger and fired the round.

POP!

Only a moment passed before the target dropped behind the berm and was quickly raised with a white spotter in the center of the bull's eye.

Stunned, Dan looked at the PMI as the instructor admonished him, "Don't tell me you weren't jerking the trigger."

Dan learned another lesson that day. Never question a sergeant.

Qualification Day is typically on a Friday. The day before is Pre-Qualification Day. If Qualification Day is a rain-out, Thursday's scores are used. Therefore, Pre-qualification day is taken just as serious.

It is also the one day the platoon was provided some entertainment. The platoon was permitted to view the 1949 Oscar-nominated war movie *The Sands of Iwo Jima* starring John Wayne. (Well, who did you expect? Nelson Eddy and Jeanette McDonald?)

by James E. Bulman

The highlight of the film was a cameo appearance of three of the surviving Iwo Jima flag-raisers, PFC Rene Gagnon; PFC Ira Hayes; and U.S. Navy Medical Corpsman Pharmacy-mate Second Class John Bradley. (After a lengthy inquiry, the Marine Corps informed the public in June 2016 that John Bradley was not one of the flag-raisers. The newly identified flag-raiser was PFC Harold Shultz.)

Unfortunately, some recruits were not allowed to watch the ultimate Marine war movie. Any recruit who did not receive a minimum passing score during prequalification shooting on the rifle range that day could not view the film. Oh, they could sit in the small gymnasium-turned-theater, but they were not allowed to watch the classic. Instead, they were instructed to put their thumb and index finger together (like the "okay" sign). Then, simulating the front and rear sight of the rifle, they were to focus on their big toe while looking through the "hole" created by their fingers. In addition, they were to silently repeat the mantra "Sight Alignment; Sight Picture" for the next hour and forty minutes.

Dan fired a 211 on Qualification Day. Disappointed at not achieving the Expert badge, the new sharpshooter was quite relieved that he avoided the dreaded "toilet seat."

One recruit wasn't so lucky. Private "Ski" Baratoski, seemed to miss more than he hit and scored a 189... one point below the requisite passing score of 190. His score was officially recorded as "Unqualified'.

The drill instructors did not take kindly to having a member of their platoon going "UNQ."

As the senior drill instructor reviewed the scoresheets that evening, his eyes zoomed in on the big, red "UNQUALIFIED" stamp emblazoned across Baratoski's score card.

Baratoski was a tall, lanky New Englander whose hunched posture and extremely large proboscis provided the drill instructors with an easy target for ridicule. Add to that, the senior drill instructor, born and raised in rural Alabama, always struggled with Baratoski's surname. That alone earned Baratoski a rather dubious sobriquet.

"BUZZARD!" the senior barked.

Without an instant delay, a "Yes, Sir!" was shouted from the communal showers.

"I'm not inventorying assholes, Buzzard. Get your non-shooting carcass out here."

Rushing naked from the showers into the open squad bay, "Buzzard" snapped to attention with a dripping-wet "Yes, Sir!"

The drill instructor began berating the gangly recruit.

"Buzzard," he began, "You're one big screw up."

"Yes, Sir!" Buzzard agreed.

"You could fuck up a shit sandwich."

"Yes, Sir!" Buzzard agreed again.

"You are one fucked-up buzzard."

"Yes, Sir!"

Deciding to have some fun with this recruit, the drill instructor continued.

"You enlisted on an aviation guarantee, didn't you, Buzzard?"

Baratoski had never been asked that by any of the drill instructors.

"Yes, Sir!" He replied wondering where the drill instructor was going with this line of questioning.

"Y'know what? You need to let everyone know how screwed up you are. Flap you wings, Buzzard!" the drill instructor ordered.

Obediently, Baratoski stuck his thumbs into his armpits and began flapping his arms.

"Fly around the squad bay, Buzzard. Tell everyone how fucked-up you are."

Always obeying orders, Baratoski "flew" up and down the center area of the squad bay, stark naked, flapping his "wings" and shouting, "I'm a fucked-up buzzard! I'm a fucked-up buzzard!"

None of the other recruits laughed. They knew, *"But for the grace of God..."*

After three or four times around the squad bay, the drill instructor shouted, "Buzzard! Get your wet ass over here."

Snapping to attention in front of the drill instructor, the senior Marine ended the "lesson" with a startling announcement.

'Buzzard, it looks like it's your lucky day," the drill instructor informed Baratoski, 'I just spotted a math error in your score card. You shot a 199... you're a qualified Marksman."

Without any thought of apologizing, the drill instructor looked at Baratoski and said, "So get your naked ass back in the shower."

Baratoski obeyed.

One good thing came out of the drill instructor's impromptu lesson. Private Baratoski was never called "Buzzard" again.

The evening before graduation from recruit training, Senior Drill Instructor Gunnery Sergeant Raymond held his final school circle. He warned the young Marines not to become complacent once they arrived at their permanent duty station.

"There are plenty of shit birds out there. Don't become one of them." Then he added, "Remember what you have accomplished. Remember your Marine Corps heritage. Always be the Marine you wanted to be the day you signed your enlistment contract."

After concluding his lecture, the senior drill instructor began informing the recruits of the Military Occupational Specialty (MOS) they had been assigned. All ears were tuned to the senior drill instructor. Each recruit hoping and praying for some choice assignment.

As the senior drill instructor called out the names in alphabetical order he would announce the MOS. Drill Instructor Staff Sergeant Washington had a cross reference sheet to decipher the nearly 500 different job titles encoded in the four-digits.

0100 series were Administrative Clerks; 0200 series Military Intelligence; 0400 Logistics; and so on.

Of course, being "real Marines", the drill instructors would cheer each time an infantry assignment was announced.

Infantry MOS's were in the 0300 group. A basic rifleman was classified as an 0311 (a.k.a. "Oh-Three-Eleven or simply "Oh-Three"). A machine gunner was an 0331. A mortar man was an 0341, and so on.

(The recruiting story goes like this: A prospect walks into the recruiting office and informs the Marine recruiter that the Army, Navy and Air Force each gave him a choice concerning possible MOS's.

"The Marine Corps does, too," the recruiter advised the surprised young man. The recruiter quickly rolled a fresh contract into the typewriter, typed in the necessary personal data, pulled it out and showed the prospect where he could enter his choice at the bottom of the enlistment agreement.

"What do you want to do in the Marines?"

"How about Nuclear Energy?" the man asked.

"Nah! Too much radiation. You'll never have any kids," the recruiter advised.

"How about Computer Science?"

"Nah! All those ones and zeros. You'll go nuts," the helpful non-com counseled.

"How about Environmental Studies?"

"Say, that sounds great!"

Both recruit and recruiter smiled broadly.

The recruiter instructed the young man, "That was your third choice, right?"

"Yeah."

"So just put 'Oh-Three' in that space on the contract.")

When the senior drill instructor announced the first of the aviation MOS's, he added a special note for one group of graduates.

"And for you recruits who enlisted with an aviation guarantee... don't think life is going to be any easier for you Air Wingers. If you think you're going to "Swing with the Wing," remember "Every Marine is a basic rifleman!"

When you get to Vietnam, (Notice he said 'When' not 'If.') you'll all end up as helicopter door gunners and get your ass waxed going into a hot zone. You had better have paid attention here and you better pay attention during Infantry Training at Camp Geiger."

As the drill instructor finally reached the K's, Dan listened intently, "Keegan – 6212... What, the hell, is that?" the stupefied senior Marine demanded. The other drill instructor hurriedly fanned through the 14 pages of numbers to finally arrive at page 11, "6212," he informed the senior, "Aircraft Communication Systems Technician."

"I don't know what, the hell, that is, Keegan," the senior drill instructor admitted with a smile, "but you're still going to Vietnam!"

Dan knew that was probably the truth.

by James E. Bulman

CHAPTER FIVE

Assault on the Marble Mountain Air Facility - July 1970

And there Dan was. Just as his drill instructor has predicted... in Vietnam, attempting to conceal himself under a Schramm tractor in the middle of one heck of a battle.

Two near-simultaneous explosions bounced our two Marines several inches off the ground. Dan's head hit the underside of the tractor.

Recoiling from the blow, Dan rubbed his injured noggin only to realize his helmet was also missing. He shouted, "Where's my damn helmet?"

On the edge of panic, he patted himself down to confirm he still had his rifle magazines, first aid pouch, canteen, and bayonet.

Refocusing on the immediate situation, both Dan and Ski were beginning to grasp the fact that this was more than a simple sapper attack. Sappers typically infiltrated their enemy's encampment, threw a few satchel charges at targets of opportunity, and high-tailed it home. It appeared that these folks planned on hanging around awhile. There were over a dozen helicopters burning.

Focused on the runway, the pair was startled to hear quick-paced footsteps to their rear. Ski spun around onto his back, intent on killing the fast-approaching intruder. Shooting from the hip while lying on your derriere under a tractor wasn't exactly a practiced technique learned during infantry training. Regardless, Ski was confident he would be the winner of this little confrontation.

"Don't fire!" Dan shouted, "It's Jason."

Ski quickly lowered the muzzle of his weapon.

Corporal Jason Walsh half fell, half dove under the tractor.

"Holy shit!" was his opening remark, "I thought you were going to shoot my ass!"

"Your ass wasn't where I was aiming," Ski responded.

"You guys okay? I've been looking all over for you." Jason informed the well-hidden sentries.

"Been right here the whole time," Ski answered matter-of-factly for both them.

Dan was relieved to have Jason there. He knew Jason would somehow get them out of this mess.

Jason was about a year older than they were and quite a bit more mature. He had enlisted in the Marine Corps several months before the rest of their clique. Jason was recently meritoriously promoted to corporal ahead of his peers but had not let it go to his head. He was still Jason...at least when there were no officers or other NCOs around.

As today's Corporal of the Guard or COG, Jason was responsible for keeping the various sentries awake and alert. Jason was good at that. He was known for maintaining a watchful eye over his charges.

A typical COG would make his rounds once, maybe twice each night. Not Jason. He would post his guards and check up on them numerous times throughout the evening. He would sometimes make his rounds and return just a few minutes later to ensure the young Marines hadn't decided to take a nap in his absence.

Jason strictly obeyed the Marine Corps' eleven General Orders memorized by all Marines and he expected Marines in his charge to obey them to the letter. The second General Order begins, "To walk my post in a military manner, keeping always on the alert..."

On this night, Jason was focused on the final General Order (the 11th) that compels sentries to be "especially watchful at night and during the time of challenging..."

"Charlie's all over the place and the Officer of the Day (the OOD or simply the OD) says they may be coming from any direction. Any direction!" he repeated to ensure they understood.

"Get your weapon and get to the H&MS hangar. We need every man we can muster to stop this. Understood?"

Stunned by the gravity of the situation, the junior enlisted men replied in unison, "Understood."

He gave a quizzical look at the unarmed, un-helmeted Dan then, amazed, asked, "Where's your gear?"

Both Dan and Ski looked mournfully towards the flight line.

"Out there... somewhere," Dan admitted.

"How, the hell, are you going to go into battle without your weapon?" Jason asked, knowing the answer.

Dan shrugged his shoulders as Jason commanded, "Find a weapon somewhere!"

Jason stormed off shaking his head in bewilderment at Dan's predicament.

Dan wasn't concerned about going to battle. All he could think was, *"How am I going to get my weapon?"*

Mustering all his courage, Dan Keegan developed a simple game plan for retrieving his gear.

"You cover me," he directed Ski.

"And where are you going?"

With a big gulp, Dan nodded towards the runway, "Out there."

"Out there? Are you nuts?"

Ignoring Ski's plea, Dan continued, "If you see anything that looks like a VC...shoot it dead. Got me?"

Stunned by his friend's intrepidity Ski simply replied, "Gotcha."

Dan knew if he hesitated he would never leave the tractor. Without so much as a "by your leave", using cover and concealment tactics, Dan ran from his somewhat meager fortress to a nearby Conex container located at the edge of the flight line... then to the next... and the next.

Skirting the open tarmac itself, his eyes scanned the interlocking steel Marsden matting covering the flight line.

Nothing in the immediate vicinity. He looked back at Ski.

Ski gave a thumb's up and pointed in the direction of the runway.

I know where the runway is!

Carefully contemplating his next move, Dan's senses were peaked.

The creak was nearly imperceptible.

Oh, shit! Dan's inside voice quivered.

Dan's mind flashed back to Infantry Training Regiment. He quickly concluded that the one day of hand-to-hand combat training at Camp Geiger was grossly insufficient, and if he survived the next few minutes, he would write a nasty letter to the Commandant of the Marine Corps informing him of such.

Very slowly, Dan turned to confront his enemy.

"Are you looking for this?" Jason was holding an M-16.

"Jesus Christ, Jason, you need to knock off sneaking up on people." Dan demanded. "You're liable to get your ass shot."

Exasperated, Jason replied, "And what are you going to shoot me with? Your..."

Jason's snappy comeback was interrupted by a thump.

Both Marines stopped breathing.

After a moment, Dan asked, "What was..."

Jason immediately put his hand over Dan's mouth.

Silently, the Corporal of the Guard handed the wayward rifle back to its owner with a pantomimed command... "Lock and load."

While Jason silently slid his .45 caliber pistol from its holster, Dan tapped the bottom of the twenty-round clip as noiselessly as possible, to ensure it was properly seated in the magazine well of the M-16. Gradually he pulled the charging handle to the rear. He pressed the upper portion of the bolt catch to release the bolt which immediately slammed a 5.56 mm round into the chamber with a loud "Ka-Chang!"

Both he and Jason winced at the noise.

With a sheepish shrug, Dan lip-synced a soundless "Sorry!"

Dan tapped the forward assist to make certain the round was inserted all the way. He nodded his head to Jason indicating he was ready.

Jason started to provide additional instructions but was interrupted from doing so by a sneaking suspicion. He reached over to Dan's weapon, twisted it so he could view the three-position, SAFE-SEMI-AUTO switch.

Shaking his head, Jason rotated the switch from SAFE to the next position with the muted rebuke, "Can't kill anybody with the safety on!"

Another silent "Sorry!"

Thump.

With only a moment's thought, Dan rotated the three-position switch one more position... AUTO.

Both sentries were straining to determine the origin of the unexplained noise.

"Sounds like someone bumped into a Conex container," Dan whispered.

Jason nodded his head.

Dan could see Jason's mind racing as he contemplated the options. Dan patiently waited the few moments for the senior Marine to finish developing his plan of attack.

Using hand signals, Jason directed Dan to go around to the left of the suspicious sound. Jason indicated that he would move to the right.

Pause.

Jason looked Dan square in the eyes. Realizing this was most likely Dan's first face-to-face encounter with the enemy and would probably shoot at anything that moved... including Jason... the senior Marine quickly changed plans.

"You come with me."

Relieved, Dan obliged.

by James E. Bulman

CHAPTER SIX

Infantry Training Regiment - 1968

Working from the premise that "every Marine is a basic rifleman," the day after graduation from Recruit Training, the newly-minted Marines from Parris Island were immediately transported by chartered bus to Camp Geiger near Camp Lejeune adjacent to Jacksonville, North Carolina for infantry training.

Here's where the recruits soon realized the difference between infantry Marines and aviation Marines.

Those assigned to one of the various infantry specialties would be provided general training in that specific area of expertise. In addition, they would be given extensive instruction on their individual job skills.

For example: Mortar men received general training on infantry weapons systems and small unit infantry tactics. Additionally, they received several weeks of training in the Mortarman Course at the School of Infantry. The course focused on the assembly, set up, and repair of the mortar. It offered detailed instruction on topographical map reading and radio communications. Also included were field exercises simulating radio communication with a Forward Observer (FO) who would call in adjustments to each mortar crew after they fired a round. This enabled the crews to quickly zero-in on the target. Finally, there was hands-on, practice firing the mortar culminating with live fire exercises.

On the other hand, Marines who enlisted with an aviation guarantee were destined for the Air Wing. They were provided four weeks of generalized infantry training at the Infantry Training Regiment (ITR). They received abbreviated instruction on small unit tactics, personnel mine countermeasures, camouflage and concealment. They also received training on each type of weapon they might be required to use in combat. Typically, they were provided an hour or two of instructor-led classroom training on each weapon system followed by an abbreviated hands-on session of live fire.

Some weapons were so dangerous or so costly that they were not allowed to handle them. Weapons like the M-72 LAAW (Light Antitank Assault Weapon) or the M2-2 flame thrower were demonstrated for the aviation-bound Marines. No hands-on by the Marine trainee was allowed.

If the weapon was intended for use by an individual (i.e. M-16A1 rifle, M-61 hand grenade, the M-79 grenade launcher) the aviation Marines were allowed to practice firing the weapon using live rounds.

If the weapon was crew-served (requiring more than one person to operate) like the M67 recoilless rifle, the M-2 60 mm mortar and the M-1 81 mm mortar, the aviation Marines were provided the opportunity to witness a team setting up, loading and firing the weapon.

The M-60 Machine Gun and the M-20 "Super Bazooka" were different. Although these were considered crew-served weapons, the air-wingers-to-be were trained to load the weapons and fire live rounds.

Dan thoroughly enjoyed this portion of his training. He was spot-on target firing the M-79 grenade launcher (a.k.a. "The Blooper"). He kicked ass shooting the M-60 machine gun and throwing the M-61 hand grenade. The bazooka, however, was another thing.

After classroom training, the Marines were told to "pair-up" with a buddy. Each team was assigned to a sand-bagged firing pit. With a coach at their side, one Marine would load the rocket into the rear of the bazooka. The other Marine would aim the shouldered weapon and fire at the target a couple hundred yards away.

As soon as Dan and his partner entered the firing pit, he saw that the coach was a sergeant.

"You guys air wingers?" he asked

Surprised by the question, Dan answered, "Yes, Sir."

The sergeant smiled and said, "Good... and drop the 'sir' crap. I put my pants on the same way you do."

Unsure how to deal with the friendly NCO, Dan kept quiet.

The sergeant continued, "See that tree about 25 yards out?"

"Yes, S... Yes," the surprised Dan responded.

"I've always hated that tree. Adjust your sights for 25 yards."

"What about the intended target?" Dan asked hesitantly.

Now with a stern voice the sergeant seemed to change personalities, "Your intended target IS that tree 25 yards out. Do you understand me, Private?"

Dan fell back on the tried and true, "Yes, Sir!"

by James E. Bulman

Taking careful aim at his new target, Dan was jostled slightly as his partner gingerly removed one arming strap from the rocket and inserted it part-way into the rear of the tube. Dan's partner undid the second arming strap from the rocket and inserted the rocket into the weapon. When it was fully seated, he tapped Dan on his helmet signifying the bazooka was armed and the back-blast area behind the bazooka was clear.

Dan awaited the signal from the range officer to fire.

Finally, he heard the range officer roar, "Firing Line!"

The young second lieutenant paused to ensure he had everyone's attention.

Then he shouted, "Ready on the left?"

The coaches on the left side of the fifteen-foot-high tower threw their right arms up signaling all was safe.

"Ready on the right?"

Arms went up on the right side of the tower.

"All ready on the firing line," he confirmed followed by, "Commence firing!"

Each pit unleashed their weapon with remarkable accuracy... with one exception. Dan's "intended target" (a.k.a. the tree) exploded into a thousand splinters.

"Cease fire! Cease fire!" the range officer screamed, "Safety all weapons."

"Pit Number Five report to the tower, NOW!" the fuming second lieutenant ordered.

Nonchalantly, the sergeant gathered up his two privates and headed to the tower. "Let me do the talking," he ordered.

When they arrived at the base of the range tower the second lieutenant was seething with anger. Leaning over the railing, looking down at the trio, the officer demanded, "Where, the hell, were you aiming, Private?"

Before Dan could answer, the sergeant stepped forward, "It was my mistake, Sir." He continued, "Just as the private was about to fire I saw the loader's hand was near the back of the tube. I smacked his hand away to prevent an injury inadvertently knocking the bazooka in a manner that caused the private to miss his intended target. It was just coincidence that he hit the tree."

After a moment's thought the red-faced officer appeared mollified.

"In that case Sergeant, I understand your actions completely. I don't want anyone getting hurt on my range."

Turning to the gunnery sergeant next to him, the lieutenant added, "Gunny, I want a Letter of Commendation for this sergeant on my desk ready for signature in the morning."

The gunny knew the sergeant's enlistment was up in a few weeks. He also was pretty sure the sergeant was bullshitting the second lieutenant but with a roll of his eyes he decided not to object. The gunny thought to himself, *I've always hated that tree, anyway.*" The gunny simply answered, "Yes, Sir."

As they walked back to Pit Number 5, the sergeant saw the confused look on the faces of the two young privates. He explained his attitude towards senior Marines.

"If you can't blind them with your brilliance; baffle them with bullshit." He dismissed them with a sly wink and a parting comment, "That's the way it's done."

Although Dan enjoyed firing the different weapons during infantry training, he did not enjoy the method of transportation used to get from his barracks to the various firing ranges. Forced marches.

A "Forced March" is intended to get the unit to its destination as quickly as possible. There is no cadence. The Marines march at "Route Step" (not in step with each other). It should move no slower than four miles per hour. Ten-mile forced marches were the norm with an occasional twenty-miler thrown in to keep the Marines on their toes (pun intended).

The old story goes: Upset with the unit's lackluster performance, the commanding officer orders the sergeant major to take the men on a 20-mile forced march.

"What shall we do when we finish?" asked the sergeant major.

The commanding officer replied, "Turn around and come back!"

Of course, infantry training included hand-to-hand combat and use of the bayonet.

Using a mannequin, the martial arts instructor demonstrated a handful of jujitsu moves that enabled the Marine to use the enemy's own forward momentum against himself. Pairs of recruits practiced the moves on each other. Dan caught on

by James E. Bulman

fast. He figured out that the trick was to pair-up with a guy smaller than himself. That way Dan could throw his partner more easily than his partner could throw Dan.

They were taught how to sneak up on a sentry from behind and choke him to death with only your bare hands using a hold called the "Naked Strangle." Dan and his partner practiced this repeatedly on each other.

Truthfully, they practiced this fighting maneuver up to the point of nearly strangling one another other to death.

Dan felt that the "take away" lesson from the hand-to-hand combat training was the use of "Weapons of Opportunity."

Weapons of Opportunity can best be described as whatever, the hell, you can get your hands on to distract, injure, or kill the enemy. Throwing sand in the eyes, using your water canteen as a hammer on your opponent's face, or beating your opponent with your helmet was allowed. Biting, kicking, and scratching may be "No Fair!" in a schoolyard fight, but it was "No Holds Barred!" during mortal combat.

Dan understood that this was not the movies. He would soon be going to Vietnam where he could be killed. There are no playground rules. This was war!

Bayonet training was an adjunct to the hand-to-hand combat instruction.

The instructor demonstrated how to position yourself if you are attacked by one or more of the enemy with bayonets. Being attacked by a single enemy soldier would necessitate turning your body 90° to the attacking enemy soldier. This would to present the narrowest portion of your torso to the aggressor. An attack by two assailants would require the single defender to move to their flank. This positioned the attackers so only one attacker at a time can reach the defender.

All of this lead up to the grand finale of the classroom portion of instruction. To impress upon the trainees that there are no rules in hand-to-hand combat, the instructor grabbed one of the loose bayonets and stabbed the mannequin in the top of the head. The visual of the mannequin with a bayonet sticking out of its head was the sight Dan would remember forever.

To simulate fixed-bayonet combat, some sadistic Marine designed the pugil stick. It consisted of a four-foot metal pipe with heavy padding surrounding each end. It looked like a 48-inch cotton swab. Each recruit was provided a pugil stick, an over-sized football helmet, and a double-extra-large padded crotch protector. (And when I say double-extra-large, I mean DOUBLE – EXTRA – LARGE!) Dan was swimming in the thing. He moved about as if he had a load of crap in his pants. Combine that with the helmet spinning around on his head blinding him and you can guess how this story ends.

Always seeing the humorous side of things, Dan decided that pugil stick fighting was the ultimate "Rock, Paper, Scissors" game. Each "player" had to try to accurately predict what move his opponent was going to make and instantly counter that move. The downside was instead of just losing a point, you would get your head bashed in.

The final score was Pugil Sticks-2; Dan-0.

To put it bluntly, Dan got his ass kicked… not once but twice.

The first time, his randomly-selected opponent turned out to be tall drink of water standing about six-foot-thirteen! Dan went down in less time than the 60 seconds Sonny Liston lasted in his fight against Cassius Clay in 1964.

The second time when facing two opponents, Dan stumbled in his oversized jock strap and was unable to move to their flank. The two opponents were on Dan like white on rice. Dan was hit so many times he could not fall. Dan was never so grateful when his legs finally gave way, and he crumpled to the ground.

Following the classroom training and the pugil stick activity, came the actual use of a fixed bayonet on a rifle. Attaching the bayonet to the muzzle of the rifle was simple. Gaining the coordination to use each of the moves was another issue all together.

Holding the rifle (with sheathed bayonet) at "Port Arms." (left hand on the barrel hand guard; right hand on the stock.) Dan, along with other Marines in his platoon, practiced each of the bayonet offensive and defensive maneuvers step-by-step.

THRUST your bayoneted rifle directly towards the center of the enemy's body.

SLASH it across his body.

PARRY the opponent's thrust aside using the barrel-end of your rifle.

HORIZONTAL BUTT STROKE was intended to hit the opponent in his head with the butt-end of your rifle in a sweeping motion.

by James E. Bulman

And finally, the coup de grace. The VERTICAL BUTT STROKE where you attempt to hit the enemy's gonads so hard with the butt-end of your rifle that he won't be able to swallow.

Following practice, it was onto the bayonet assault course. This was a series of stations where each of the learned moves could be demonstrated by the Marine with the unsheathed bayonet. The stations consisted of rudimentary obstacles simulating enemy soldiers.

Dan thrust his bayonet into the center of one sand-bagged enemy soldier. He horizontal-butt-stroked a second enemy soldier's head made from a piece of a car tire. He vertical-butt-stroked the rubber-tired crotch of another.

Everything was going well for Dan until he was caught wrong-footed as he stepped forward with his left foot and parried the enemy's "broomstick rifle" to his left. This resulted in the enemy's "bayonet" hitting Dan in his own crotch.

The instructor didn't miss a thing. Dan cringed as the gunnery sergeant shouted, "Oh, that's just fucking great, Keegan. Cut your own balls off. Just fucking great!"

Personnel mines (land mines) were of great concern during the Vietnam War. In 1968 more than a third of Marine casualties in Vietnam were caused by a detonated land mine. Learning how to find them, avoid them, and protect yourself from them required specialized training.

Classroom instruction focused of the types of mines that the Viet Cong were using. Mines that were triggered by tripping a loose wire. Mines that were triggered by cutting a taut wire. Pressure sensitive mines that were triggered by stepping on them.

They were using mines based upon the World War II German "Bouncing Bettys." When triggered, the "Bouncing Betty" would leap about three feet into the air before exploding. Instead of blowing off one or more of your legs like typical land mines, a Bouncing Betty would take out your mid-section.

The lesson stressed that mines could be triggered by moving the booby-trapped body of a fellow Marine or an enemy soldier. Mines could be hidden under war trophies like swords or other ornate military accoutrements.

The instructor ended the lesson by stating, "Experience has shown that an alert Marine, aware of what to look for and where to look, is the most effective mine detection device."

As the Marines were leaving the classroom area for a break, the instructor asked Dan to bring two nearby jerry cans to the podium for the next portion of the class. Always willing to help, Dan picked up...POP!

Dan instantly recognized the sound of a spring-loaded blasting cap. It seems the cans had been booby trapped by the instructor.

Pleased with his own deviousness, the instructor repeated his parting line, "Experience has shown that an alert Marine, aware of what to look for and where to look, is the most effective mine detection device."

The instructor called Dan to the front and berated him, "I just instructed you on mines and booby traps. Why didn't you inspect the can before you moved it?"

"No excuse, Sir," was his only defense.

As punishment for Dan's lack of vigilance, the instructor took a spring-loaded blasting cap and placed it between Dan's right thumb and forefinger. Cautioning him not to release the spring, the instructor removed the arming pin. He performed the same action with Dan's left thumb and forefinger.

Dan now had two apparently live blasting caps in his possession. He was instructed to return to his place in the class on the bench seats.

Dan quickly learned who his friends were. The Marines who had been sitting near him silently slid farther and farther away from the booby-trapped Dan.

Not sure if the blasting caps were "live" or not, Dan struggled to prevent them from opening. In the back of his mind he rationalized that the instructor would never put a student in harm's way. Therefore, the blasting caps were probably inert... probably.

Dan's mind changed when, after a few minutes of straining to hold the deadly mechanisms closed, the instructor took pity on Dan and re-inserted the arming pin into one of the blasting caps. As he was attempting to re-insert the pin into the seconded blasting cap, Dan's fingers twitched. The spring began to open on the potentially explosive device. As Dan's fingers twitched, the instructor appeared shaken and nervously ordered Dan to, "Hold still. Hold still!"

After the pins were re-inserted, the instructor continued the class, often referring to Dan as a bad example throughout the remainder of the class.

Dan would never know if the blasting caps were live or not but while sitting on that bench, Dan was not going to take a chance.

by James E. Bulman

Finding hidden mines is difficult in the daylight. At night, it involved moving at an excruciatingly slow pace. The Marines were taught to carefully use their arms in a sweeping motion to gently touch any tripwires that may be in front of them. If a tripwire was located, the Marine should, in a whisper, notify the Marine immediately behind him who would continue the notification process.

In addition, the Marines were instructed, if a land mine explodes, to freeze in place. If they were to dive for cover they might trip yet another mine.

That evening the Marines experienced their first live-fire night exercise in locating land mines. While there were no actual mines in use, the blasting caps used to initiate mines were live. Wanting to spice things up, one of the instructors rigged a handful of medium-grade fireworks into the mix to simulate exploding land mines.

The Marines were instructed to belly-crawl down a thin dirt path. Separated by thirty-second intervals, the Marines carefully swept their hands through the pitch-black darkness. Several tripwires were located and Marines who followed were warned. Climbing over or crawling under the tripwires was tricky business.

The exercise seemed to be going well until Dan "tripped" one of the wires and the distinct "POP!" of a blasting cap was heard. An instant later, an old-fashioned bottle rocket soared into the air and exploded in a shower of colorful sparks.

Startled, nearly every Marine on the path did exactly what they had been told NOT to do. They dove for cover.

Dozens of blasting caps along the path exploded in rapid-fire succession.

What ensued was colorful and bright. The night sky lit up like a small town Fourth of July fireworks display. Roman candles soared. Bottle rockets showered the area with a fountain of sparkles. The 5-inch "Super Shell" with 60 grams of gunpowder "finale" had everyone wincing.

Every blasting cap that earlier had been meticulously hidden by the instructors exploded. The entire activity was destroyed. The instructors were beside themselves.

Knowing that they could never determine who had initiated the multi-colored extravaganza, Dan kept his mouth shut but deep inside he was thinking, *That was so cool!*

One good thing about ITR was that the trainees were allowed a bit of freedom. Not too much, mind you. Just a bit.

SWING WITH THE WING

During their limited free time the Marines could check out of the barracks area and go to the Post Exchange (PX), the post office, the base library or the disbursing office. The "slop chute" (a crude nickname for any establishment that serves little else but beer) was off limits.

Even more special, on Tuesday evenings Dan's company could go as a unit to the outdoor theater and watch a movie (or "flick" as they were called by many Southerners).

The outdoor theater may need some explaining. Envision an old-fashioned drive-in movie theater without the cars or the pole speakers. Instead, there were rows of wooden benches. Several large bullhorns blasted the audio across the gap between the projection booth and the screen. The quality of the audio was quite poor, but it served its purpose.

There was even a concession stand that sold peanuts, popcorn, Co-cola (a.k.a. Coca-Cola) and other pogey bait (candy). Each platoon was assigned one evening each week to attend... whether you wanted to or not.

If you didn't like the feature, you would move to the rear of the outdoor theater and shoot the breeze with your like-minded buddies.

Believe it or not, on multiple occasions when his platoon was not assigned to attend, Dan would sneak out of the barracks area and enjoy an evening alone at the movies. The trick was sneaking back into the barracks before lights out (2200). (Still having a hard time with this? That would be 10 PM.) If the movie ran long and the fire watch had already been posted, Dan had a couple of choices. Everything depended upon who was assigned as Fire Watch. If Dan was in good standing with the Fire Watch, the Fire Watch would simply turn a blind eye to Dan's return.

On the other hand, if Dan was on the "outs" with the Fire Watch, he would use cover and concealment tactics to evade and avoid capture.

On more than one evening Dan barely escaped discovery by diving fully clothed... boots and all, into his bunk and covering himself with his blanket as the NCO in charge of the barracks checked to see if anyone was missing.

Dan was never caught.

Although Infantry Training was designed to take four weeks, the Marine Corps couldn't let pass an opportunity to screw with the Marines' brains.

by James E. Bulman

Yes, the training was scheduled for four weeks but thirty days of mess duty was tacked onto the schedule. After all, why should they hire civilians to operate their mess halls when they had perfectly good privates to fill the billets.

So, of course, you can also add a couple weeks of interior guard duty and your four weeks easily becomes ten to twelve weeks.

Unfortunately for Dan, it would last a bit longer. During one of the ten-mile hikes Dan severely twisted his right ankle. Curled up in pain, Dan was ambulanced to the Naval Hospital at Camp Lejeune where he was laid up for several weeks.

September flew by and October slowly became November. The thought of going home on leave for the upcoming Thanksgiving holiday was on everybody's mind... including Dan's.

Then a miracle happened.

The Navy captain in charge of the hospital decided that all ambulatory patients could have liberty over the four-day weekend. Not leave, mind you, but liberty. That meant Dan didn't have to use up any of his accrued leave time.

The Wednesday afternoon before Thanksgiving Day, all hands within earshot of the hospital loudspeakers were informed in the traditional Navy fashion.

"Liberty Call. Liberty Call," announced the disembodied voice, "Liberty to commence at Wednesday, November 25th at 1600 (4:00 PM. Are you civilians catching on yet?) until Monday, November 30th at 0730. (You are on your own from here on out.) Now, Liberty Call."

Dan had never been on liberty and, for that matter, he had never been off base. Dan asked the Navy medical corpsman in charge of his ward if he was authorized to go on liberty with the other "walking wounded" patients.

"No problem, your ankle is healed. Heck," he continued, "the doctor told me you will be discharged on the Monday after Thanksgiving."

Excited about going home, Dan threw a few toiletries into his AWOL bag (gym bag for you civilians) and headed for the door.

"Don't forget to sign out in the log book," the corpsman reminded Dan.

So, in his rush, he quickly filled in his data under the columns in the one of those ubiquitous 8-½" x 11" green military log books.

Name; Rank; Service Number; Service; Destination; Time Out; Time Return.

Dan quickly scribbled: Keegan (forget the initials); Pvt (he abbreviated); 2617703 (almost unintelligible), MC (he abbreviated), Lib (he abbreviated); 1600. The last column he would complete upon his return.

Dan rushed out of the hospital and made a mad dash (as best he could on a weakened ankle) for Swooper's Circle.

Swooper's Circle was located beneath the immense base flagpole on a traffic island in the middle of the main drag on Camp Lejeune. It was a gathering point for Marines with personal vehicles willing to share a ride with fellow Marines lacking transportation. The car owner would put a cardboard placard with his destination in the front window of his car. Marines heading in the same basic vicinity would team up, agree to split the cost of gasoline (after all, gasoline was 28 cents a gallon!), agree on a rendezvous point for the return trip, and the swoop was on!

Dan found a driver heading to Massachusetts. He agreed to drop Dan off at a highway truck stop in New Haven, Connecticut, where Dan called his brother to complete the first half of his journey.

On his first night home, as he and his immediate family sat around the kitchen table, Dan had a grand time regaling his brothers and sisters with stories of Marine Corps boot camp. He even demonstrated some hand-to-hand combat techniques on his older brother, but he stunned his family into silence when he responded to a question from his mother.

A bit distressed by the seemingly endless stories of the harshness of recruit training, his mother waited for a pause in the "oohs" and "ahs" to ask, "Do they actually hit you?"

All heads turned towards Dan.

Dan answered his mother in a flash, "Fucking-A!"

Dan instantly turned a bright shade of red, as he tried to extricate himself from his embarrassing predicament.

"Er... I mean... er... yes... Sorry."

The awkward silence that followed soon turned into roaring laughter from his family... except from Mom.

Dan was able to redeem himself when he agreed to attend Thanksgiving Eve midnight mass with his elderly mother.

The laughter quickly returned when his mother added an additional request.

"Will you wear your... er... your... er...," she struggled as the word escaped her.

Eventually the thesaurus in her 70-year-old mind kicked in, "... your... er... your costume?"

Dan's Navy and Air Force brothers were especially pleased and continued to remind Dan how good his "costume" looked.

by James E. Bulman

Several days later, waiting at the New Haven truck stop at the agreed upon time for his ride back to Camp Lejeune, Dan soon realized his Marine limo driver was nowhere to be seen. One hour late turned into two which became three.

Realizing he was going to be in deep trouble if he was not in his hospital ward by 0730 the next morning, Dan began thinking of options.

There were none.

With few options, he did what every young man in 1968 would have done. He decided to hitchhike the 648 miles to Camp Lejeune in North Carolina.

Standing at the entrance ramp to Interstate 95 South, Dan was soon offered a lift from a big-rig trucker who took him as far as Baltimore where a second trucker took sympathy on the exhausted Dan. After a few moments of conversation, Dan fell asleep.

Somewhere between Petersburg, Virginia and the North Carolina state line, Dan awoke only to find himself travelling down a two-lane blacktop.

"What happened to I-95? Where are we?" the disoriented Marine asked.

"U.S. 17 near Norfolk which is as far as I go."

Dan knew U.S.17 is the road that runs through Jacksonville, North Carolina, home of Camp Lejeune.

"Thanks. You can drop me off anywhere along here," Dan instructed the driver.

As the old country song goes, *"If it weren't for bad luck, I'd have no luck at all."* Dan was having no luck at all. Of course, trying to hitch a ride in the middle of nowhere at three o'clock in the morning was not the best of ideas. Quite aware of the inherent dangers of riding with strangers, Dan was put in several awkward situations.

Dan was offered rides by inebriated good-ole-boys, stoned long-haired-hippy-dudes, and a local cop.

He gracefully declined their offers by telling the drunk or stoned drivers that he was just going to the next intersection. He would thank them. They would drive away wishing him a safe journey.

The Chesapeake Police Officer wasn't so easily put off.

Dan climbed into the patrol car. After a few pleasantries, he was barraged with a series of questions that seemed more like an interrogation than idle curiosity. Eventually, the constable asked to see Dan's leave papers.

None were to be had.

"How about your liberty pass?"

Again, none was to be had.

With a firm voice the officer asked to see Dan's military identification card.

Luckily, Dan's drill instructors had impressed upon him the importance of always keeping his ID on him.

After verifying Dan had no "Wants and Warrants" with his name on them, the sheriff gave Dan a stern lecture concerning leave, liberty, and proper documentation. He dropped Dan off at the city line.

Eventually arriving in New Bern, North Carolina, after multiple short hops through Virginia and North Carolina, Dan flagged down a passing taxi and paid for the last 38 miles of his journey "out-of-pocket."

Dan finally returned to the hospital ward where he had begun his holiday trek 109 hours earlier. Dan was a bit late for the 0730 Monday morning muster... about six hours late.

Upon entering his ward, Dan could not find the log book to sign himself in as having returned.

"Where's the log book?" Dan asked the corpsman.

"The Master-at-Arms has it and he wants to see you right now!" the corpsman informed Dan, "You are in a world of shit."

Dan put on a fresh uniform and trudged to the MAA's office.

The Master-at-Arms is like the local sheriff for the Navy. In this case, this Master-at-Arms was a Navy Master Chief whose job it was to deal with all the problematic Marines and sailors attached to the hospital.

It was about two in the afternoon (1400 for all you Marines out there) and there was a line of servicemen queued up outside the MAA's office.

Busy weekend, Dan mused.

Dan could not help but overhear through the open door the stories as each defendant plead his case to the gruff military constable. Their excuses always began with, "This is no shit, Master Chief." And the Master Chief was buying none of it. His typical judgement began with an abrupt, "Bullshit!" followed by his recommendation for punishment which ran the gamut from stripping the guilty SOB of any future liberty privileges to recommending courts-martial.

Dan realized he was in dire need of a really good story that didn't begin with the phrase, "This is no shit, Master Chief."

After what seemed to be an eternity, Dan's moment of reckoning arrived. And he had no idea what he was going to say in his defense. Dan entered the small office and reported.

"Private Keegan reporting to the Master-at-Arms, as ordered," he announced from the position of attention.

"So, what's your story, Private?"

"Sir, I have no story. I don't know what I'm supposed to have done wrong."

"Bullshit, Keegan!"

Not a good start, Dan thought.

"I've got you dead to rights. You signed your own death warrant."

by James E. Bulman

Brandishing the green log book taken from Dan's hospital ward, the Master Chief rotated the official Navy document. Dan could see his Wednesday entry.

Keegan; Pvt; unreadable numbers, MC, Lib; 1600. The last column was blank.

The MAA continued, "You signed yourself going on liberty... L.I.B... Liberty. I'll tell you what you are guilty of!"

The senior sailor stood and leaned across his desk. He pushed the official log book closer to Dan.

"You went on liberty Wednesday without obtaining your liberty card from the senior Marine's office. Therefore, you have been AWOL since Wednesday at 1600. That's nearly five days over the hill, Private. That's a court-martial offense. Now what do you have to say for yourself."

The MAA flopped back into his desk chair grinning like a small-town prosecutor who had just won his first case. Dan expected to hear the Master Chief shout, "The Navy rests its case!"

Dan's head was spinning. He didn't know he was supposed to check out with both the hospital ward AND the senior Marine. He didn't even know what a "Liberty Card" was. He simply didn't know! Dan was bright enough to know, true as it may be, that story wasn't going to fly. Ignorance of the law is no excuse.

Glancing down at the entries in the log book, Dan had an epiphany... and he began his tale.

"Master Chief, I have no idea what you are talking about. I never went on liberty."

The master chief's face scrunched up as if ready to pounce but all he could summons was a weak, "What?"

"I checked out to go to the library. He spelled it out, "L. I. B. ... 'library'. I simply forgot to sign back in Wednesday evening."

The Master Chief had no answer. His next phrase did not begin with "Bullshit!"

"Then where have you been at morning musters all this time?

"Jogging. I've been jogging every morning since my ankle cast was removed. The corpsman in my ward will attest to that."

Shuffling through his stack of papers, the MAA found what he was looking for.

"Your regular corpsman went on liberty this weekend. A different corpsman was assigned to your ward."

Dan had the MAA on the ropes but decided to let him off easy.

"Master Chief, I guess it is my fault for not informing the replacement corpsman of my daily routine... and forgetting to sign back in when I returned from the library Wednesday evening."

"Okay, Keegan. I've got bigger fish to fry. Next time keep everyone informed of your whereabouts and don't forget to sign back in. You're dismissed."

"Yes, Sir."

Dan did a perfect about face and exited the MAA's office.

As Dan walked past the remaining members of the queue, he thought of the bazooka instructor's advice, *"If you can't blind them with your brilliance, baffle them with bullshit!"* He gave the group a sly wink and said, "That's the way it's done."

by James E. Bulman

CHAPTER SEVEN

Getting There - January 1970

Lance Corporal Keegan had been travelling all day from the east coast with connections in Chicago O'Hare International Airport to Los Angeles International Airport. Tired and a bit disheveled he arrived via shuttle bus at the departure terminal on Norton Air Force Base in San Bernardino, California. It was 2310 (Figure it out yourself.) on a warm winter night in 1970. He was ordered to report by midnight for his flight to Vietnam with a layover on Okinawa courtesy of the U.S. Air Force's Military Airlift Command (MAC).

Dan was surprised to find the departures area to be as large and as busy as any fair-sized city airport. (I guess that tells you something about our involvement in Southeast Asia.)

Navigating through the maze of duffle bags, flight bags, guitar cases, and cardboard boxes wrapped with heavy twine, he stumbled over, around, and on the somewhat irritated supine soldiers, sailors, and airmen who seemed to fill every square foot of floor space in the waiting areas.

Looking around the area, Dan suspected that most of the servicemen (there were no women that Dan could see) had spent the earlier part of the evening frequenting one (or more) of those establishments of less-than-admirable repute previously mentioned. The sober ones, (yes, there were a few) were killing time by playing spades or hearts. Many were reading the Raquel Welch interview in the latest edition of Playboy magazine. (Well, they could have been reading but we all know they were most probably ogling the centerfold of Jill Taylor, the latest Playmate of the Month.)

Dan continued to run the gauntlet of the neatly arranged sleeping warriors-to-be until he found himself in the hardly moving line designated "Marine Check-In."

As he slow-stepped his way forward along with fellow Marines, his eyes focused on the arrival and departure schedule posted on the wall behind the check-in counter. The removable, inch-high, white letters listed three outbound flights. There was only one inbound flight. (That, also, should tell you something about our involvement in Southeast Asia.)

All three of the departures were heading for either mainland Japan or for Okinawa which, depending on your branch of service, were waypoints for the trek to South Vietnam.

Dan's flight was departing at 0130 and destined for Kadena Air Force Base, Okinawa via Elmendorf Air Force Base, Anchorage, Alaska.

It seemed strange to him that they would use Alaska as a way station to Southeast Asia, but who was he to question the wisdom of the United States Air Force Military Airlift Command. (Of course, being the inquisitive type, he did question their wisdom only to learn that the route flown to Okinawa from San Bernardino was known as the "Great Circle Route" and was, indeed, the shortest distance between the two points... on a globe.)

Looking past the counter, Dan zeroed in on the unevenly spaced letters on the sign, his departure (let me rephrase that) ... his outbound flight was the next aircraft to begin boarding. The "T YpE A/C" was listed as a "DC 8ST RETC H" and the "CA RRIER" was "FTL."

When Dan's turn came at the check-in counter he unzipped his leatherette portfolio, withdrew the stack of papers that were his traveling orders and handed them over to the disinterested Air Force check-in clerk who accepted them without looking up.

He placed his sea bag (duffle bag to you soldiers out there) on the scale next to the check-in counter. Dan had deciphered most of the schedule on the wall. Type Aircraft: Stretch DC 8 (a longer version of the reliable DC-8) but the carrier was still a mystery.

"What's FTL?"

"What?" the corporal responded with an irritated look.

"What's FTL?" Dan repeated. "You know, 'Carrier: FTL' on the schedule." He clarified by adding a pointing finger.

Cocking his head toward the wall behind him, the airman's eyes lit up in understanding,

"Oh... FTL. The Air Force charters civilian carriers for many of its overseas flights. That's Flying Tiger Lines," he said matter-of-factly.

Now it was Dan's turn to ask for clarification.

"What?"

Seeing the surprise on the young Marine's face, the flyboy grinned as if he'd just been given a 96-hour pass.

by James E. Bulman

"Yep, that's Flying Tiger Lines: leather flight helmets on their heads, white scarves around their necks, shark teeth on the nose of the aircraft, and John Wayne in the pilot's seat!"

Unsure of what he had heard, Dan asked, "Are you shitting me?"

Leaning over the counter the clerk placed a tag on Dan's sea bag then whispered, "Would I shit you? Hell, Lance Corporal, I wouldn't shit you," he said reassuringly, "You're my favorite turd!" He laughed heartily.

Dan wished he could have thought of a snappy comeback to the crude joke, but the corporal did outrank the lance corporal even though the jokester was in the Air Force. Dan's jaws tightened but he kept his mouth shut.

"Eat shit and die, ass wipe!" a fellow Marine interrupted.

Startled at the retort, the airman glared at Dan's defender.

"Knock off the bullshit and get this line moving, Corporal," the Marine gunnery sergeant demanded.

Seriously outranked and firmly put in his place, it was the airman's turn to bite his tongue.

He quickly stamped Dan's arrival time on his orders, initialed several pages, retained a few copies, stapled his baggage receipt to his orders, and slid the remaining pages back across the counter. He added a terse admonishment, "Gate Seven. Your flight departs at 0130. Don't be late!"

The Air Force corporal grabbed the green canvas sea bag by its handle and heaved it onto a conveyor behind him. All of Dan's worldly possessions slowly disappeared into the three-foot-high hole in the wall.

Acknowledging the inter-service victory, Lance Corporal Keegan smiled at the gunnery sergeant.

"Have a good flight, Gunny."

The senior Marine returned the smile, "You too, Marine."

As Dan walked away gathering the jumbled documents into his portfolio, he heard a familiar voice.

Power-hungry, piece-of-shit flyboy! He'll probably spend his entire enlistment behind that counter harassing the real fightin' men like us. What he needs is a good ol' ass-whooping! Right, Danny boy?"

But as far as him being a "real fightin' man", the truth was Lou Archer, like most of Marines arriving at Norton AFB on that night, was an air winger. He was a jet engine mechanic. Dan was an avionics technician. The average citizen would hardly classify them as "real fightin' men."

They accompanied each other on the mini-quest for their departure gate.

"Too bad there ain't a bar around," Lou lamented, "I could use a cold one."

"...or three." Dan added.

They both chuckled.

"What, the hell, is so funny, Lance Corporals?" a stern voice demanded.

The lance corporals both spun around expecting to encounter a sergeant or an officer only to recognize Corporal Jason Walsh.

From Ohio, Jason was level-headed and slow to burn. Although he had no college education, he seemed to understand why people acted the way they did. His calm demeanor and great (some say, "vicious") sense of humor encouraged his friends to relax. Within minutes they would recount their life stories and confess their inner most secrets. Having a bartender's ear, Jason could typically be found in a one-on-one discussion with another Marine who needed to drown his sorrows in his beer (preceded by a shot of Jack Daniels, of course). When the night's festivities concluded, Jason would be the one ensuring the less-than-sober Marine made it back to the barracks safely. You could always count on Jason.

The pair eagerly greeted Jason with handshakes and a couple of snide references to his recent promotion.

"Boy, they'll promote anyone these days!" Dan chided.

Jason responded with a loud, "Boy?"

"BOY?" (Quite a bit louder this time.)

"Lance Corporals, I'm here to tell you I've been around the world, fought in two wars, made love to a thousand women... (pause for effect) been to three county fairs and I've even been to parts of Arkansas... and you have the nerve to call me BOY!"

He continued, "Why I ought to rip your arm off and beat you over the head with it, boot!"

Although they had heard Jason's monolog many times, the junior Marines were laughing like fools.

As the trio arrived at their departure gate, they caught sight of more of their buddies.

Spotting the newcomers approaching the group, "Catfish" Haroldson's eyes lit up. He quickly wolfed down the remains of a jelly doughnut. With his mouth stuffed full of the USO staple, he wiped his strawberry jelly-laced fingers on a tiny napkin. Grinning, he critiqued the confection with, "So good, makes you want to slap your Grandma!"

Acting as if he had just realized Dan, Jason and Lou had joined the crowd, Catfish continued, "Well, who, the hell, left the gate open?"

The laughing streak continued.

"What does that mean?" a confused Brian Walker interjected.

They laughed even harder.

"I don't get it," Brian announced.

Of course, he didn't. Brian never got it. Although he had the highest IQ of any of his compatriots, Brian never got it.

by James E. Bulman

The story goes like this: Brian applied for an appointment to Officer Candidate School. Admission hinged on the positive recommendation of his current commanding officer. During the requisite interview, the commanding officer commented on Brian's off-the-charts IQ. Brian responded by saying, "Yes, Sir, but everyone says I don't have any common sense."

He was right and, unfortunately, the commanding officer agreed. Brian was not recommended for OCS and was, therefore, on his way to Vietnam with the rest of the Neanderthals.

"Ski" Baratoski (Dan never did learn his first name.) was, of course, the late one of the bunch.

Ski had recently lost a stripe for repeated offenses regarding tardiness. While his friends were quite distressed over his actions and the inevitable repercussions, it didn't seem to bother Ski in the least. His reply concerning his stripes was a matter-of-fact, "They come off as easy as they go on."

The best aircraft mechanic for his limited years, Ski was quick to learn. If it had an engine, a transmission, or a drive shaft, Ski was the "go-to" guy. He loved anything mechanical.

Ski was nowhere in sight... as usual.

They had been at the departure gate for some time when an Air Force sergeant began announcing the boarding procedures. As the devil dogs queued up, Dan glanced out the large pane-glass window onto the flight line.

There, big as a...well, big as a Stretch DC-8, was their ride to the Orient. And, sure as shit, the shark's teeth were missing from the nose but painted on the tail was a blue circle with an orange bull's-eye containing a large white capital "T." Dan scanned the fuselage and muttered, "Flying Tiger Line."

"Guess that Air Force corporal wasn't shitting you, after all," Lance Corporal Archer commented with a smile.

Meanwhile, all eyes were desperately scanning the terminal for their wayward Polish prince. He was spotted attempting to stuff his wad of orders into his portfolio while running the low hurdles over the various service members.

They heard a lot of, "Excuse me. Sorry, 'Scuse. My fault. Gangway. Oops."

When he arrived at the gate, he was greeted warmly by our band.

As they shook hands, Dan spoke for the group, "Glad to see you, Ski."

"I'm glad to be seen," he grinned, quickly adding "... given the circumstances."

The flight from San Bernardino to Okinawa was uneventful. During the layover at Elmendorf AFB outside Anchorage, Alaska, military safety regulations mandated that the passengers disembark the "Stretch-8" while it was being refueled. This required the Marines to walk across the tarmac to the terminal. (Does walking across a flight line on a remote air field in the middle of Alaska at "oh-dark-thirty" constitute being "in" Alaska?)

The entire terminal was closed except for one small book store. Dan stepped into the line of jarheads and eventually purchased a crossword puzzle magazine, a spy novel, and a postcard for his girl back home. So much for his exciting visit to the Land of the Midnight Sun, eh?

When the refueling process was complete, they re-embarked on their aircraft and continued their journey westward. Next stop: Kadena AFB, Okinawa Prefecture, Ryukyu Islands, Japan.

Upon landing at Kadena Air Force Base, they were quickly bussed to Marine Corps Base Camp Butler named for Major General Smedley D. Butler who was awarded the Medal of Honor ...twice!

"Oki" as most Marines call it, was the staging area for all things going "West Pac - Forward." Military talk for "Western Pacific – As close as you can safely be to the front lines."

During the two weeks with the staging battalion, our small troupe was readied for their upcoming combat tour.

While on Oki, they were issued their camouflaged utility uniforms (a.k.a. "jungle utility uniforms" or simply "jungle utes"). Their white undergarments were replaced with green socks, green tee-shirts and green boxer shorts (No briefs, just boxers). Their stateside green sateen utility uniforms were gathered up along with their civilian clothes and packed in a footlocker-sized cardboard box. They were instructed to pack all their dress uniforms into the container except one full set of dress khakis.

"Just in case you get a medal or something," they were advised.

Dan wrote his name, rank, service number on the box...which he never saw again. (I often wondered what the Marine Corp did with the thousands of footlocker-sized cardboard boxes that were never retrieved. (Again, a sign of our deep involvement in the Vietnam conflict.)

by James E. Bulman

The staging process included inoculations... lots of inoculations. The "real fightin' men"-to-be received inoculations against every kind of virus, bacteria, and bug imaginable.

From Dan's point of view, medical injections could be classified into three categories.

The first is a shot in the arm using a hypodermic needle. Those he can handle.

The second is a shot in the arm using a jet injector. That's a type of injecting device used to inoculate large groups. It uses a high-pressure, narrow stream of the serum instead of a needle to penetrate the skin. It looks like a Buck Rogers hand-held ray gun. It's not exactly pleasant when it rips through your epidermis but, so long as you don't make any sudden moves, it is tolerable.

The third is a buttocks injection. Most notorious was the gamma globulin or "GG" shot right in ye ol' gluteus maximus. Those he couldn't handle.

Scuttlebutt (pun intended) was that the GG shot was intended to thicken your blood, accelerating the clotting process if you were wounded. Dan instantly realized how stupid that was. That was just the cover story. Any thinking man had to have known that the GG shot was to protect you against "The Black Syph."

(I can hear you now, "The black what?")

Dan could speak with some authority because he had received the word from one of his friends who knew a Navy medical corpsman who told him the true story about the dreaded disease.

Black Syphilis was so untreatable that, once contracted, the Secretary of the Navy would simply send a telegram to your family informing them that you were MIA. You would be confined to a secret medical facility in Saigon and never be allowed to leave Vietnam ...for the rest of your life!

Several of his buddies figured that the Black Syph was a rumor started by the Department of Defense to reduce sexually transmitted diseases. Dan knew better.

Personally, he didn't care who started the story. Whether it was true or false, Dan made the decision as he was dropping his trousers and leaning over a table in a medical tent on Okinawa that his tally-whacker was staying in his pants for the next thirteen months.

They hit him with the GG shot.

As Dan leaped about a foot off the ground, the corpsman announced, "We've got ourselves a jumper over here!"

A good round of laughter ensued... at Dan's expense.

Marine Lance Corporal Dan Keegan fell silent as the chartered Boeing 707 made its final approach into Da Nang International Airport in the Republic of Vietnam. Dan's group left the Flying Tiger crew and their aircraft in Okinawa and had departed on a different civilian carrier two weeks later. The Boeing 707 in which they were now flying was an older aircraft belonging to a charter airline Dan had never heard of, Air America. He was just pleased that the four Pratt and Whitney JT3D turbofan engines had hummed smoothly throughout the flight across the China Sea.

As he viewed the vividly blue South China Sea, he had visions of his aircraft being shot from the skies by a Viet Cong on a sampan with a rocket propelled grenade or maybe with a lucky rifle shot. He had even heard rumors that American aircraft had been shot down by bow and arrow.

While he rationalized that all of this was just some oft-repeated war story and probably wasn't true, he still scoured the sea for enemy vessels. How he would recognize an enemy sampan from the dozens in the water below was irrelevant. He was going to maintain a watchful eye.

Although he was not a nervous flier per se, he had an uncomfortable feeling ever since he checked in at the Military Airlift Command counter at Norton Air Force Base back in San Bernardino, California.

The approach into Da Nang was quiet as they crossed the coastline of South Vietnam and slowly turned north.

"Feet dry!" he heard a passenger say.

Obviously voiced by a helicopter crew chief trained to inform his passengers when they could remove their floatation vests.

The earth steadily neared.

The aircraft was filled to the brim with Marines. Front to back. Port to starboard. Floor to ceiling.

As the seven-oh-seven continued its descent, the typically boisterous soldiers of the sea fell silent, each in their own thoughts.

Jerry was calculating the number of days in a thirteen-month tour.

Catfish was wondering what kind of fish were in the South China Sea.

Lou was figuring out the best way to transfer to an infantry unit.

Jason was locked in conversation with Brian who was busy drafting an appeal to his former commanding officer concerning the denial of his OCS request.

Ski was asleep.

by James E. Bulman

Dan was more of a worrier. He was convinced a sniper was ready to put an AK-47 round between his eyes as soon as he stepped off the aircraft.

As everyone peered out their windows, they saw the coastline pass under them. They could hear the whirr of the electric actuators adjusting the ailerons and flaps on the wings as the pilot readied the aircraft for landing. A few minutes later they flew over the perimeter fence surrounding the airport followed immediately by the edge of the black runway.

Touchdown, any second now...

Suddenly, the engines increased in power. The pilot pulled back on the yoke as the aircraft veered to the right in an obvious "go-around."

The silent cabin came to life.

There was more than one "What the fuck?" Several "Jesus Christs!" And quite a few "Holy Shits!"

The stewardesses attempted to calm the passengers as the Boeing realigned itself for a second attempt at landing. The engines settled down. The ailerons and flaps were reset. The landing gear deployed and... the landing gear deployed? They had not deployed the landing gear!

The murmur of "The landing gear!" was repeated Marine after Marine followed by more than one "What the fuck?" Several "Jesus Christs!" And quite a few "Holy Shits."

The pilots in the front of the plane were shaking their heads in disbelief at their blunder and repeating the comments being heard from the passengers.

"What the fuck?" the pilot demanded.

"Jesus Christ!" the co-pilot responded.

"Holy Shit!" the stewardesses muttered en masse.

Extending the landing gear, the now-properly "dirtied up" flying machine passed over the small shack near the end of the runway housing a single young Marine holding a pair of field binoculars. Grinning like Gomer Pyle upon graduation from boot camp, the Runway Wheels Watch heard his AN/PRC-25 radio crackle, "Good job, Wheels Watch."

Pleased with himself for saving an aircraft full of fellow Marines from experiencing a potentially deadly wheels-up landing, the Marine was more pleased with his pending reward. He would be first in line for the next flight out of Da Nang taking Marines on R & R.

"Hong Kong, here I come!" He said aloud.

CHAPTER EIGHT

Assault on the Marble Mountain Air Facility - July 1970

Creeping through the dozens of Conex containers, the two leathernecks each had a different vision of what was about to happen next.

Dan was confident that a sapper would surprise them and kill them both before either could react.

Jason was confident that at the first sight of Charlie, he (Jason) would get shot in the ass by Dan. Quite confident.

Unexpectedly, there was a loud shuffling noise to their rear. Both Marines spun around with full intent of unloading both of their magazines on the interloper. They came within microseconds of completing the task when they both recognized Catfish.

Simultaneously, Jason and Dan yelled, "Jesus Christ, Catfish, you need to knock off sneaking up on people. You're liable to get your ass shot."

Ignoring their comments, Catfish described the chaos while huffing and puffing as if he had just run the hundred-yard dash.

"If VC were cars, this place would be a dealership." Then added, "They're all over the place."

Jason's radio crackled, "Corporal of the Guard, muster all sentries at the armory immediately." The order was repeated several times.

"Shit!" Jason thought aloud, "If they hit the armory we're fucked."

"Get to the armory. NOW!" he commanded.

Dan and Catfish did not hesitate. They both realized it was time to circle the wagons. As Dan and Catfish departed, Ski approached.

"Where, the hell, have you been?" Jason demanded.

by James E. Bulman

"I thought you guys had forgotten about me. I started looking for you but..."
Another explosion rocked a nearby revetment.
"Christ, they're everywhere!" Jason shouted.
Ski sensed that Jason was becoming unnerved.
Ski put his hand on Jason's shoulder and in a calming voice assured him, "It'll be okay."

CHAPTER NINE

In Country - January 1970

As the Marines exited the aircraft, the air crew's customary stateside goodbyes were dropped entirely. "Thank you for flying _____ (fill in the blank) Airlines," and "Have a nice stay in _____ (fill in the blank)" were simply inappropriate.

More supportive farewells were exchanged.

"Be safe" and "Good luck" were the departing sendoffs.

Dan hesitated at the doorway. He remembered the sniper with the rifle aiming between Dan's eyes, and with a gulp, he stepped onto the mobile stairway.

There was no gunshot. There was no sniper.

But something else hit Dan between the eyes... right in his olfactory organs.

The smell.

It was the smell that Dan would never forget. With his nose scrunched up, his inside-voice asked *What is that foul stench?*

Dead fish. Answering his own question.

Thirteen months of smelly, dead fish is going to be rough.

This is going to be worse than I imagined.

Oh, well. Better get used to it.

Beginning the day-long arrival process, our illustrious team was funneled through Da Nang International Airport Customs.

"Who would smuggle anything ***into*** Vietnam?" Dan wondered aloud.

"Money," replied an Air Force Customs Agent.

"What?"

"Your money," the agent repeated.

"You want my money?"

"Hey, you're catching on, Marine."

by James E. Bulman

Seeing the shocked look on Dan's face, the airman quickly explained. "You have to exchange your money for MPC."

"MP what?"

"MPC, Military Payment Certificates. You can't bring hard U.S. currency into the country. It weakens their currency and disrupts their economy."

Dan nodded as if he understood and was directed to a Disbursing Officer sitting nearby who ensured Dan exchanged his cash for the new scrip.

The team was shuttled to the Marine Wing Headquarters Squadron – One (MWHS-1) affectionately referred to as "MUSH-1" for "further assignment." From there, they were trucked southward across the Han River bridge towards the Marine Aircraft Group-16 (MAG-16) headquarters south of Da Nang at the Marble Mountain Air Facility.

Although on edge ever since touchdown, Dan quickly realized that this area was relatively safe. The only security assigned to the M39 five-ton "six-by-six" truck carrying Dan and his buddies was one driver with a 1911A1 model Colt .45 caliber pistol loosely strapped to his hip, and a rather inattentive Marine riding in the passenger's seat carrying an M-16... with no magazine inserted. The rifle-toting Marine seemed more interested in telling war stories than in watching the road.

Having never been outside the continental United States, the truck bed full of passengers was amazed at the chaos on the streets of Da Nang.

As their "six-by" rumbled down the thoroughfares of Da Nang city center, they witnessed what to them was a wild scene. Commerce was everywhere.

It made Dan think of the hustle and bustle of downtown Christmas shopping in his own home town except it wasn't Christmas. This was a thriving center of the South Vietnamese economy, not the war-torn shambles televised every night on *The CBS Evening News with Walter Cronkite*.

"Where is the war?" one rookie passenger muttered to nobody in particular.

One veteran passenger, a gunnery sergeant, responded ominously, "It'll catch up to you when you least expect it."

"You've been here before?" Dan asked.

"Third tour," was his brief answer.

All heads turned in his direction. The gunny had their full attention.

"Don't get complacent. It'll bite you in the ass every time."

"Hell," one mournful Marine observed, "it looks like there's no war left for us."

Lou added, "We're in the rear with the gear at Marble Mountain, anyway."

"Don't get too anxious, Lance Corporal. There's plenty of war left in this country for everyone."

"Even at Marble Mountain?" Dan asked.

"Even at Marble Mountain," the gunny reassured his listeners.

He related a tale that had his audience spellbound.

"Back in '65, sappers hit Marble Mountain with a vengeance. They destroyed thirteen of our UH-1Es and damaged 35 more aircraft. We lost three Americans including a Navy corpsman," he continued, "The VC knew exactly how to breach the perimeter and exactly where to go to do the most damage." As the gunny shook his head in sorrow there was mixture of, "No shit?", "Really?" and "Wow!" from his audience.

"How did they know all that?" one Marine asked.

"Spies. One of the base barbers was a spy," he said sadly. "So, don't drop your guard, even for a moment," he cautioned the newbies.

"How many did we kill?" was asked from the group.

"Close to 50," he responded matter-of-factly.

"That's pretty good?" one of the Marines blurted.

The gunny's ire was raised. "Tell that to the parents of those dead Marines!" he admonished the commenter.

The Marines realized they had crossed a line and had angered the gunny. They went silent and returned their focus on the surroundings.

The streets were near chaos. Local drivers ignored traffic lights and stop signs. Horns were honking. Bicycle bells were ringing. Curse words (in Vietnamese) were flying. Police whistles were screeching. Pedestrians risked their lives jaywalking across streets without a thought to the mass of vehicles racing in both directions. There seemed to be no rules of the road, except "Watch out!"

Brightly colored stores with pastel facades announced their purpose with signage in both Vietnamese and English.

The only outward indications that there was a war going on were the occidentals carrying side arms...either the Colt .38 revolver in a shoulder holster or the trusty Colt .45 pistol strapped to their hip.

Several of the passengers pulled Kodak Instamatic cameras from the cargo pockets of their jungle utilities and began snapping 3" x 3" Kodachromes of the colorful businesses, the billboards advertising American products, the three-wheeled bicycles, and, most of all, the beautiful South Vietnamese women.

Crossing the Han River, exiting the city proper, their "taxi" turned onto Highway 538 heading south.

The rookie Marines began to see the more rural areas of South Vietnam. The rice paddies tended by women in traditional black pajamas topped with conical straw hats, water buffalo guided by young boys bearing stick switches, thatch covered huts alternating with small wooden structures capped with corrugated metal roofs. This looked more like the panoramas seen in the travel posters (assuming anyone would want to travel to South Vietnam for vacation in 1970).

The children along the roadside waved at the grinning Marines. Peeking from their doorways, the young women smiled coyly which added mystery to their beauty.

by James E. Bulman

Every few hundred feet small store fronts would appear. These were stores no bigger than a front porch with locals hawking American products. Dial soap, Head n' Shoulders shampoo, Camel cigarettes, anything American.

During the staging process on Okinawa, Dan and his fellow newbies were warned against purchasing foodstuffs or cigarettes from the locals. Poison, crushed glass and other deadly contaminants were a possibility.

Continuing their short journey, our travelers realized that the buildings and huts were becoming fewer and fewer. Highway 538 widened, and the military traffic intensified.

As the newcomers scanned the area for more sights of interest, all eyes soon focused southward. On the horizon, a cluster of five near-vertical mountains jutted abruptly from the landscape. As a group, they were called the Marble Mountains. To the natives, they were known as the Mountains of the Five Elements of the Universe (Ngu Hanh Son).

Dan had heard about these geologic quintuplets during staging. The Vietnamese traditionalists believed each formation represented one of the five basic elements. There was Metal Mountain (Kim Son), Wood Mountain (Moc Son), Water Mountain (Thuy Son), Fire Mountain (Hoa Son), and finally, the tallest at 345 feet, Earth Mountain (Tho Son).

The mountains themselves consisted of marble and limestone.

Transfixed, Dan muttered, "Beautiful."

The sudden combination of a low-pitched roar and high-pitched whine of a Lycoming T53-L-13 engine mixed with the unmistakable "chop-chop" of rotor blades sent all eyes skyward. A single-engine, UH-1E Iroquois (a.k.a. "Huey") buzzed their vehicle.

The abrupt increase in the number of aircraft overhead made it quite apparent that the air facility was nearby. The tour was over. The driver and his partner straightened their uniforms, adjusted their sateen caps, and extracted their military identification cards from their pockets.

The passengers stopped their chatter. They knew it was time for business.

Now 1430, the large plywood sign emblazoned with stenciled scarlet and gold lettering (Not "red and yellow" but the official colors of the Marine Corps... scarlet and gold. There's a difference.) assured the passengers that they had most definitely arrived at the Marble Mountain Air Facility, Marine Air Group-16, 1st Marine Aircraft Wing, FMF WPAC (i.e. Fleet Marine Force, Western Pacific).

Located between China Beach and the Marble Mountains themselves, the air facility's address could have continued with "Quang Nam Provence, Republic of Vietnam."

At the gate, the guards motioned the driver to stop his vehicle. Each passenger was instructed to show his military identification card.

Dan looked up at the two guard towers straddling the entranceway. Surrounded by sandbags, the elevated bunkers each had a Marine keeping a watchful eye with an M-60 machine gun. They smiled at the newly-arrived Vietnam veterans.

"Boots," one sentry mumbled in feigned disgust to the newcomers.

Staring directly at Dan, the opposing sentry shouted, "Better watch yourself. Charlie's going get your young ass."

His partner chuckled as did the gate guards.

Passing through the checkpoint, the truck continued only a few hundred feet to the Marine Aircraft Group-16 Headquarters building.

Surrounding the building was a sandbagged blast wall approximately five feet high.

Like most of the other structures on the airfield, the Group Administration office (G-1) was a one-story 20' by 40', wooden hut raised about three feet off the ground. There were no windows as you might expect. As with all the buildings on the air facility, the glass in the "windows" was replaced with screens that could be closed to the weather using shutters made from sheets of plywood that were hinged at the top of the screen just below the eaves. The openings ran the entire length of both sides of the building and were held open by a simple length of wood placed between the bottom of the shutter and the bottom of the screen.

After a moment of contemplation, Dan understood the reason for the lack of glass windows. Flying glass would be a serious injury hazard if they were attacked... if they were attacked!!!

Oh, shit, he realized.

I'm in a combat zone!

Jumping from the "six-by," Dan's boots sank into the sand.

Sand?

When the average American thought of Vietnam, they inevitably pictured jungles and rice paddies. It took Dan a minute to realize that the Marble Mountain Air Facility was on the coast. Wherever the East China Sea, Da Nang Bay to be more specific, meets the shore, you'll find... sand.

The handful of forested marble and limestone projections jutting up only a few miles to the south provided anyone willing to hike to one of the summits with a spectacular view of Non Nuoc beach and of the air facility.

by James E. Bulman

Caves pockmarked the ancient cliffs. Hindu temples and Buddhist pagodas dating from the 1600's filled the grottos and caverns of the sanctuary. If it was not for the war it would be an idyllic setting for a movie starring Yul Brynner and Deborah Kerr.

The vista was quite impressive from the ground, Dan thought.

Observing Dan's transfixed stare, the driver commented, "Looks kind of pretty from here, doesn't it?"

"Yes. Bet there's a great view from up there."

"Yeah, Charlie thinks so, too. It won't seem so beautiful when they start lobbing mortar rounds on you from up there."

Incredulous, Dan asserted, "We should be able to take them out pretty quick, I would think."

"Religious temples. Need special dispensation from the Pope or something. By the time we get that, Charlie has already cleared out."

"We send patrols up there daily, but Charlie always seems to know when we're coming," the driver added.

Spies, Dan reminded himself.

The driver shook his head in disgust and climbed back into his truck. As he shifted into gear he glanced over his shoulder at Dan. As if in a moment of weakness, the driver tossed Dan a piece of advice.

"Keep your head down and your flak jacket on, Lance Corporal."

"Will do," Dan replied.

Now filled with trepidation, our small troop proceeded to check into the MAG-16 G-1 (Group Administration).

After a cursory review of their travel orders, the administrative officer, a young first lieutenant, tore our clique asunder.

Disregarding the vigorous protestations by each member, Jason, Jerry, Lou, Brian, Catfish, Ski, and Dan were each assigned to different squadrons.

Resigned to their fate, they agreed to meet at the enlisted man's club (Didn't even know where it was, but they were confident there was one.) at 1900. Each newbie was given walking directions to his respective unit. Dan was directed to the Squadron Administration office (S-1) of Headquarters and Maintenance Squadron-16.

As he trekked through the air facility towards his goal, he spotted few "permanent" buildings. Most were temporary wooden structures.

Dan was relieved to see the showers were in a cinder block building, although he was somewhat shocked to see Marines walking butt naked into and out of the communal facilities.

He was pleased that the Enlisted Club was also of brick and mortar construction. From the outside, it looked like any E-club on any Marine Corps base stateside.

And it didn't surprise Dan that the H&MS-16 aircraft hangar was a permanent structure. After all H&MS personnel performed in-depth repair and maintenance on the choppers. The helicopters were often torn down to "parade rest" during repair. Protecting the disemboweled aircraft from the elements was a major concern. The availability of cranes, external electricity, pneumatics, hydraulic power, the dozens of pieces of electronic test equipment, and the myriad tools required to maintain the choppers were additional reasons for constructing steel hangars.

On the other hand, the aircraft revetments were temporary, as were the personnel living quarters.

After a few wrong turns and several dead-ends, our trusted lance corporal located the H&MS-16 squadron administration office.

"Is this where I'm supposed to check in?"

The administration corporal smiled broadly from behind the counter.

"Yes, it is," he added, "Welcome to H&MS-16. We'll get you settled in as quickly as possible. Your orders?"

Dan handed over his written orders to the corporal.

While the corporal thumbed through Dan's paperwork, Dan eyeballed the office in search of the corporal's name. He spotted it on the nameplate on the corporal's desk. Corporal Blaine.

In turn, the admin corporal provided Dan with a list of dozens of NCOs and officers he needed to inform of his presence. The corporal made Dan believe that everyone on base was well aware of his arrival, and they were all eager to greet him in person... or the war would be lost!

"You have 24 hours to complete your check-in process. It's easier if you follow the list in order. Start with the sergeant major then work your way down the list. Skip and move to the next on this list if you can't complete any of them but you must have the list completed in 24 hours. 24 hours." he repeated, "Is that understood, Lance Corporal?"

"Yes. Where's the sergeant major's office?"

"He has his own private office just outside the hangar." The corporal added, "You can't miss it."

Corporal Blaine flashed a friendly smile and offered his advice, "Keep your flak jacket on and your head down. Only twelve months and 29 days to go."

Dan half-smiled at the gallows humor and hesitantly exited the admin office, paused, and turned around. With a worried look he informed the clerk, "I don't have a flak jacket."

"You will," he added wryly, "... within 24 hours."

The corporal seemed like a nice guy. He tossed in another bit of advice.

"Make sure you announce yourself properly before entering the sergeant major's office. He's a real stickler for military protocol."

by James E. Bulman

The admin corporal was surprised when Dan responded, "Will do. Thanks, again, Corporal Blaine."

I'll have to buy him a beer at the club, Dan decided.

Making his way outside, the young Marine spotted a semi-permanent, free-standing raised wooden hut. Several steps led to the door. Dan looked around to see if the building was marked with the sergeant major's name only to discover there was a set of steps on the other side also leading to a door.

Two doors? Maybe two offices? Maybe the sergeant major had his own clerk?

Dan shrugged, "Who knows?"

Before climbing the few steps, Dan used his hands to press the wrinkles out of his uniform as best he could. He took a deep breath and readied himself to announce his arrival.

Reminiscent of waking his drill instructor in recruit training, Dan positioned himself properly, standing perpendicular to the door. Using the palm of his hand Dan banged on the door jamb three times (as instructed in boot camp).

Bang! Bang! Bang!

With a loud, clear Marine Corps voice, shouted "Lance Corporal Daniel Keegan reporting for duty, Sergeant Major."

Hearing a clear, bellowing "En... TER!" from inside, Dan swung open the door.

"Sergeant Maj..."

Facing Dan was a smiling young Marine with his trousers around his ankles, sitting on one of two toilet seats on this side a "four-holer," a four-person outhouse.

Holding back his laughter, the seated Marine offered his advice, "Uh, there's no sergeant major in here but I think there may be one on the other side."

Realizing he was the butt (pun intended) of a practical joke, Dan was not smiling.

Banging on the adjoining wall, the jocular Marine shouted, "Hey, Sergeant Major, you in there? There's a boot camp Marine who wants to check into the squadron."

Bang! Bang! Bang!

"Hey, Sergeant Major?"

Shrugging his shoulders, the seated Marine overacted his regrets with a "Sorry, devil dog. No sergeant major there, either. You might try again after supper. I'm pretty sure the mess hall is serving Mexican tonight."

More laughs from outside the "office." It seems Corporal Blaine had assembled an audience. Dan could only smile and shake it off.

Dan wouldn't be buying the corporal a beer, after all. He decided Corporal Blaine was an asshole.

As for the four-person structure, Dan learned it was built by the Sea Bees (Naval Construction Battalions – CB's, get it?) to provide a modicum of privacy for Marines carrying out certain bodily functions. A thin wall of plywood separated one pair of seats from the second pair on the other side. (I know, I know. Envisioning yourself taking a crap while sitting next to some other grunting and groaning guy was not all that appealing to any of us either but, to paraphrase Walter Cronkite, "That's the way it was.")

The entire structure was on a raised platform just high enough to slide a 55-gallon drum under each seat to catch the... um... hazardous waste. Each day, disinfectant was sprinkled into each partially-filled container.

If you think that was a shitty job (I couldn't resist.), every so often the drums had to be removed, doused with gasoline and burned. I can tell you unequivocally it was not the Marine of the Month who was given that glorious responsibility!

Dan went from point to point like a dutiful Marine following the check-in list in sequence, as directed.

At each stop the sick Marine Corps humor was ever present. Dan ignored the routine cracks at every waypoint on his check-in list,

Dan had heard the jibes before.

"Boot on the quarterdeck!"

"I smell newbie!"

"Stateside Marine on deck!"

The list seemed endless.

At the Motor Transport garage Dan was asked if he could drive a stick shift. After an affirmative reply, he was immediately issued military driver's license Form OF-356. No written test. No hands-on road test. Just a simple "yes" was enough.

The Special Services clerk simply initialed the check-in sheet and handed it back to Dan.

The uninterested Enlisted Club NCO did the same.

Squadron Operations Officer was at least polite enough to ask where he was from. Frowning at Dan's reply, the lieutenant simply initialed the sheet.

The Legal Officer repeated the trend.

The Squadron Training NCO asked if Dan was qualified on the M-16.

"No, Sergeant. We used the M-14 in boot camp and at ITR (Infantry Training Regiment). We did have one live-fire exercise with the M-16 but I missed it because

I was donating blood to a Marine's dependent daughter who had been in a car wreck that day."

Interrupted with a terse, "I didn't ask for your life story, Lance Corporal. A simple yes or no would do!"

"Yes, Sir."

"So, 'Yes' you have used the '16."

"No, Sir."

"Well, which, the hell, is it?" the irritated sergeant barked.

"No, Sir! The lance corporal has never fired the M-16."

Dan was immediately scheduled for the rifle range.

"But I don't have a rifle," Dan reminded the NCO.

"You will..." the sergeant began.

"Yes, I know..." Dan added, "... within 24 hours."

The sergeant couldn't help but smile, adding, "You're catching on."

Next on the list... the barber shop.

Dan thought it a bit strange that he had to check in with the civilian barber shop on base. Upon entering the establishment, the giggling trio of Vietnamese barbers were more than happy to offer him an open chair.

For sixty cents, he figured, *Why not?*

Quickly snapping the barber's cape around Dan's neck, the yellow-toothed barber fluffed the cape over Dan's chest. Using the standard electric clippers, most of Dan's hair was gone in seconds.

Then came the trim typically accomplished with a straight razor... but not here. Dispensing shaving cream from a red, white, and blue-striped can of Barbasol, the barber lathered Dan's nearly non-existent sideburns, the hairline around the back of his ears, and across the nape of his neck. The barber proceeded to use a plastic disposable BIC razor to remove the remaining follicles.

"No straight razor?" Dan asked a waiting customer.

Sensing a rookie, the Marine replied, "No. they won't let them use straight razors. The base CO is afraid they'll cut your throat... or worse."

Dan paled, remembering the gunnery sergeant's warning during the ride from Da Nang, *"One of the base barbers was a spy."* Dan sat frozen in the barber's chair.

After the grinning barber completed the trim and rubbed after shave lotion over the affected area, he immediately grabbed Dan by the head, snapping left... then right. The barber began thumping Dan's trapezius and deltoid muscles with rhythmic gusto.

Believing he was under physical attack, Dan threw off the barber's cape, and scampered out of the chair towards the exit.

Hearing the laughter behind him, Dan halted his "escape" as he came to the realization that he had been the recipient of an unsolicited but rather highquality neck massage.

He sheepishly handed the barber one dollar (MPC, of course) and told him to keep the change. Rubbing his neck, Dan appreciated the work done. Dan left embarrassed but smiling.

Checking in at the post exchange was next. The long walk to the extremely small "PX-in-a-Tent" was hardly worth the effort. Located on the opposite side of the runway, it was so far out of the way most of the air facility's residents rarely visited the place, but when a Marine needed a few moments to himself, a hike to the PX was a way of killing some time. You never know, they may have received a batch of recent magazines. On rare occasions, the trek would culminate with the PX officer opening a new shipment of eight-track tapes or audio cassettes from artists only a senior citizen could love. (Who is Johnny Ray, anyway?)

The lonely PX officer greeted Dan warmly, and handed the newbie an inch-thick catalog for his keeping.

"You can place an order by mail and have it shipped here or to your hometown," he enthusiastically informed Dan.

Dan thanked the second lieutenant then continued his check-in mission.

The next stop seemed just as odd. The soda mess.

The walk from the post exchange (PX) to the soda mess was much longer than he had anticipated. He eventually found himself back in his squadron area.

This cramped closet of a store was in a small room just off the work area in the hangar. Product choices were few, but Marines could buy a pack of cigarettes and some chewing gum. On a metal sales rack was a small display of candy bars (quantities were limited). Of course, the full-sized refrigerator behind the counter held Coke, Pepsi, Diet Rite, or Mountain Dew at twenty-five cents MPC per can.

In the spirit of economic freedom, the commanding officer authorized this small venture with a big caveat. Each week the PX officer would balance the books. When the soda mess receipts covered the cost of its merchandise (purchased from the Post Exchange at Freedom Hill in Da Nang) and paid the young Vietnamese lady to operate the enterprise her weekly salary of $10.00 U.S., she was required to clear all her shelves of product in an end-of-the-month giveaway to the troops. Sales were halted as soon as the enterprise broke even. No profit was to be had.

by James E. Bulman

The petite Vietnamese national managing the store was a friendly face in an otherwise dreary day. Dan quickly learned if you had the twenty-five cents MPC you could purchase a Coke, engage in a bit of conversation, and get a whiff of her perfume. As he offered the young lady his check-in sheet for her signature, she asked Dan where he was from, what his job was, and if he had a girlfriend back home. She seemed to express a genuine interest in the young Marine.

Dan hadn't spoken to a woman since they left Okinawa when he asked the flight attendant for the arrival time for Da Nang. Dan found himself telling the "Soda Mess Lady" (that's what she was called) his life story (albeit a rather short story). He handed her twenty-five cents MPC for a can of Coke, but she refused payment.

"First one free!" she announced.

Dan soon became a regular customer as did most of his pals.

Continuing his check-in journey, Dan headed for the supply warehouse. He had saved this stop for next-to-last because knew he would be issued the mother lode of combat equipment. He was...two sea bags full!

The supply clerk rattled off the items in a rapid-fire staccato as Dan checked their condition.

One steel helmet, one helmet liner, one helmet cover (reversible).

One entrenching tool, one entrenching tool cover.

One mosquito net.

One mess pan kit containing one set of field mess utensils (one fork, one spoon, one knife).

One knapsack.

One shelter-half. (That would be one-half of a two-man tent. The other half is supplied by another Marine.)

Three tent poles, five tent pins. One length of tent line.

One wool blanket.

One poncho, one poncho liner.

One haversack.

One canteen, one canteen cup, one canteen cover.

Four magazines (M-16), four magazine pouches (M-16).

One bayonet, one bayonet scabbard.

One first aid kit with assorted contents.

One cartridge belt, one set of cartridge belt suspenders.

One armored vest (a.k.a. flak jacket).

One M-16A1 rifle, serial number 256245.

And one rifle cleaning kit.

After signing his life away on the Department of Defense Standard Form NAVMC-782, Receipt of Individual Combat Equipment, and donning his ten-pound flak jacket and steel helmet, Dan packed as much of his *"seven-eighty-two"* gear (the acronyms and military slang don't get any better) as he could cram into his haversack, knapsack, and two sea bags.

Balancing the remainder of his *"deuce gear"* in his arms, Dan waddled and stumbled towards the barracks area.

Along the way, he heard and ignored the wiseacre remarks from his fellow Marines.

"Hey, Mac, you got a match?"

"You dropped something."

"The supply officer says you forgot to sign for some of that 'deuce' gear. You need to go back to the supply warehouse."

Covered in sweat, he arrived at the barracks area and quickly located the NCO in charge.

Lou, Brian, Jerry, and Catfish were waiting inside the duty hut anticipating their hooch assignments. As usual, Ski was nowhere to be found.

As a corporal, Jason was assigned to a hooch in the NCO section of the barracks complex.

The sergeant in charge of hooch assignments (the Barracks NCO) issued each Marine a complete set of linens, a pillow, a pillow case and a fart sack (a large bag-like covering for the mattress).

"Lucky for you we have the new hooch just about completed... or maybe not so lucky," he added with a smirk.

The team looked at each other in confusion.

"I don't get it." Brian voiced more of a question than a statement.

This time, Brian's brethren was in sync with Brian.

"What do you mean 'not so lucky'?"

Deciding he had played the game long enough, the Barracks NCO explained "Your hooch-mate, Corporal Hodges ..."

He was interrupted by a chorus of, "Corporal?"

"Let me explain. Let me explain."

The group muffled their queries.

"Corporal Hodges, at the time Lance Corporal Hodges, was asleep in his hooch along with seven other Marines when, without warning, a mortar round struck the hooch and exploded. The hooch was destroyed. All seven of his hooch-mates were killed. Hodges woke up rolling in the sand wondering what, the hell, had just happened."

The Barracks NCO had the full attention of the small band.

"When the hooch was being rebuilt Hodges asked the sergeant major if he could be assigned to the new hooch even though he had been promoted and should be quartered with other NCOs. Superstitious, you know. The sergeant major agreed without hesitation."

Having finished his mini-biography of Corporal Hodges, the Barracks NCO warned the group, "Don't get too comfortable," the NCO cautioned, "Things can get shitty real fast."

The new arrivals were silent.

The Barracks NCO pointed towards their new abode.

"Hodges is over there now monitoring a group of female civilians hired to rebuild the blast wall around the hooch."

In unison, the Marines did an "eyes right" towards the activity around the mini-construction site.

The NCO continued. "He's been monitoring them all day. You've got to keep an eye on them. They'll vanish, go wandering about and enter nearby hooches and steal you blind. Got to keep a sharp eye on them," he repeated.

The young Marines gathered their belongings and trudged to their new abode.

Corporal Hodges spotted them and with a broad smile and a firm handshake welcomed each of them to their home away from home.

After the routine niceties, Hodges reminded everyone that it was nearly dinner time. He asked for one Marine to volunteer to monitor the Vietnamese working party while he invited the rest to dinner.

"My treat!" he added with a broad smile.

Everyone laughed except Brian.

"I don't get it. The chow should be free."

Everyone laughed harder.

Dan explained to Brian that it was a joke. The chow was free.

Hodges had a quizzical look on his face and asked, "Is he for real?"

All heads nodded in the affirmative.

Dan offered to stay behind as Jason enlightened Hodges concerning Brian's unique personality traits.

As the group turned towards the mess hall, Catfish asked, "Anyone know what they're serving?"

Smiling to himself, Dan shouted, "I'm pretty sure it's Mexican."

Now everyone was looking back over their shoulders at Dan wondering why he was grinning.

Hodges reiterated, "Keep an eye on 'em. Don't let them drift away. They'll steal you blind."

"Roger that," Dan replied.

He heaved himself on to a neighboring blast wall and began his vigil. Dan did a quick head count. He observed that the thirteen ladies had split into three four-person teams. One team member held the empty sandbag open, one worker shoveled it full of sand, another tied the filled bag closed, while the last worker methodically stacked the bags like bricks around the hooch. The thirteenth member of the workers was an older woman who apparently directed the labor force.

Thinking about home, his trek across the Pacific, and his current situation, Dan's mind wandered. He must have dozed off.

He was startled awake by a young Vietnamese girl tapping his leg vigorously.

Annoyed with himself for his failure to maintain a watchful eye, Dan snapped, "What?"

"Me got to go," she informed our less-than-vigilant overseer.

"No, you're not allowed to leave this area," he informed her.

"No. Me got to go."

"I'm sorry. You can't leave one at a time. You have to wait and leave together."

Exasperated, the young girl took her complaint to the older lady who marched over to Dan.

"She got to go now."

"NO!" Dan stated emphatically, "She cannot go."

Now several ladies gathered around jibber-jabbering at Dan. Tongues were lashing, hands were waving, and tempers were elevating. Lance Corporal Dan had a full-fledged mutiny on his hands, but being the Marine, he was, Dan stood his ground. "No. No! NO!" he insisted.

As the crowd's furor increased, Dan's firmness intensified.

Luckily, a beautiful young Vietnamese girl rode up on a bicycle. Quite well dressed in her native garb, it was obvious that she was the area supervisor/translator of some sort.

She approached the hostile group and they immediately gave way. In Vietnamese, the older worker explained the problem to the supervisor who seemed to understand the miscommunication.

Without introducing herself, the supervisor faced Dan and repeated, "She has to go."

Frustrated, Dan continued his opposition.

"No, she has to stay here."

Searching for the appropriate words and phrases in English the supervisor implored, "No. No. She got to go."

Dan maintained his stand.

Equally frustrated, the supervisor resorted to pantomime. She squatted, put both hands on her butt checks and repeated, "She got to go...Poop! Poop! She got to go!!!"

"You mean, she's got to take a shi...," interrupting himself. Realizing how stupid he must have looked to these women, he instantly relented, "Go. GO!"

Relieved (pun intended) the young worker ran off. The area supervisor shook her head and returned to her bicycle. The workers mumbled their way back to the blast wall, talking amongst themselves. They returned to their task, whispering to each other, occasionally glancing at Dan and shaking their heads.

They may not have been speaking English, but Dan knew exactly what they were saying.

I must look like an idiot.

He was quite thankful when Catfish jogged up to him a relieved him of his duties.

As he walked towards the mess hall he looked back at the working party.

They were watching him depart and shaking their heads.

After chow, the newly arrived leathernecks began the arduous task of stowing their "782" gear into their wall lockers and foot lockers.

"Dang," Catfish exclaimed, 'It's like trying to stuff ten pounds of pig shit into a five-pound sack."

Everyone chuckled in agreement. Even Brian.

As they were nearing the completion of their mission, three loud knocks interrupted their progress.

"Hey, dumb shits," Jason shouted from outside, "I thought we were hitting the club?"

"Holy shit, yeah!" Dan answered.

"Damn! Is it that time already?" Jerry asked.

Catfish countered with, "As my old Uncle Spurgeon would say, 'It's always time for beer.'"

As if on command, they began cramming the remaining items into every nook and cranny of storage space they could find.

"Dang!" Catfish complained, "I had all of my uniforms laundered and pressed on Oki. Now their full of summer creases."

"Summer creases?" Brian had to ask.

"Yeah," the team responded in unison, "Some are here, and some are there."

The laughter continued as they set course for the club.

The enlisted club was a brick and mortar facility whose exterior resembled any other military club back home. Inside was another matter.

The décor was stark. A few Marine Corps re-enlistment posters hung from the walls. They featured the cartoon character, Mac Marine, touting his mantra, "It's a good career. Stick with it." Most junior Marines repeated a slightly different version, "It's a good career. Stick it!"

The tables were stained and wobbly. The chairs were torn and did not match. There was no pool table, no shuffleboard, no foosball. Nothing except a bar and a juke box which was strategically located behind the bar.

Upon inquiry, Dan learned that each form of entertainment purchased for the club had been destroyed during the numerous barroom brawls that had taken place in the austere establishment. The base commanding officer was fed up with the shenanigans and removed all the machines.

So, off-color jokes, war stories (real and imagined), good-natured teasing filled the void.

At 25 cents MPC per beer, nobody was complaining.

The young Vietnamese waitresses flirted demurely with the sex-starved jarheads. Dan soon learned that one such maiden did not discourage a little "touchy-feely." The larger the tip, the longer she would linger.

Dan assumed the first time her knee "accidentally" glanced his hand was indeed an accident. After the third encounter Dan got the message.

Dan rubbed her knee. On the next visit, knee became thigh. Thigh became inner thigh. Inner thigh became cheek. Cheek became full butt...

"Whoa!" Dan snatched his hand back when the young lady's cheek unexpectedly escalated, not to a full buttock as he had anticipated but to another Marine's hand!

It seems some other Devil Dog had landed on that beach before Dan had.

Dan's eyes immediately traced a path from the trespasser's hand to his arm to his shoulder to the shocked face of none other than Lou Archer.

"Oh, shit!" Dan figured he was about to get his ass kicked until he saw Lou's shocked face turn to laughter.

"Hell, Danny Boy!" Lou apologized loudly, "If I'd have known you had planted a flag on that piece of heaven, I wouldn't have tried to take the territory for myself. Sorry, Danny Boy"

Between the laughter, each Marine offered to buy the other a beer.

by James E. Bulman

As the evening slowly became night, the newcomers upheld the highest traditions of the Marine Corps. They toasted their squadrons, the Corps, the Commandant, and the President. They toasted Ski's late arrival. They toasted everything and everyone. They even toasted people and units vaguely related to their current situation. They continued their toasts until they were informed by the club manager that the club was closing for the evening. Their last toast was to themselves for being the last patrons to leave the war-zone honky-tonk.

They were now all knee-walking, commode-hugging, snot-slinging drunk.

Their trek to their hooch was filled with ribald jokes with loud punch lines that were followed by roaring laughter.

Lou began singing the Marine Corps Hymn at the top of his lungs as they stumbled to the barracks area. His drinking partners joined with gusto. Lou's six-man back-up chorus was doing just fine until they reached the second stanza of the hymn. At that juncture, each member of the magnificent seven took a different lyrical path. The chorus started sounding more like a cacophony.

Their enthusiastic rendition of the Marine Carps hymn was interrupted by a colony of critics trying to sleep. There was more than a chattering of catcalls, a gaggle of "give-me-a-breaks", and an assortment of "shut-the-fuck-ups!" In addition, several empty beer cans were tossed in their direction.

Hearing the disturbance, the Officer of the Day soon arrived on the scene.

"What, the hell, are you Marines doing? Don't you realize there are Marines trying to get some sleep?"

Without hesitation Jason took charge.

"Yes, Sir. Just a little too much Tiger Ale, Sir. I'll get them to their bunks, Sir."

The second lieutenant was not mollified. "I ought to write every one of you up!" he threatened.

Seeing an opening, Jason leaned close to the young officer and whispered some guidance.

"Sir, that wouldn't be a very good idea."

"And why not?" the lieutenant asked indignantly.

"I suspect," Jason continued, "the commanding officer would not look kindly on a junior officer reporting a group of hard-charging Marines for singing the Marine Corps Hymn. You have to admit it sounds pretty silly."

"Yeah," Lou chimed in, "You ought to write up every one of these sleeping Marines for not coming to the position of attention when the hymn is being sung!"

Jason hushed Lou and turned to the second lieutenant who was now smiling.

"Get them in their hooch and shut them up."

"Yes, Sir."

Jason started pushing the barely controllable mob towards their hooch. It was like herding kittens. Just when he thought he had them heading in the right direction, one or more would stray from the herd. Finally, they arrived at their destination.

After tucking his drinking buddies in for the night (figuratively... not literally), Jason quietly departed, leaving his intoxicated friends to their dreams.

Sleep came slowly. Each woozy Marine took turns trying to stop the hooch from spinning. One by one, they would extract a leg from under their blanket/poncho liner and slap their foot to the floor. It didn't work. The world continued to spin until they eventually dozed off.

Dan was the last to fall asleep. He listened to what sounded like the rumble of thunder. Even in his drunken state Dan understood it was not a distant storm but an artillery barrage. The 155mm rounds from the M114 Howitzers would occasionally pause, awaiting corrections from the forward observer. The silence was inevitably followed by additional salvoes.

Raising himself up on one elbow to clarify the artillery's origin, Dan heard a soothing voice.

"It's outgoing. It'll be okay." Ski advised Dan.

Dan lay back down and silently thanked his hooch-mate.

Several silent minutes passed.

Suddenly, Catfish screamed like a school girl and lurched from his bunk. Curse words poured from the Southerner.

"Jesus Christ Almighty! God Damn! Son-of-bitch!"

All hands were on deck.

"What the fuck?" was the most common phrase heard from his friends.

Someone switched on the lights.

Catfish was standing on his bunk holding a broom like a baseball bat.

"It's a little late for field day," commented Lou Archer referring to the Marine Corps' traditional weekly cleanup.

"Well, what the fuck?" was repeated by several groggy Marines.

Regaining his composure, Catfish informed his buddies of the problem.

"A rat just ran across my chest."

Five Marines leaped to their feet and jumped onto their bunks as if they about to be physical attacked. All together the brave Marines demanded information.

"How big was it?"

"Where is it?"

"You sure it wasn't a mouse?"

"Did you get it?"

"Is it still alive?"

"Which way did it go?"

"Are you sure it wasn't a dream?"

by James E. Bulman

Searching the hooch for the rodent, the Marines scoured every corner of the wooden structure to no avail. Eventually our sextet surrendered and lay back down in the hot night...with their poncho liners pulled over their heads.

In the silence, someone muttered, "It'll be okay."

Eventually, they slept.

Someone shouted, "Incoming!"

Dan heard the aural warning, but in his drunken stupor it meant nothing. He felt the forceful shoves from his hooch-mates as they evacuated their living quarters, but the physical stimuli also meant nothing. He felt the ground shudder when a mortar shell impacted less than 100 feet from his hooch. That meant something.

Forcing himself into a sitting position on the edge of his bunk, Dan shouted, "What the fuck is going on?"

There was no reply other than the screen doors on both ends of the hooch slamming shut. Dan struggled to regain his senses. He scanned the hooch only to discover it was empty.

Another round slammed into the earth nearby. Dan's senses quickly returned.

"Holy shit! Incoming!"

His training kicked in.

While on Okinawa, his instructors warned against rushing to the shelters without your combat gear. They emphasized donning your boots, helmet, and flak jacket during such a crisis.

Following those instructions, Dan grabbed his boots with one hand and with the other hand threw his helmet over his newly-barbered hair. He attempted to slip on his flak jacket only to discover the boots wouldn't fit through the arm-hole.

"Fuck!" he shouted at himself.

Switching his boots to his other hand, he donned the armored vest as his helmet began to slide off his head. Dan scrambled to reposition his helmet while holding his boots which hit him squarely in his face.

Another explosion shook the ground.

And another.

And another!

Frustrated by the seemingly impossible task of donning his combat gear, Dan dropped his boots, let his helmet fall where it may, and scurried from his sleeping quarters.

Like the lead-off man stretching a double into a triple, Dan slid into the doorway of the bunker only to realize he was the last to arrive. The Marines were packed in like passengers on a discount airline... assholes to belly buttons.

"Sorry, Mac, there's no room at the inn," one Marine informed Dan.

Another impact shook the earth. It was close.

Making the best of a bad situation, Dan hunkered down between the shelter and the neighboring hooch.

He reassured himself by repeating, "It'll be okay. It'll be okay," until the bombardment stopped.

by James E. Bulman

CHAPTER TEN

Assault on the Marble Mountain Air Facility - July 1970

"It'll be okay," Ski assured the senior Marine. Realizing his doubts were beginning to show on his face, Jason forced himself to regain his composure. "The armory. Let's get to the armory…Now!"

With Ski in the lead, they both ran like the wind. Upon arrival at the now heavily fortified armory, they could see four teams setting up Browning M-2, .50 caliber machine guns at the four corners of the armory. Jason was stunned by the realization that they were constructing a redoubt, a last defensive position.

A vision flashed across Jason's mind.

"Holy, shit," his whispered. "It's the fucking Alamo!"

Ski spotted the remainder of their band standing in a line collecting ammunition from an armorer.

Like a bartender on Super Bowl Sunday, the armorer was flinging and slinging. Handing bandoliers of 5.56 mm rounds to Marines armed with M-16's, heaving ammo cans with .50 caliber rounds to the operators of the M-2 Browning, tossing boxes of .45 caliber rounds to the senior NCOs, and boxes of .38 caliber rounds to the pilots. Many of the pilots and senior NCOs were foregoing their assigned weapons and opting for the increased fire power of an M-16 rifles instead.

Just tell the armorer what you wanted. He gave it to you. No questions asked, no ID cards, no signatures. It was "shitting and getting" time.

Several armorers were standing at makeshift work benches repairing malfunctioning weapons and expediently returning them to their relieved owners.

Dan was issued his 5.56 mm rounds. The armorer handed over two bandoliers of one hundred rounds each to the surprised young Marine.

"Holy shit!" Dan exclaimed, "How much shooting do they expect?"

A seasoned Marine behind Dan interjected, "You'll be wishing you had more if the shit really hits the fan."

"You mean it hasn't hit the fan, yet?" Dan asked in amazement.

by James E. Bulman

CHAPTER ELEVEN

In Country - February 1970

A s a non-rated Marine (private, private first class, or lance corporal) the adage that "shit rolls downhill" held true. They were assigned the lowliest, most menial tasks one could contrive. The most common assignments were barracks detail, interior guard duty, and mess duty.

Barracks detail was the most coveted of the three. It was typically a 0730 to 1630 assignment. Steady hours repairing damaged hooches, getting the weekly linen issued, generally doing whatever the Barracks NCO needed. Assigned for a thirty-day period, additional tasks included making improvements to the blast walls and ensuring the 55-gallon "pissers" were sanitized daily. Also included was raking the "Marine Corps grass." (It's not what you think!) To the casual observer, it would appear to be raking lines into the sand, but not so to the Barracks NCO. To him it was a beautification project designed to convert disorganized beach sand into organized, straight-lined "Marine Corps grass," and nobody was about to argue. Stepping on Marine Corps grass would bring the wrath of the gods upon the trespasser.

Most of the junior troops were assigned interior guard duty (meaning inside the confines of the air facility). Every night these junior Marines took turns standing watch. It worked out to be about once a month. But, like a fireman's tour of duty, it was hours of boredom punctuated with moments of terror. Typically, the hardest part of interior guard duty was staying alert.

The Fire Watch patrolled the barracks area for fires or disturbances. He also ensured "lights out" at 2200.

The Armory Watch ensured the security of the weapons and ammunition. It was referred to as a "dead man's post" since all an intruder had to do to gain access to the armory was to shoot the guard. But, there was an additional armed Marine inside the armory just in case that situation ever occurred.

The Revetment Watches maintained a presence in and around the aircraft parked in the various squadron areas.

While each watch was broken into two-hour shifts, the tedium made it seem much longer. It was difficult not to fall asleep.

On the other hand, Marines assigned to the mess hall had steady albeit long hours. Mess men assisted with preparing meals, serving food and cleaning the mess facility between meals, 0430 until 1900 every day, seven days a week for thirty days.

It was Dan's unlucky day when he was ordered to report to the mess cook. He issued Dan three pairs of white trousers, three white jackets, and a paper hat. To make matters worse, Dan was directed to the scullery where he was instructed in the proper loading, operation, and unloading of the dishwasher. (There were no actual "dishes." Rations were served on the iconic, six-compartment, metal dining trays.)

The mess men were fully occupied keeping up with the thousands of individual meals served every day. Early chow for flight crews. Breakfast, lunch, and dinner for everyone else, then midnight rations (mid-rats) for the night shift.

Up at 0400 and in the rack by 1930.

There was little to entertain those assigned to mess duty, but most Marines have a sick sense of humor and can always find a laugh when needed.

One night after mid-rats, Dan was escorted by another Marine to the rear door of the dining facility. The guide turned off the inside and outside lights. After a few moments passed, he quietly opened the door. Peering out to the piles of bagged garbage, the Marine snapped on the outside spotlight.

Dan was horrified. Hundreds of rats immediately stopped foraging through the trash and froze as if commanded to do so.

Dan's buddy suddenly lurched forward as if to charge the rodents. They scattered to the four winds. Remarkably, two extremely large members of the "rear guard" remained until the horde was safely evacuated. His co-worker laughed like a lunatic until the mess cook abruptly pulled the door shut.

"Looks like the two of you have too much time on your hands."

Both Marines shook their heads in the negative.

"I have just the job for the two of you," the mess cook, a staff sergeant, said with an evil grin.

"Follow me."

The idle Marines obeyed.

The mess cook walked directly to the spud locker where the vegetables were stored and prepared for the next day's meals. Dan had visions of Beetle Bailey peeling mounds of potatoes while Sarge laughed maniacally. Dan snickered.

"Oh, we think this is funny, eh?" the Cook asked. Dan had forgotten the lesson he learned in boot camp. Again, both Marines shook their heads vigorously in the negative.

"No?" the mess cook offered. "Do you really think I'd have you peeling potatoes?"

Without pausing for an answer, the sergeant continued, "Potatoes are too good for you."

Not good enough for potatoes? Dan snickered, again. The mess cook glared at Dan.

There was no stopping him now. He was on a roll.

I wonder if that covers all potatoes. Maybe it's just Idaho potatoes. Are we good enough for sweet potatoes? Dan's mind flashed back to Popeye cartoons, *"I yam what I yam and that's all that I yam."*

Dan struggled to hold back his smile.

"Plus, tomorrow's dinner is spaghetti. We don't need no stinking potatoes."

(*... or badges*, Dan recalled the line from Humphrey Bogart's *Treasure of the Sierra Madre*.)

Dan was losing the battle.

"What we need are..."

Without completing his sentence, the mess cook pointed to two 50-pound sacks of sweet, Vidalia onions.

Dan and his cohort kept straight faces until the mess cook departed the spud locker... then Dan and his partner in crime both began laughing at the thought of peeling 100 pounds of onions.

"This tops Beetle Bailey!" Dan asserted.

Dan's accomplice correctly described the task before them. "This beats everything!"

The mess cook could hear them laughing but said nothing. He had a hard time holding back his own laughter.

Now I know how Sarge in the Beetle Bailey comics feels, he giggled to himself.

As soon as they began the process of peeling the onions, the eyes of the two Marines welled up with tears until they both were crying like housewives watching their favorite soap opera. After a few minutes, the free-flowing fountains acted as liquid barriers and the onions no longer burned their eyes but they both continued to laugh throughout the evening.

As the days passed, our team got down to the business of fixing helicopters. There were many long hours and a lot of sweat spent patching bullet holes, splicing wires and swaging new hydraulic tubing. Within weeks they became experts at combat field repairs.

The maintenance crews were divided into three shifts. More often than not, the off-going crew stayed late to assist the oncoming crew. After all, the aircraft needed to be repaired quickly, and there wasn't much else to do at Marble Mountain anyway. A Marine with time on his hands would soon discover there were additional duties to be fulfilled at the whim of their NCO.

Work, chow, the club, and sleep filled the days.

When not working on the aircraft or not actually on watch, there was little for entertainment.

An outdoor theater showed recent theatrical releases. Unfortunately, the choice of movies was determined by higher authority. The censored films were referred to as "be no" movies.

There "be no" anti-war messages. There "be no" racially provocative storylines. There "be no" drug scenes. There "be no" controversy, and most regrettably, there "be no" nudity. Often the movies had been edited to the point that there "be no" plot.

Corporal Hodges was a true American entrepreneur. He was a problem solver who knew how to make a profit.

Always looking for a way to make a fast buck, Corporal Hodges counted down the days until the end of each month. At which time, he and his hooch-mates would race to the soda mess in the hangar and grab as many free cans of soda as they could carry. He would chill them in his dormitory-sized refrigerator he had purchased on the cheap from a Marine rotating back to the states. He would sell the soft drinks for fifty-cents a can during the hours the soda mess was closed for business. One hundred percent profit.

The lack of any sexual relief was paramount on everybody's mind, but wherever there is a problem, there is a solution that will not only satisfy the consumer but will make money for the entrepreneur who discovers it.

Upon his return from R & R in Hong Kong, he let it be known that he was in possession of a veritable library of smuggled... er... exclusive adult... er... artistic... er... newly discovered Super 8mm skin flicks.

Every other Friday, for a five-dollar cover charge, the patrons were allowed entrance into Corporal Hodges' hooch where a variety of erotic pleasures could be viewed. Blue movies from the fifties (white jockey shorts and black socks included), bondage, S & M, Asian porn, and almost anything else you can imagine.

Hodges's fellow hooch-mates were exempt from the fee. That sounds rather magnanimous of Corporal Hodges but after the third or fourth viewing, even pornography gets old. At the unanimous request of his fellow-hooch dwellers, Corporal Hodges decided to limit the dates of his shows. He quickly learned that manipulating the supply of a product increased its value. It was soon twenty dollars per viewing once a month.

Corporal Hodges supplemented his soft drink and box office incomes by hosting late night poker games. For a very small fee, he would supply the cards, the poker chips, the table, some snacks and the most sought-after commodity... hard liquor.

As with all things Marine, rank has its privileges. Junior troops were not allowed to have any alcohol in the barracks area. NCO's could have beer in the barracks but no distilled beverages. Senior NCO's could have anything they desired.

Of course, any Marine with a little initiative, good connections, and a few dollars could easily locate a source of liquor for poker night. Corporal Hodges was that Marine.

On the other hand, loans were not very easy to come by in a combat zone. After all, you might not be around tomorrow to pay it back. It was table stakes. You bought your chips from the house, Hodges took his cut, and you played until you lost all your... er... chips, or until lights out.

It was straight poker. None of that "red-deuces-one-eyed jacks-and-suicide-kings-are-wild" crap. No "Indian poker" or "no-peak." It was five-card stud, seven-card stud, or five-card draw poker.

Most attendees left empty handed at the end of the night. One or two left smiling.

As for Corporal Hodges, he was always smiling.

By agreement on some nights and by ponying up an extra fee for the house, the games would go late into the night. The additional fee was purported to be for the "guards" posted at opposite ends of the hooch. Their singular task was to notify the players when the Officer of the Day or Staff Duty NCO was in the area.

Of course, some officers were wise to the late-night goingon and simply turned a blind eye to the infractions. Others played it by the book.

Then there were a few who had a sense of humor about it. First Lieutenant Waverly had such a sense of humor.

On this poker night, Waverly made his way stealthily through the barracks area. Keeping low, he wormed his way around each hooch, taking cover behind blast walls, pausing to ensure surprise.

Without warning he plopped himself down next to one of the "guards" sitting on the hooch steps. With one index finger to his lips, he ordered the bewildered sentry to maintain his silence. Dan had no choice.

"The corporal up in the admin office says they play for money. Is that so?" the OOD asked Dan in a whisper.

"I don't think so," Dan stuttered his falsehood.

Smiling at Dan's lie, the Officer of the Day rose and made a "Gangbusters" entry into the hooch.

"How's it going, Marines?" he boomed in a drill-instructor voice.

All heads spun towards the door. The table went silent. Corporal Hodges was quick to react.

As if nothing was amiss, Hodges responded, "Just fine, Sir. Want to sit in a few hands?"

In unison, the players' heads snapped towards Hodges. They all had the same thought. *Is he nuts?*

Impressed with Hodges brazenness, Waverly smirked. "Running a little late, aren't we?"

Straight-faced, Hodges looked at his wristwatch and informed the officer, "My watch must be running slow. I have 2145, Sir." He offered his watch-bearing wrist as evidence of their innocence.

He's good, the officer thought.

"Any money involved?"

"Oh, no, Sir. That would be against regulations," Hodges reassured the OOD as his right foot nudged the cigar box full of cash under the nearby bunk.

"So, you're just playing for chips. No money."

All heads nodded in agreement continuing the lie.

"Just chips. No money," each player agreed.

"You're sure there isn't any money involved?"

"Positive, Sir" Hodges said straight-faced.

All heads shook back and forth in agreement. No money involved.

"Well, that's good," the officer commented as he elbowed his way between two players, scooped up each player's chips and piled the combined loot on to the center of the table.

He concluded with, "Have a good evening, Marines."

by James E. Bulman

As he neared the door, he stopped and cocked his head toward the card players, "You have ten minutes until lights out...Corporal." He departed the hooch quite satisfied with his trickery.

Sitting on a nearby blast wall, Dan was surprised to see the OOD exit the hooch with a smile.

Spotting Dan, the OOD approached and heaved himself up onto the stacked sandbags next to the not-too-diligent sentry.

"This ought to be interesting," Lieutenant Waverly predicted.

"What happened, Sir?" Dan asked nervously.

As the OOD explained his actions, Dan saw the players slowly depart the makeshift poker parlor. Most glared at the OOD. Corporal Blaine from admin waved to the officer with a loud, "Thank you, Sir!"

Sliding off the blast wall, the OOD commented, "Well, I guess they figured out a solution without killing one another."

"Yes, Sir," Dan replied as he excused himself and made a bee-line for the hooch.

"What, the hell, happened?" his curiosity demanded of Hodges.

Hodges provided the details.

"Nothing, at first. After they realized the situation, some wanted to start all over from their initial stake, others claimed to know how much they had and tried to extract their portion from the pile of chips. So, I decided they would play one hand for the entire pot... nearly $500."

"Holy, shit!"

"Corporal Blaine won it all," he continued, "with two pair... tens and fours."

Mail was of the highest importance. Letters from home were worth their weight in gold.

Hometown news, family status reports, along with paper-clipped family photos and, of course, love letters from sweethearts arrived daily at Marble Mountain. (Another advantage of being in the rear.)

Each afternoon, around 1400, the squadron mail orderly (a.k.a. Corporal Blaine) would arrive with a Santa-like bag hoisted over his shoulder containing the welcomed envelopes and boxes.

"Mail Call!" was a motivating announcement.

Packages from home were an extra special treat. Personal care products, home-baked goods, and fresh reading material were the most desired items.

Unfortunately, nothing was private. It was an unwritten rule that CARE packages were to be opened with every Marine within a fifty-yard radius leaning over the recipient's shoulder, witnessing the grand unveiling of its "top secret" contents.

Prior to opening the box, the recipient could lay claim to a few specific items. Friends could also claim items with the childish, "Dibs on... (whatever)."

It was the edibles the crowd desired. After all, Mom expected you to share her homemade delicacies with your friends. Cakes, cookies, homemade fudge were lusted over and reluctantly divided amongst the rubberneckers.

On one occasion, Corporal Blaine arrived accompanied by the squadron sergeant major. This was an ominous sign.

The unit's most senior enlisted Marine was not smiling. Of course, he seldom smiled. It was rumored that the sergeant major only smiled on days that did not end in "Y." Unfortunately, today he was even more dour than usual.

With a bellowing "Lance Corporal McCoy, front and center!" the sergeant major made it clear who was the target of his visit.

The other Marines breathed a group sigh of relief.

Corporal Blaine pointed to Jerry.

"There he is, Sergeant Major."

The unlucky Jerry scurried to within a few feet of the sergeant major. Skidding to a stop, he snapped to attention with a "Yes, Sergeant Major?"

"Is this yours?" referring to a package being held at arm's length by the admin corporal.

As Jerry reluctantly leaned forward to read the recipient's address he got a whiff of something unusual. Sniffing once, twice and a third time, the odor quickly registered in the unfortunate Marine's brain. The lance corporal slowly looked up at the towering sergeant major.

Booze. The package reeked of hard liquor. And not just any liquor but the good stuff. Before admitting ownership of the contraband-laden box, Jerry attempted to stutter a disclaimer.

"Sergeant Major, I never asked anyone..."

"Open it."

"But Sergeant Major, I didn't..."

"Open it!" the sergeant major insisted.

"I..."

"Open it!!" the sergeant major ordered.

"Yes, Sergeant Major," Jerry meekly surrendered.

Unenthusiastically accepting the package from the mail orderly, Jerry noted the parcel was from his older brother in West Virginia. *I'll kill him when I get home*, Jerry promised silently.

by James E. Bulman

"Sergeant Major..." Jerry attempted one last plea.

"Open it."

Jason unsheathed his government-issued TL-29 aviation pocketknife and proceeded to slit the yellow masking tape. As he bent back the flaps of the unwanted container, he viewed a glass bottle of Jack Daniel's Tennessee Sour Mash Whiskey with the neck broken. The glass container was empty.

Retrieving the two-piece empty vessel, the sergeant major married the broken neckpiece to the body the bottle. Satisfied that McCoy would not partake in any unauthorized drinking, the sergeant major was mollified.

"Inform whoever sent this to you that it is against regulations..."

Interrupting the sergeant major, Jerry blurted out, "Not to fucking worry, Sergeant Major. I'm going to kick his fucking ass when I get home."

The sergeant major couldn't help but smile to himself. The senior Marine nodded his head, did an about face, and departed the area with a very disappointed Corporal Blaine from admin.

Jerry's fair-weather friends now felt safe approaching the accused and congratulated him on his narrow escape.

"I thought you were toast."

"I figured you were going to wet your britches."

"I thought he was going to shit himself."

"You sounded like Porky Pig," mocking Jerry's nervousness, "'Buh... buh... but Sergeant Ma...ma...major... I... I... I never..."

The laughter continued until one Marine asked, "Hey, Jerry. Anything else in the box?"

All eyes focused on the package with renewed interest.

"I don't know," Jerry replied.

Slowly reexamining the remaining contents of the box, Jerry removed a pair of now-worthless slippers.

The disappointed crowd booed.

Jerry continued his search.

"Aw, man!" seriously upset Jerry continued, "my mother's brownies... they're all soaked..."

The crowd frowned.

"... in Jack Daniels."

The mood of the crowd turned from disappointment to jubilation. Momma's home-baked brownies never tasted so good.

Several days following McCoy's near miss with the sergeant major, the mail orderly delivered another surprise package for one of our young studs.

Soon after the orderly completed his rounds handing out the day's mail, he returned with a sea bag heaved over his shoulder.

A second mail call? everyone thought.

Well, sort of. It was a second mail call for one Marine only. That would be none other than Catfish Haroldson!

All hands gathered around to see what goodies they might soon be sharing. Catfish kneeled over the canvas sack and slowly opened the mailbag only to discover there were no packages... just letters. Lots of letters. Hundreds of letters!

"What the hell?" the dumbfounded Catfish wondered aloud as he plucked a letter at random from the sack. After quickly scanning the contents, Catfish snatched another letter. Then a third.

"Holy shit," he said in realization. "Holy shit!"

"Well?" one Marine prodded.

As if awakening from a dream, the dazed Catfish explained his windfall.

"My father is the state commander of the American Legion," he began slowly.

"Well? several Marines insisted.

"It seems," he continued, "my father had my photo inserted in their national magazine as a Marine wanting to correspond with young ladies." Looking up at his colleagues, Catfish waved his hand across the satchel like Roxanne introducing a prize on Beat the Clock, "and these are the replies," he ended matter-of-factly.

"Holy shit!" the group agreed in wonderment.

"Damn, Catfish, are you gonna have to answer all of them?" one Marine asked.

"Bet his Daddy substituted a picture of some movie star because that face couldn't be the one they published!" another Marine observed.

Everyone laughed. Even Catfish chuckled.

After obtaining permission to take his windfall to his hooch, Catfish invited Dan and Jerry to accompany him.

Upon arrival at their hooch the young Marines discussed several sorting methods. By state? By postmark dates? By the amount of perfume added to the letter? By the length of the letter? By how well written the letter?

They finally settled on three obvious categories:

Pile One: No photo enclosed.

Pile Two: Photo enclosed.

Pile Three: Nude photo enclosed!

The roommates enjoyed drooling over the X-rated Polaroid photos. Corporal Hodges offered to broker a deal to sell the photos for five bucks a pop with the two Marines splitting the profit.

Catfish declined the offer.

by James E. Bulman

Ever the negotiator, Hodges counter-offered to rent the photos at two dollars an hour. Appalled by the offer, Catfish again declined.

Always the southern gentleman, Catfish spent time each night for the remainder of his thirteen-month tour responding to those letters.

Work, the club, and sleep took its toll on all the leathernecks in Vietnam. Boredom was rampant. Anything that might break up the monotony was welcome.

The boredom finally reached a level that caused Dan to break the cardinal rule of all the services. A rule understood by all servicemen and women, and (I might remind the reader) reiterated by retired Marine Master Sergeant Santiago in Grand Central Station.

"Never volunteer for anything!"

On a Wednesday afternoon, Dan was informed that there was a "bird run" heading up to Da Nang on Saturday morning.

Sounds interesting, Dan mused.

Dan submitted his name.

He was ordered to muster at the H&MS hangar Friday after evening chow for a meeting that would explain everything. He was instructed to bring his rifle for a cursory rifle inspection.

"What the heck is a 'bird run' anyway?" he asked a bit too late.

Corporal Hodges explained, "With the war supposedly 'winding down' (which he emphasized with a pair of invisible, finger-written quotation marks) under Nixon's 'Vietnamization of the War' (another set of fingers), some units are rotating back to the States."

One of those units had already prepared its twelve aircraft for the long voyage home. The helicopters were to be towed from Marble Mountain behind "six-by's" to the deep-water pier in Da Nang where they were to be loaded aboard a transport ship heading for Hawaii.

Therefore, on Saturday, Dan would be riding shotgun on one of those "birds."

Sounds easy enough, Dan rationalized.

Like the good Marine he was, Dan checked in at the muster point on Friday evening with his weapon only to discover the rifle inspection was a ruse. They were heading out now!

Directed to the armory, each Marine was issued two bandoleers of 100 rounds each of ammunition.

What have I gotten myself into? Dan's inside voice quivered.

Reassembling at the muster point, the "bird run" was explained.

A team of eight Marines would be assigned to each of twelve helicopters. The driver and a radioman would ride in the cab of each "six-by" truck being used to tow the aircraft. Two would ride in the bed of the truck. One Marine would sit on each fuel sponson projecting from the sides of the CH-46 Sea Knight. The Sea Knight, being a tandem rotor helicopter, would require one Marine to ride atop the forward rotor blade hub and one on the higher position atop the aft rotor blade hub. The rotor blades had been removed earlier and were stowed inside the cocooned cargo helicopter.

Since the convoy was not travelling the traditional route to Da Nang, the latter two positions had the added responsibility of lifting any power lines that may droop over the roadway and contact the helicopter. Provided a meager broomstick to push aside the highly-charged lines did not bring comfort to Dan who, of course, was assigned the loftiest position.

The briefing continued.

If a mechanical breakdown should occur, they were informed, a maintenance crew would bring up the rear loaded with anything and everything that might be necessary to repair the derelict vehicle or aircraft. During a breakdown, the eight-man towing teams were instructed to form a perimeter around the stopped aircraft and prevent any civilians from approaching. The Marines were cautioned to be especially watchful of children carrying a "present" for the G.I. That present could be a hand grenade.

While travelling, if an attack should occur, the teams were informed that the military police accompanying the convoy would provide defensive cover. The drivers were instructed to increase speed and get the hell out of Dodge. At no time were the Marines to open fire without a direct order from the convoy commander.

Great, Dan thought, *I'm going to get shot at, electrocuted, or blown to bits without returning fire. What, the hell, kind of war was this anyway?*

Remembering the mantra, Dan repeated to himself, "*Every Marine is a basic rifleman.*"

Who came up with that idea? Probably some basic rifleman, he surmised.

Riding atop the CH-46 Sea Knight, Dan had a panoramic view of the villages they passed through. Mostly tin huts and a scattering of wooden structures, he felt he was witnessing the "real" Vietnam. He could tell this was not the routine route between Marble Mountain and Da Nang. They were obviously taking a more circuitous path to outwit any would-be attackers. The villagers were very curious and quite surprised to see the line of helicopters passing by their front doors.

Conversely, the enemy also had a clear view of Dan doing his Statue of Liberty impersonation with his torch-like broom handle guiding the electrified wires over the chopper.

POP!

POP!

Two distant but distinct gun shots.

POP!

POP!

Two more... a bit closer.

Dan tried to determine the direction of the shooter.

Ka-chang! Ka-chang! Ka-chang! Ka-chang...

The sound of dozens of M-16 charging handles slamming shut, one at a time, began at the head of the column and quickly travelled to the rear. Like a pianist thumb-brushing across the keys, each Marine in the convoy took the cue from the Marine directly preceding him and chambered a round.

Nervously, Dan laid his broomstick aside, tapped the bottom of his magazine and followed the lead of the Marine on the forward hub.

Ka-chang!

The ripple continued through the convoy until all weapons were locked and loaded. It took only a few seconds.

Slowly becoming aware that he was the easiest target in the area, Dan lay on his back and slid down between the open clamshell-like doors that cover the aft transmission. It was a feeble attempt on his behalf to look like part of the helicopter. The aircraft skin constructed of thin aluminum sheet metal would not protect Dan from any projectiles, but it might provide some cover.

All eyes scanned the village they had just entered. Any movement was suspect. Any movement could be an aggressor.

"Oh, shit!" was heard from the Marine seated on the forward hub.

Dan looked his way and quickly realized the Marine had no helmet.

"Where's your helmet?" Dan shouted across the chasm between the forward and aft hubs. The man pointed straight down.

"Where?" Dan repeated.

"It fell into the tow bar." The hapless Marine replied.

Suddenly, Dan felt the aircraft lurch upward a few inches as if it hit a speed bump.

"Oh, shit!" the Marine on the forward hub exclaimed a second time, "It just went under the forward wheel strut!"

The loud scraping noise made it was apparent that something was terribly wrong with the nose wheels.

The helmetless Marine gained the attention of the two Marines in the bed of the six-by truck. Leaning over the edge of the bed towards the front of the truck, one shouted into the passenger side window and informed the radioman of the situation.

After notifying the convoy commander, the radioman received orders for the driver to pull to the side of the road and the eight-man crew to establish a defensive perimeter around the chopper. The driver obeyed as did the rest of the team. The remaining aircraft in the convoy continued as if nothing had occurred.

Facing outward at port-arms, the Marines forming the meager perimeter could hear the other aircraft parade pass them.

They were now face-to-face with local villagers. Most of the locals peeked from their doorways or through curtained windows. Very few stood outside their huts.

Oh, shit! Dan muttered to himself.

A toddler, no more than two years old, waddled naked toward the aircraft.

"No, kid. Don't come any closer," Dan ordered.

There was something in the child's hand.

Searching for a word a two-year-old Vietnamese child might understand, Dan scrambled, "Stop. Halt. Cease. Desist!" Dan waved his arms frantically.

Nothing was working.

"No, kid. Stop! Please!" Dan pleaded aloud.

The giggling child continued onward.

Please, God almighty, No! Dan prayed.

Near panic, an older woman, probably the child's grandmother, scurried to the infant and scooped him up. Bowing over and over to Dan, the old lady understood the Marine's fear and offered her apologies in Vietnamese while scolding the child. Dan didn't understand a word she said but he understood her intent. Relieved, Dan awkwardly returned her bow.

As the woman retreated, two jeeps crowded with military policemen arrived on the scene. They positioned themselves alternately between each of the Marines on the perimeter.

The maintenance crew arrived moments later. Dan recognized some of the mechanics. The repair crew attacked the forward pair of wheels. In no time at all, both wheels were removed and replaced with new.

"Good to go!" a senior maintenance man shouted as he jumped back into the jeep.

Acknowledging his report, the military police cleared an opening for the now-tardy vehicle-aircraft combo to re-enter the convoy. Dan's crew climbed back onto the aircraft and repositioned themselves in their previously designated posts.

Well, not exactly as before. Dan regained his position atop the rear rotor hub, maybe not quite as high as earlier, and he continued to do his best to look like part of a helicopter.

Thinking of the child, Dan breathed a sigh of relief.

I had never anticipated anything like this, Dan's inside voice whispered.

CHAPTER TWELVE

Entertainment - July 1970

The most well-known form of military entertainment is the USO camp show. Founded at the request of President Roosevelt in 1941, the non-profit United Service Organization combined the best of the best to provide morale-boosting recreation for service members and their families. The Salvation Army along with the YMCA, the YWCA, the National Catholic Community Service, the National Travelers Aid Association, and the Jewish Welfare Board worked together to accomplish the mission assigned to them by the commander-in-chief.

Yes, Bob Hope did big productions every Christmas over several decades. Bob Hope, himself, supplied the stand-up comedy poking fun at the military food, the accommodations, the lack of female companionship, and the military in general as well as the generals in the military. A typical Bob Hope USO Show included an A-list country-western artist or the latest pop singing sensation, a troupe of leggy dancers, a sports celebrity (e.g. Super Bowl MVP or Heisman Trophy winner), the most recent national beauty contest winner, and finally, the latest buxom bombshell to hit the silver screen. Ann-Margret, Joey Heatherton, Connie Stevens and Raquel Welch were crowd favorites.

Yes, they were much appreciated.

Yes, Bob Hope should be applauded for his dedication to the soldiers, sailors, airmen and Marines but he wasn't the only act that played "in country."

Two of the first entertainers to visit the troops in Vietnam were cowboy and cowgirl movie superstars Roy Rogers and Dale Evans. Roy and Dale actually met during a stateside USO camp show in the 1940's.

Comedienne Martha Raye made numerous trips to South Vietnam. Paying for many of the trips herself, she did much more than entertain. There are multiple accounts of Raye rolling up her sleeves and assisting medical personnel treating wounded soldiers.

Many lesser known, less publicized artists risked the perils of performing in the middle of a war zone. Newly-formed musical groups and single artists from stateside honed their talents and perfected their performances in front of eager military audiences before returning stateside to much tougher crowds.

Entertainers from other countries also toured Vietnam. Some with official USO sponsorship. Some without. Some were simply earning a living performing at various military bases.

Groups from the Philippines, Japan, and Australia that performed in less spectacular productions before tiny audiences at more extreme outposts were as welcome as the big acts. Typically, the songs were more rock-and-roll than pop. The jokes were bawdier. And, most importantly, the female entertainers were much more flirtatious.

The biggest problem with each of these shows was security. Showtimes were not announced until the day of the performance, or on rare occasions, the day before.

At the Marble Mountain Air Facility, the rumors started several days earlier. There was a USO show coming to town!

It was impossible to keep it "hush-hush." The enlisted club manager was responsible for setting up the stage and the equipment. The details may have been a mystery, but the scuttlebutt ran the gamut. Would it be Bob Hope? Joey Heatherton? Ann Margret? The speculation ran wild, but if you needed to know anything about anything, the soda mess lady always had the inside information.

She let everyone know the band was "*The Rock and Roll Review*" out of Australia. The show was to be a standard all-male rock-and-roll quartet (drummer, lead guitarist, bass guitarist, and rhythm guitarist.) The rhythm guitarist also performed vocals and acted as the front man. It would begin immediately following evening chow at approximately 1830 on Friday at the outdoor theater.

Unfortunately for Jason, he was assigned Corporal of the Guard that night. Dan and Ski were just as unlucky having been assigned to revetment watches. They would walk their posts to the rhythm of distance rock and roll music.

When the day arrived, Marines started gathering at the venue just after lunch. The supper meal at the mess hall was near empty as showtime neared. The crowd grew larger and larger. Several scuffles broke out. It seems there were Marines squeezing through the crowd trying to get a better view.

The military police were called in to control the increasingly rowdy assemblage. There were several pushing and shoving matches going on until the base commander announced from the makeshift stage that the show would not begin until the crowd settled down.

Calm quickly returned to the group as fellow leathernecks hushed one another and threatened misbehavers with sure death if they caused the show to be delayed or cancelled.

After conferring with the Officer of the Day, the club manager asked for volunteers to relocate a couple speakers to enable the Marines in the distant seating area to enjoy the performance. This further calmed the crowd.

About 45 minutes late, the musical group made their entrance, plugged in their guitars, and prepared their instruments as the front man welcomed the leathernecks with, "G'day, Yanks. We're the *Rock and Roll Review* out of Sidney, Australia."

Applause and whistles let the Aussies know they were quite welcome.

The lead singer looked over the crowd apparently searching for something.

"Hey, mates..." acting shocked, "where are all the women?"

The crowd hooted and hollered answers.

"What women?"

"Stateside!"

"The Army's got them all!"

The lead singer shook his head in disappointment.

"Damn, I guess I'll have to take matters into my own hands!"

The Marines roared with laughter.

The lead man then shouted, "Are you ready to rock?"

The Marines cheered enthusiastically.

The group lead with Sam the Sham and the Pharaohs' monster hit "*Wooly Bully*" beginning with its famous countdown:

"*Uno. Dos. One. Two. Three. Quatro!*"

The crowd sang along to the nonsensical lyrics:

"*Mattie told Hattie*
'Bout a thang she saw
With two big horns
And a wooly jaw" (or "*wooly dog*" to at least half of the crowd).

The entertainment continued until intermission. The band was critiqued by all comers as the best band ever to play at Marble Mountain.

The second set opened as night approached. Spotlights had been installed for the occasion. The lead singer stood in silence a few feet from the microphone for several seconds. This dramatic pause encouraged the crowd to settle down. The silence fed on itself as the audience quieted.

Stepping up to the mic the lead singer emoted his most mournful expression and with a deep voice began singing Eric Burden and the Animals' hit, which became an anthem in Vietnam:

"*In this dirty old part of the city*
Where the sun refused to shine

by James E. Bulman

People tell me, there ain't no use in trying."

The crowd mumbled the next few lines anticipating the call-and-response buildup to the chorus with the jarheads shouting, more than singing:

"Work! Work! Work! Work!
We gotta get out of this place.
If it's the last thing we ever do.
We gotta get out of this place.
'Cause girl, there's a better life for me and you."

The song had everyone singing at the tops of their lungs. Marines were dancing with other Marines. In 1960's parlance, it was a "happening." Everyone was having a grand time... until three loud explosions interrupted the festivities. Sirens immediately overpowered the music. The Australians seemed unsure as to what was occurring. Electricity was quickly cut off and the air facility went dark.

One by one, individuals broke away from the impromptu block party and rushed to the shelters. Larger groups followed until mass confusion reigned. Unsure of the location of the closest shelters, Marines were running in all directions. Some Marines ran towards the shelter in their living quarters dozens of yards from the stage. The first three mortar rounds exploded near the van complex on the beach.

It was every man for himself.

Squeezing into a nearly full shelter Lou, Jerry, Brian and Catfish were barely concealed but at least had some protection. All sat quietly each knowing the next round could impact their shelter.

Lou was the first to break the silence, "Damn! Jason's got the duty tonight. He's probably knee deep in shit about now."

Catfish chimed in. "Dan and Ski are both on revetment watch, and it's hotter than a Billy goat's ass in a pepper patch out there."

"What's that mean?" Brian asked but nobody answered.

"We need to get out of here and find them. They'll need all the help they can get tonight." Lou assumed the three would not hesitate to help out their buddies in a tight situation.

He was correct.

They left the somewhat secure confines of the bunker in search of Jason, Dan and Ski.

Jason reported to the Officer of the Day who was, himself, gathering .38 caliber rounds from the armory.

"Are all your sentries accounted for?" the first lieutenant asked.

"Yes, Sir, I..."

The first lieutenant cut him off.

"Good. Get every man you can and set up a defensive position at the rear of the van complex."

Jason was incredulous. *The Viet Cong don't attack from the sea! Marines do!*

"They're coming from the beach?" a stunned Jason asked.

"They're coming from every fucking where, Corporal!" the Officer of the Day shouted. "Get your men on the beach. Let me know immediately if you see anything. Don't let one Goddamn VC through. Do you understand me? Not one Goddamn VC. Got it?"

"Yes, Sir! Got it." Jason's voice was starting to quiver.

"GO!" the Officer of the Day commanded.

Jason's sentries were gathering at one corner of the armory along with a mismatched bunch of air wingers... aircraft mechanics, avionics technicians, welders, hydraulics men, and to top it off, Corporal Blaine from admin. Upon the arrival of Lou, Jerry, Catfish and Brian, all were lance corporals except for Jason and Corporal Blaine. Of course, in Ski's case, one Private First Class.

Jason motioned the motley crew to gather around.

"School circle!" he ordered. The ad hoc team edged closer.

"Has everyone been issued ammo?" All hands nodded in affirmation.

Trying to appear calm, Jason kept his words to a minimum.

"Charlie may be coming in from the beach..."

There was a murmur of astonishment from the Marines.

Jason ordered his small band to double-time to the rear of the van complex. Jason planned to position his men behind anything that might offer protective cover.

"Follow me to the rear of the vans."

"Whoa, Mac! I'm an admin clerk... a Remington Raider... a clerk typist. I'm not supposed to get my ass killed playing fucking grunt!" Corporal Blaine protested.

Before Jason could respond, Lou Archer snatched the senior Marine by the collar with his left hand and forced him backwards against the armory wall. Clearly and succinctly he explained to the corporal, "If you want to live to see tomorrow, you'll do what the Corporal of the Guard says. Tonight, we're all fucking riflemen. Understood?"

Catfish, Jerry, Brian, Ski, and Dan stepped closer to ensure the admin corporal understood.

The corporal nodded his understanding.

by James E. Bulman

Three mortar rounds impacted in quick succession striking the H&MS hangar. More helicopters were damaged. Probably more Marines injured.

The situation was not looking good.

Upon arrival at the rear of the van complex, Jason positioned each of his Marines as best he could.

Several additional Marines scampered up to Jason seeking guidance.

"The OOD told us to join your unit," one of the latecomers informed him.

Unit? Jerry thought. *This is no unit. It's a hodge-podge of inexperienced air wingers. What am I supposed to do with these rookies? Hell,* his thoughts continued, *I'm a rookie at this shit, too!*

Having been a squad leader in boot camp gave him some idea about military leadership but his training was very basic. (Hence the title "basic training.")

Four weeks at Camp Geiger at the Infantry Training Regiment gave all aviation Marines an hour or two of training on each weapon they might use during an actual attack. Unfortunately, that little bit of experience with the Marine Corps arsenal was one thing. Leading men into battle was a whole different matter.

Jason used the newly-arrived men to plug the gaps in his defensive line.

Suddenly several flares illuminated over the beach.

Were they ours or theirs? Jason feared the worst.

Blinded by the bright light, all eyes squinted towards the water.

Nothing.

Then a loud "FUCK!" came from one of his troops followed by similar expletives from numerous Marines.

Seeing nothing, Jason decided not to take any chances.

"Lock and load! Lock and load!" He commanded.

Most of the crew had already done so on their own volition but a few tardy "Ka-changs" could be heard.

"Steady," Jason cautioned his soon-to-be-warriors. "Steady."

Scanning the field in front of him, Jason's mind was racing.

Where, the hell, are they?

What kind of war was this anyway? Dan questioned. *Jason's in charge of a rag-tag group of stragglers who have never seen the enemy, never been in battle, and never fired their weapons in anger.* Dan continued his thoughts. *Hell, neither has Jason!*

Looking up and down the line Dan could see the trepidation on the faces of Jason's young charges. Tension smothered the re-assigned aviators like a fog.

Every sound, every creak, every snap of a twig brought a dozen rifles to bear, maintaining their aim until the noise was identified and the immediacy of battle subsided... for the moment.

Any whispered word was immediately hushed by nearby Marines.

They were well-aware of the stakes. Now was not the time for idle chatter or gallows humor.

This was real. This is what they had trained for.

This was why all Marines are indoctrinated in the Marine Corps mantra, "Every Marine is a basic rifleman."

I never anticipated anything like this. Dan's mind raced. Drawing on all the tactical knowledge gained from his Marine training, all the military books he had read, all the history lessons he had attended, and all the John Wayne movies he had seen, he could add nothing to Jason's game plan... if Jason had one.

All Dan could think of were movies like *The Alamo*, *Gunga Din*, *Bataan*, and *Beau Gueste*. All movies about fighting to the death. They were not very encouraging at all.

Everyone could see that Jason was gaining confidence in his defense plan.

It seemed apparent that the powers-that-be didn't believe the beach was the point of attack. If they thought that it was, they (the powers-that-be, that is) would have placed more seasoned ground units to this sector, Dan rationalized.

But, this could be the site of a diversionary attach by the enemy to draw forces away from the main assault somewhere else. This may very well be where the battle is to begin.

Battle. Dan thought, *I'm about to go into battle. We will all soon be battle-hardened Marines... or dead ones.*

Of course, the harshness of boot camp and thoroughness of infantry training prepared young Marines for just this moment. Marines are indoctrinated to believe that it's the other guy who will die. It reminded Dan of the old story of the general briefing the ten Marines who volunteered for a dangerous mission.

"We expect 90% casualties," *the general warned them.*

Each Marine looked up and down the line thinking the same thought, "Damn, I'm going to miss these guys!"

by James E. Bulman

Dan could see Jason looking up and down the line. He, too, saw the nervousness on the faces of the young men on the line.

This was, in reality, why many of these young men had chosen the Marine Corps over the other services... the allure of testing one's mettle under fire.

Each Marine was in his own thoughts. Some had visions of medals being pinned to their chests for gallantry above and beyond the call of duty. Most had hopes of simply making it through the night's ordeal without looking like a coward. Of course, there were others on this defensive line who feared the worst...dying in a firefight halfway around the world, in a God forsaken country nobody had ever heard of, on an obscure patch of earth nobody cares about and being shipped home in a flagged-draped coffin.

"I hate this place!" one Marine vented loudly.

CHAPTER THIRTEEN

Staff Sergeant Wordsworth - March 1970

All servicemen and women complain. It's natural. Marines are no different. Marines complain about the food, the living quarters, the pay, and the lack of _____ (fill in the blank).

The difference between Marines and members of the other services is Marines only complain to each other and only to Marines of the same pay grade. Privates complain to other privates. Corporals complain to other corporals. Sergeants complain to other sergeants. You seldom hear a Marine NCO complaining to junior troops. And you rarely hear a senior NCO complaining about his superiors.

Staff Sergeant Wordsworth was the exception. Unfortunately for him, his reputation preceded him. When made aware of Wordsworth's pending arrival, the commanding officer of the squadron commented to the unit's senior enlisted man, "Sergeant Major, if Ho Chi Minh walked through this air facility's front gate right now, arm-in-arm with Staff Sergeant Wordsworth, half of the Marines in this squadron would groan, 'Oh, shit! Here comes Wordsworth!'"

Staff Sergeant Wordsworth could not relay an order without ensuring everyone understood that it wasn't his idea, unless there were successful results. Then, of course, it was all his doing.

The opposite also held true. If the outcome of one of his own ideas was not up to standards, Wordsworth would find a junior Marine to blame.

Oh, he preached a good sermon. Integrity, leadership, loyalty, but he was loyal to only one entity... himself.

by James E. Bulman

When Wordsworth first arrived at the Marble Mountain Air Facility, the sergeant major had been forewarned by other sergeants major. One summed up the staff sergeant's leadership skills by commenting, "Hell! He couldn't lead a train through a tunnel."

The junior troops quickly figured him out, as did the senior NCOs and officers.

The day he checked into Dan's unit, Wordsworth gathered up all his subordinates and began a monologue of his life story, including all his military achievements. Claiming to be the Marine Corps' finest helicopter mechanic, his self-aggrandizing lecture culminated with a Purple Heart and Bronze Star heroics. It was certainly impressive... if it was true.

Wordsworth's braggadocio left most of his men quite skeptical. True heroes don't brag. They don't have to.

"Probably shot himself in the ass playing 'quick-draw'," one Marine whispered.

"More likely fragged by one of his own men," another suggested.

It didn't take long before the troops set out to prove whether Wordsworth was as good as he claimed. Feigning ignorance on every problem that came their way, junior troops would search out the staff sergeant for guidance.

It became evident the senior Marine knew very little about helicopter maintenance and repair. It was also evident he had most likely gotten as far as he did by taking credit for other Marines' efforts.

Wordsworth thought he could disguise his lack of technical ability by employing one of his favorite tricks. He would "test" the younger Marines about an aircraft problem.

"I'm just checking to see how much you know," he would begin. "If you were to tackle this problem what would you do first?" Translation: "I haven't a clue where to begin. I need you to show me."

The use of this not-so-subtle ploy soon became obvious and Marines would purposefully lead him astray.

Dan was the first to prove Staff Sergeant Wordsworth's technical abilities were lacking. While troubleshooting a minor electrical problem on an aircraft that was ready to launch on a mission, the pilot asked Dan.

"How long will this take, Lance Corporal?"

"Only a few min..." Dan's response was interrupted by Staff Sergeant Wordsworth.

"You never know, Sir. Some of these electrical problems can be a bit tricky. Don't want to give you false hope but I trained my men well. Lance Corporal Kergan (mispronouncing Dan's name) will get you up and flying as quickly as possible."

The pilot and co-pilot looked at each other and rolled their eyes.

Completing his troubleshooting, Dan removed a fuse from the system and announced matter-of-factly, "Blown fuse."

Wordsworth had a quizzical look on his face, "How can you tell? It's a ceramic fuse. You can't see the filament inside, and you don't have an ohm-meter to check it."

Not missing out on an opportunity, Dan answered, "I did the "lip check."

The pilots looked at each other and wondered what Dan was taking about.

"The lip check?" Wordsworth repeated.

"You never heard of the 'lip check?'" Dan acted astonished.

"It's commonly used in combat operations," Dan informed the staff sergeant as if everybody knew.

Dan demonstrated the mystical technique by placing one end of the inch-long cylindrical fuse on his lips and tapped on the other end with his finger.

"Yep, it's bad."

"Bullshit!" the staff sergeant blurted out.

"Well, if you want to verify it, let's go to the shop and see if I'm correct or not."

When they reached the shop, the indignant staff sergeant snatched the suspect fuse from Dan's hand. Placing the meter leads on opposite ends of the fuse, Wordsworth was amazed that the meter proved Dan to be correct. The fuse was most certainly blown.

Continuing his ploy, Dan grabbed a replacement fuse from the new parts cabinet and performed the "lip check" one more time.

"Yep, this one is good."

The disbelieving staff sergeant snatched the replacement fuse from Dan's hand. Placing the ohm-meter leads on opposite ends of the fuse, Wordsworth was again amazed that the meter proved Dan to be correct. The replacement fuse was indeed good.

Still not truly converted, Staff Sergeant Wordsworth informed Dan, "I'll take it to the aircraft. You finish up the paperwork." Translation: *You stay back here so I can take credit for troubleshooting and repairing the system*, Dan realized as he shook his head.

Dan gathered together his compatriots and informed them of his little "lip check" trick.

"I don't get it," Brian said, once again, "You can't check a fuse that way."

Dan quickly explained.

"Look, I've troubleshot these systems before. The fuse in the aircraft was most likely blown. So, it "lip checked" bad. The replacement fuse came out of the new parts cabinet. It was most likely good. Therefore, it "lip checked" "good."

The trickster and his band of troublemakers crammed to look out the small window facing the flight line to witness Wordsworth walking out to the awaiting aircraft... with the one end of new fuse in his mouth while he continually tapped the opposite end of the fuse.

by James E. Bulman

The team roared with laughter.

It quickly became a contest as to who could best reveal Staff Sergeant Wordsworth's technical incompetence. They tried all the routine tricks. He wouldn't fall for most of them. He wouldn't fetch "flight line" (It's not rope but the area where the aircraft are parked) or "prop wash" (It's not detergent but the propeller-generated wind behind the aircraft), or "rotor wash" (same as prop wash but from helicopter rotor blades). He didn't fall for the "left-handed monkey wrench" or the "reverse rivet." Just when you thought he had figured out all the gags, he would fall for another.

One afternoon Staff Sergeant Wordsworth informed the gunnery sergeant in charge of the shop, he was going to the head "to take a crap."

Jerry chimed in with, "I heard they finally received the new combat toilet paper."

"The combat what?" Wordsworth took the bait.

A nearby gunnery sergeant overheard the conversation. He knew how this gag would end. The gunny thought about halting the prank but decided to let it run its course. He considered Wordsworth's behavior shameful. The gunny forced himself to remain expressionless and made a strategic retreat to avoid witnessing the punch line.

Acting surprised, Jerry asked, "You haven't heard?"

"No," Wordsworth responded, "I just arrived in country," was his excuse.

"Well," Jerry explained, "the new combat toilet paper eliminates any odor from your... er... your... your feces." He continued his lesson, "They plan on introducing it first to the ground-pounders, so the enemy can't use bloodhounds to track patrols or downed pilots."

Skeptical, Staff Sergeant Wordsworth asked, "Then why do we have it?"

"Testing before they issue it to the field," Jerry answered matter-of-factly.

Shaking his head, the staff sergeant trotted to the nearest four-holer to take care of his... (How shall I put this?) ... his business.

Twenty minutes later the staff sergeant strode up to Jerry and announced, "That combat toilet paper does not work!"

Envisioning Wordsworth with his nose in his recently-soiled toilet paper, sniffing as hard as he could, Jerry told the staff sergeant he would report his finding to the CTPO.

"The who?"
"The CTPO. The Combat Toilet Paper Officer."
More stifled snickers.

One morning, the staff sergeant "tested" Lance Corporal "Catfish" Haroldson's troubleshooting skills by starting the day with his typical opening.

"I'm just checking your knowledge of the system. What would be the first thing you would do to resolve this problem?"

Catfish spotted the opening, teed one up, and hit a hole-in-one by responding, "If it were me, I would use an I.D. – 10T."

Appearing to be helpful, Catfish pronounced it phonetically. "eye-dee-ten-tee."

Never having heard of an "I.D. – 10T" yet unwilling to admit it, Wordsworth continued to pretend to be the teacher.

"Where would you go to get one of those... er... I.D. – 10T's?"

"There should be loads of them in the tool room. They had a bunch, but it takes a Staff NCO to check one out."

Eager to flaunt his seniority, Wordsworth marched to the tool room demanding an "eye-dee-ten-tee."

The young Marine minding the squadron's tool inventory explained that there were no more in the tool room. They had all been moved to Maintenance Control. Maintenance Control apologized because they had just moved them to Metal Shop who transferred them to... well, you get the picture.

After making the rounds of nearly every shop in the squadron, Wordsworth entered the Avionics shop. Avionics finished with the coup de grace.

"We just saw some upstairs in the pilots' Ready Room this morning. There are plenty of them up there."

Grumbling about the squadron's lack of tool control, Wordsworth entered the Ready Room filled with pilots who were being briefed on the day's mission.

"Are there any 'eye-dee-ten-tees' in here?" he bellowed.

After a short pause, the pilot's all began to chuckle.

One responded, "Only one, Staff Sergeant." (emphasis on "Staff Sergeant")

More laughter.

Seeing the "what-the-hell-are-you-talking-about" look on Wordsworth's face, the Officer of the Day took pity on the staff sergeant and pulled him aside.

"'Eye-dee-ten-tee', Get it?"

by James E. Bulman

Nothing but a blank stare.

The officer led Wordsworth to the chalk board. In big, bold letters he wrote the letters and numbers: I... D... 10... T.

Still not getting the joke, Wordsworth nodded as if he understood but the OD saw the confused look and continued his lesson.

"'I. D. 10. T,' Put them all together," the officer coaxed.

Nothing.

Finally surrendering, the officer revealed the answer.

"It spells 'IDIOT'."

The Ready Room erupted in laughter. The O.D. quickly hushed the jovial crowd.

"It's just a prank played on all of the boot... er... new arrivals," the officer explained.

It was apparent Staff Sergeant Wordsworth could not take a joke.

"All in good fun, Staff Sergeant," the O.D. cautioned.

Red-faced, Wordsworth insisted that he was well aware of the prank the entire time but was just playing along. The pilots nodded their heads facetiously, trying to conceal their giggles. Wordsworth was humiliated. The troops had gotten the best of him... again.

This would not stand. The staff sergeant put on a false front and laughed it off.

It was never mentioned again... but Wordsworth had a way of dealing with Marines who made him look bad. He would remember Catfish in the weeks to come.

The gust lock is another good example. On the "heavy hauler" CH-53 cargo helicopter there is a lever in the cabin directly below the main rotor head. It is a two-position lever (locked and unlocked). In the locked position, it prevents the rotor blades from spinning freely during gusting wind conditions when the aircraft is parked. Although it is called the gust lock, there is no key (You could envision the problems if the imaginary key was lost).

One afternoon while Staff Sergeant Wordsworth was lecturing the entire shop on the intricacies of a problem he had repaired on an aircraft, Jerry walked up to the staff sergeant and asked for the key to the gust lock.

Stunned by the request, the Staff Sergeant stammered a pitiful, "I... I... I don't have it."

"You were the last one on the aircraft. You are responsible for the key. Where is it?" Jerry demanded.

The rest of the crew added background chatter.

"Holy shit, he lost the key."

"It'll take weeks to get the master key from the States."

"Glad it wasn't me."

"They're going to have to break the lock."

"Hell, they can't do that. The locking pin may never release after that."

"Glad it wasn't me."

The staff sergeant began to sweat.

Jerry quickly offered a solution. "Maybe one of the other squadrons has an aircraft with the same last three digits of the aircraft bureau number. It might be a match. The last time this happened, the other squadrons refused to hand their gust lock key to anyone except a Staff NCO."

All heads turned towards Staff Sergeant Wordsworth. The sweat was visible.

Wordsworth carefully transcribed the six-digit bureau number into his green, pocket-sized notebook (carried by all Marines) and set out to locate the "matching key." As he reached the door someone chuckled, then another, and another until everyone began laughing.

Realizing he had been made to look the fool again, he had enough. There was fire coming out of his eyes.

The laughter stopped. The room fell silent.

Now it was Jerry's turn to sweat.

"No more!" Wordsworth demanded. "McCoy, your ass is mine," he informed the instigator as the senior Marine exited the room.

Jerry was immediately surrounded by his friends who offered little, if any, words of encouragement such as:

"He was really pissed."

"You're toast, man."

"I think you went too far this time."

"Glad it wasn't me."

The comments concluded with Ski's words of advice.

"If you ever considered going over the hill... now would be a good time."

Of course, there was a time or two when Staff Sergeant Wordsworth was correct, but the young Marines would not let him know it.

by James E. Bulman

Such as the afternoon the maintenance officer, piloting a CH-53 Sea Stallion, returned from a mission with an unusual discrepancy. The multi-position, conically-shaped knob on the top of the pilot's cyclic control stick was missing. Staff Sergeant Wordsworth directed Jerry to take care of the problem.

Jerry conducted a cursory examination of the cockpit for the small "coolie hat" and came up empty. Using a small, hand-held, two-way radio Jerry radioed an order for a replacement. Staff Sergeant Wordsworth refused to place the order admonishing Jerry over the air, "It's got to be in the cockpit somewhere!"

In fact, the staff sergeant was absolutely correct. The small knob could easily roll around under the cockpit jamming a flight control stick or creating an electrical short circuit.

Reluctantly, Jerry returned to the aircraft and performed a more thorough inspection, again, to no avail.

Wordsworth ordered Dan to assist Jerry in his search, warning the two maintenance technicians, "If you can't find it, I'll go out there and find it for you!"

After some time, Staff Sergeant Wordsworth radioed, "Well?"

"It's simply not here, Staff Sergeant." Jerry explained.

"I'll find it! I'm on my way," he threatened.

Staff Sergeant Wordsworth gathered an inspection mirror, a flashlight and an assortment of other tools then departed the shop, heading in the direction of the discrepant helicopter.

At that moment, Dan triumphantly announced, "I've got it. I found it!"

Dan was smiling broadly as he walked over to Jerry. Dan dropped the "coolie hat" into Jerry's open palm.

"Is this what you are looking for?" he asked with a shit-eating smile.

Jerry played with the small black knob between his fingers while contemplating his next step.

"We're going to look like idiots," he commented. "Wordsworth will never let us forget this."

Then without a second's hesitation, Jerry threw the small knob as far as he could into the tall grass along the taxi way.

Dan was horrified, "Why did you do that?"

"He'll never find it now, will he?" Jerry responded with a menacing grin.

Staff Sergeant Wordsworth arrived with all the confidence of a champion heavyweight boxer sparring with a high school featherweight.

"I'll show you how it's done," he announced.

The staff sergeant proceeded to climb all over the cockpit area, searching every nook and cranny, climbing on, under, and over every square inch of the flight compartment and, of course, came up with nothing.

Sweating like an also-ran at Pamlico Raceway, Wordsworth exited the aircraft. With a harsh tone, the staff sergeant instructed Jerry, "Order it!" as he stormed off.

Dan was stunned by Jerry's trickery.

Jerry looked at Dan and said, "That's the way it's done."

Corporal Blaine from the admin office was another pain in the ass. Not only were his practical jokes wearing thin, but his eagerness to enhance his reputation with senior Marines by informing on anyone junior to him, alienated most of the squadron personnel.

It took no time at all for just about everyone in the squadron to figure out Corporal Blaine. He was on par with Staff Sergeant Wordsworth for self-promotion. Simply put, the admin corporal was not only a kiss ass, and a snitch, he was also a bull-shitter. He bragged about his experience in combat and the Bronze Star medal he earned but conveniently lost in a house fire. Also lost were the Combat Aircrew Wings he supposedly earned as a helicopter crew chief during an imaginary previous tour in Vietnam.

While recounting one of his fantastic combat escapades, Corporal Blaine was hoisted by his own petard. The Officer of the Day, First Lieutenant Waverly, happened to be making his rounds when he overheard the admin corporal telling one of his wartime fairy tales.

The first lieutenant interrupted the story by informing the young corporal, "You know Corporal, I need a First Mechanics/Gunner on tomorrow's mission. You're more than welcome to tag along."

Corporal Blaine knew the First Mechanic's responsibility was to assist the enlisted crew chief and, if necessary, to operate the M-60 machine gun if the landing zone was hot.

The corporal sounded like a school boy explaining why he had not completed his homework assignment.

"Um, ah, mmm, y'know, Sir, I've got to get caught up with my administrative work," he stammered.

The lieutenant leaned close to the admin corporal and whispered, "You do know everyone thinks you're bull shitting about being a crew chief. This would be a great way to set them straight."

Stuck between a rock and a hard place, Corporal Blaine relented.

"Yeah. Sure. What time is the briefing?"

by James E. Bulman

The next morning the admin corporal emerged from the hangar sporting a shiny new flight suit, flight gloves, flight boots, flight helmet and, of course, aviator's sunglasses.

Walking…no… strutting towards the assigned helicopter, he thought himself quite the rock star. Stopping in front of the aircraft, he placed his left palm on the nose and leaned close to the CH-53.

Lieutenant Waverly looked at Dan who was filling in for the regular crew chief and asked, "What, the hell, is he doing? Communing with the Helicopter Gods?" They both chuckled.

It became obvious during the pre-flight inspection that Corporal Blaine didn't know one end of the helicopter from the other. The pilot and Dan continued to glance at each other and shaking their heads in amazement.

As payback for the four-holer gag the admin corporal had played on Dan when he first checked into the squadron, Dan lead the ersatz crew chief to the forward corner of the cabin. He pointed to a funnel connected to a long tube. The tube passed through a hole in the cabin floor.

Holding the funnel, Dan explained, "This is a new feature. It is the auxiliary intercom system (ICS). If your primary intercom system fails and you can't communicate with the other crew members, you can shout into the funnel to speak with the pilot."

Corporal Blaine thanked the young crew chief for the update on new modification, "Can I try it out?"

"Sure," Dan responded.

The admin corporal placed the funnel over his mouth and shouted, "Testing. One, two, three. Testing."

There was no response. The Admin Corporal shouted into the "auxiliary ICS" several more times to no avail.

"It doesn't work."

Dan shrugged it off, "I forgot, the engines need to be running for the system to operate."

Laughing to himself as he thought *Why should it work? It has nothing to do with the intercom system. It's the piss tube used by the air crew members to relieve themselves during long flights.*

Watching the admin corporal shouting into the funnel over and over was as good as it gets. *That's the way it's done*, Dan whispered to himself.

Upon completion of the startup procedures, the helo taxied to the runway. After obtaining clearance from the tower, First Lieutenant Waverly pulled up on the collective stick with his left hand, lifting the behemoth into the air. With his right hand, he pushed the cyclic stick forward slightly tipping the nose down and rapidly gaining both airspeed and altitude.

As they passed over the air facility's perimeter, Dan removed his flak jacket, folded it neatly on the crew chief's seat, and sat on it. Aghast, Corporal Blaine ignored Dan's lead and donned his flak jacket. He buttoned it as tight as he could.

Sympathetic to the corporal's ignorance, bull-shitter or not, Dan didn't want to see anyone hurt. Dan rose from his seat and leaned close to the corporal's ear. He pulled the helmet's earpiece and shouted into his helmet, "At cruising altitude, the bullets are coming straight up. When we enter the Landing Zone we'll don our flak jackets. Got it?"

A short moment of eye-opening realization and Corporal Blaine nodded his head, folded his flak jacket and sat down like a misbehaving school boy being sent into the corner.

The flight was a routine supply run. They were to pick up a couple pallets of supplies and delivery them to a small outpost. They were not expecting any action. But the admin corporal provided enough excitement all by himself.

About twenty minutes into the flight Dan noticed the seated corporal glancing this way and that way as if searching for something. As Dan wondered what the corporal was looking for, the corporal seemed to find whatever it was. Dan tried to follow the admin corporal's gaze to figure out what his eyes had locked on to. Corporal Blaine seemed to be staring at the cabin floor near the rear of the aircraft.

There's nothing back there except the hellhole, Dan thought. *Why would the hellhole interest him? That hatch leads to the external hook.*

Then it hit Dan like a brick.

He's sick. He's going to puke!

Dan intercepted the braggart just in time.

"You puke in the hellhole and it'll come right back in your face!" Dan informed the supposedly experienced crew chief. But one look at Corporal Blaine, and anyone could see that nothing was going to stop the green-faced braggart from upchucking in the aircraft.

Panic was setting in.

Dan always carried a plastic trash can liner in the left leg pocket of his flight suit for just such emergencies. Ground troops were notorious for getting airsick. He scrambled to remove the bag but was taking too long.

The admin corporal ran to the crew door on the starboard side (apologies to the civilians out there... the right side) of the helicopter. Dan tried to warn the airsick NCO but before he could, Corporal Blaine stuck his head out the crew door window.

At a cruising speed of 159 mph, the air rushing by the aircraft was as powerful as a category five hurricane. In an instant, Corporal Blaine's shiny new sunglasses were torn from his face and his unsnapped helmet ripped from his head. Both lost forever in the South Vietnamese jungle. Immediately following the loss of his equipment came the loss of his breakfast.

Turning his face away from the direction of flight, the admin corporal let loose... again and again until he had completely emptied the contents of his stomach.

Upon landing at the supply depot, Dan stepped outside the helicopter to survey the remains of Corporal Blaine's morning meal which were smeared as thin as possible over the entire starboard side of the aircraft.

Dan was beside himself. He was responsible for this aircraft. As a routine courtesy, was required to return it to its rightful owner, the crew chief who regularly crewed this helicopter, in the same or better shape than when he accepted it. Since there was no method of cleaning the aircraft either at the supply depot or at the Marine outpost, Dan would have to wait until they returned to Marble Mountain to clean it up.

Dan fumed during the remainder of the mission. He had no intention of cleaning up some admin asshole's puke. Upon landing at home base, Dan tossed a pile of rags at the corporal.

"Clean it up!" he ordered.

Corporal Blaine being the senior Marine replied with a snotty, "In case you have forgotten, I outrank you. So, YOU clean it up! I'm reporting to sick bay."

Dan's ire was raised, "Like bullshit you will. It's your puke. You'll..."

Calmly interrupted by First Lieutenant Waverly, "Excuse me. In case you have forgotten, I'm senior to both of you."

The two enlisted Marines went silent.

"Corporal, it's your puke. You'll clean it up. Lance Corporal, you report to me when he finishes so I can inspect his thoroughness. Understood?"

"Understood, Sir." from both Marines.

Dan smiled at his victory while Corporal Blaine glared at him.

When the rainy season arrived, the sand at the Marble Mountain Air Facility turned to mud. The ponchos that were issued to our young Marines served little purpose. Every gust of wind made the poncho billow like Marylyn Monroe's dress as she stood over the subway grating in New York City. The plastic poncho barely kept the chest area dry especially with an M-16 rifle keeping you company under the supposed "rain-proof" outerwear.

The plastic raincoat designed for use with the dress uniforms wasn't much better. It did have an advantage in that it could be buttoned up. It could keep the Marine dry from about the mid-thigh to the upper torso.

Although it was intended for use with the dress uniforms and because it was somewhat better than the poncho, many Marines wore it while in the camouflage utility uniform. Unfortunately, most West Pac first-timers left the raincoat in that footlocker-sized cardboard box on Okinawa. Not Staff Sergeant Wordsworth. He ignored the packing instructions back on Okinawa and kept his raincoat.

This leads us to the next incident.

On this rainy day, the commanding officer had a technical question for the avionics officer who happened to be unavailable. At that moment, the senior man in the avionics division was none other than Staff Sergeant Wordsworth. When made aware of the commanding officer's inquiry Wordsworth was eager to demonstrate his superior technical knowledge. He figured if he didn't know the answer to the commanding officer's question, he could confuse him with technical bullshit. He threw on his raincoat and rushed to Lieutenant Colonel Reeves's office.

Upon entering the inner sanctum, Staff Sergeant Wordsworth came to the position of attention and reported.

"Staff Sergeant Wordsworth reporting for the avionics officer, Sir."

The commanding officer paused for a minute, recalling the history of this Staff NCO. The commanding officer shook his head as if saddened and instructed the staff sergeant.

"Staff Sergeant, before we go any further, go get your uniform in proper order so we can continue."

Stunned by the lieutenant colonel's mild but stinging rebuke, Staff Sergeant Wordsworth staggered out of the commanding officer's office as if suffering a heart attack. He rushed to the nearest men's head in search of a mirror. Like Snow White's stepmother, Wordsworth was no stranger to the mirror. He prided himself on his outstanding military appearance and, as one underling paraphrased Will Rogers by commenting, "He never met a mirror he didn't like."

Until now.

Positioning himself in front of the reflecting glass, Staff Sergeant Wordsworth immediately spotted the discrepancy. Someone had removed one of his black, metal staff sergeant insignia from his raincoat collar and replaced it with a silver, metal first lieutenant insignia.

Staff Sergeant Wordsworth couldn't muster the nerve to return to the avionics division where the unknown culprit probably worked. Nor did he want to face the commanding officer again. He removed the raincoat and trudged through the soaking downpour to his sleeping quarters.

Later that day after gathering up all the courage he could pull together, the staff sergeant stormed into the sergeant major's office without knocking. (The sergeant major's real office, not the four-holer described earlier.)

The breach of protocol pissed off the sergeant major, but he let it pass. He could sense Staff Sergeant Wordsworth needed to vent.

The staff sergeant uttered a stream of vulgarities, intermixed with bits of each insult to which he had been subjected, coupled with the names of the disrespectful miscreants.

"Goddamn troops... lip check... Keegan... son of a bitch gust lock... McCoy... missing key bullshit... I.D... fucking... ten... lieutenant bars... whoever!"

Exasperated with this weak-kneed staff sergeant, the sergeant major listened carefully and decided to intervene.

Upon hearing of the latest prank, the sergeant major wanted to chuckle but knew that would look as if he condoned the whole affair. Instead he decided to put an end to this, here and now.

He put on his "sergeant major face" and marched to the avionics division. Gathering the junior troops in a school circle he proceeded to explain the rank structure and the meaning of respect to his young charges. He completed his mass dressing down with, "Whoever did this doesn't deserve to call himself a Marine. Hell, it's just plain un-American."

"Damn," Catfish whispered, "They'll take away the guilty party's citizenship!"

The unknown vandal was never identified. The pranks continued.

There wasn't much for entertainment at Marble Mountain. Visiting the enlisted club, reading paperback books, reading and re-reading old magazines, and writing letters home topped the list.

Armed Forces Radio and Television Service (AFRTS) provided one radio station with "Top Forty" music and occasional sports broadcasts from the States.

"A-FARTS," as it was affectionately known by the troops, also broadcast one television channel that aired the daily news (anything controversial was simply not reported), reruns of popular stateside programming such as *Rowan and Martin's Laugh-In* (all sexual innuendo or anything detrimental to unit morale was redacted), *Bonanza*, *What's My Line*, *Bewitched*, NFL highlights, etc.

Remember, there were no such things as Sony Walkmans, no CD players, no MP3 players, no iPods, and no internet.

By 1970 audio cassettes were quickly supplanting eight-track tapes which were bulky and often became a tangled mess inside the player.

Some servicemen saved their money and purchased pricey reel-to-reel tape recorders through the Armed Forces Exchange Catalog, but the average leatherneck couldn't afford these expensive toys.

Everyone searched for something to break up the monotony. Jogging and weightlifting helped burn off some calories as well as some steam. It also helped to clear one's head. On the other hand, Staff Sergeant Wordsworth had his own answer.

Having obtained a Black Belt in karate (so he said), he organized classes for the junior troops. The senior leadership was pleasantly surprised at this ingenious idea and threw its full support into the off-duty activity.

Flyers were posted around the base. Word was passed during daily meetings. Even Armed Forces Radio and Television Service mentioned the initiative during its nightly news broadcast.

Wordsworth was quite pleased with himself. Obviously, he had something up his sleeve.

Encouraged by Wordsworth's never-ending cajoling, several of our small group joined the Karate Club. Jerry, Dan, Jason, and Catfish lined up with a dozen or so others and began learning from Sensei Wordsworth.

All went well for the first few lessons.

Wordsworth demonstrated the basic karate stances, strikes, kicks, punches and blocks. The students did their best to copy his moves.

As the days and weeks of lessons continued, some of the younger Marines were beginning to change their opinion of their sensei. He might not be as bad as they first thought.

A few weeks into their training, Sensei Wordsworth was instructing his pupils on the world-renowned karate chop. They each took turns breaking boards. It was a blast. Everyone was enjoying themselves.

by James E. Bulman

To finish the evening's lesson, the staff sergeant displayed his superior karate skills by entertaining his students with a flurry of kicks. He emphasized the position of the hips and the direction of the standing leg.

For the culmination of the demonstration, Jason and Catfish held a wooden target as Wordsworth swung his leg towards the half-inch-thick piece of wood. Unfortunately, Wordsworth missed his aiming point and kicked Catfish squarely in the face. Our North Carolinian dropped to the floor and lay unconscious for several minutes. His nose bled profusely.

The team quickly realized that this "demonstration" had been a not-so-subtle, deliberately planned means for Staff Sergeant Wordsworth to extract his revenge on Catfish.

Tending to his friend's injuries, Jerry, the doctor's son, applied pressure to stem the flow of blood from Catfish's nose. Once he came to, the troupe escorted him to sick bay for examination.

Diagnosis: A broken nose and a mild concussion.

Apologizing over and over, Wordsworth kept repeating, "Sorry, but accidents will happen from time to time."

The next morning, the entire karate class was standing at attention in front of Lieutenant Colonel Reeves. The commanding officer was not happy.

What had seemed like a morale-boosting activity had instead seriously injured one of his men. The lieutenant colonel had received a "heads up" about Staff Sergeant Wordsworth prior to his arrival in the squadron. The commanding officer had heard about the ID-10T incident and had a sneaking suspicion that Staff Sergeant Wordsworth had intentionally struck this young Marine.

The lieutenant colonel's inquiry was getting nowhere. Each Marine had the same story... the exact same story. It was an unfortunate accident. Nobody's fault. Nobody to blame.

Staff Sergeant Wordsworth stressed the point that "accidents will happen" but the lieutenant colonel wasn't buying it. The commanding officer dismissed the team but instructed Wordsworth to stay.

"If there is one more incident like this one, I will hold you personally responsible. Do you understand?"

"Yes, Sir!"

With that admonition, the lieutenant colonel dismissed the senior NCO.

As Wordsworth turned to depart, the commanding officer could have sworn the staff sergeant had the hint of a smile on his face.

"Staff Sergeant!"

Wordsworth spun around, snapped to attention, responded with a straight-faced, "Yes, Sir!"

"One more! Am I clear?"

"Yes, Sir. Crystal clear."

The junior Marines continued to do their best to make Wordsworth look bad. After much trial and error, they soon discovered his true Achilles Heel. He had a weak stomach.

This lead to a series of actions that left the staff sergeant afraid to be in the same room with our gallant gang. Most of the routines were standard Marine Corps fare:

Acting as if you are puking while pouring cream of mushroom soup onto the floor scooping it up and "re-eating" it.

Catching a fly, secretly swapping it for a raisin chewing on the "bug."

Capturing a gecko, popping its tail off (Don't worry. It grows back.), placing the wiggling tail in your mouth so it looks like you're eating the whole lizard alive.

To the delight of the Marines in his unit, Wordsworth was heaving chunks day after day.

Lou Archer came up with a slightly better routine.

One day following lunch, the staff sergeant was discussing a maintenance issue with Jason. Surreptitiously, Lou slowly edged his way towards the pair while keeping his face turned away from view. In an instant, Lou sidled up next to Staff Sergeant Wordsworth and spun around to face the startled senior NCO.

Lou had a string stuffed up his nose with the opposite end exiting his mouth. He pulled on the nose-end of the string and the opposite end would retract into his mouth. Alternately, pulling on the mouth-end of the string would cause the nose-end to shorten.

Wordsworth's eyes widened in amazement which immediately turned to disgust. He ran for the head where he deposited his lunch. He could hear the cheers in the distance.

Assuming Staff Sergeant Wordsworth was the great war hero he claimed to be, it was strange that he was a "nervous Nellie" when assigned to any task that could potentially be linked to real combat. Even something as simple as Interior Guard was too close to possible combat for the staff sergeant.

It was required that each staff sergeant in the squadron take his turn as Staff Duty NCO for a full 24-hour period approximately once every thirty days. As Staff Sergeant Wordsworth's turn neared, he would survey his fellow Staff NCO's for a volunteer to take his place. He used several tricks on a rotating basis. One month he would feign a splitting headache. Not bad enough to go to sick bay and see a doctor, of course. The next month he would insist he was needed by his squadron maintenance officer to repair a much-needed aircraft. He would offer to swap his duty day for another staff sergeant's duty day in the future. he would play the same game with another Staff NCO the next month. He figured he just had to play this scam twelve times over the next year, and he would be home free.

It only took a couple of months for the other Staff NCOs to figure out his little "bait and switch" scheme. Soon it became impossible for Staff Sergeant Wordsworth to avoid his turn as Staff Duty NCO.

When he ran out of takers, Staff Sergeant Wordsworth eventually had to assume his turn as Staff Duty NCO for the squadron. Of course, being Staff Sergeant Wordsworth, instead of personally checking posts throughout the night, he would "provide a leadership opportunity" to the Sergeant of the Guard or Corporal of the Guard by delegating his responsibility to the junior Marines on watch. As the SOG or COG departed, he would toss in, "Call me on the radio if you need anything," as he kicked back in his chair and watched reruns of *The Joey Bishop Show* on the Armed Forces Radio and Television Service.

One evening, the Officer of the Day suddenly appeared while the staff sergeant was "delegating" his rounds. The OOD was not pleased and proceeded to chew Wordsworth a new asshole.

"You cannot assign a junior NCO to a Staff NCO watch! How long have you been playing this game? Who gave you the authority to do this? Why aren't you checking posts personally?"

Wordsworth "er'd" and "ah'd" as he tried to tap dance his way out of his predicament.

Within minutes Wordsworth was checking all the sentries throughout the squadron area... and continued to do so every month thereafter. That is, when he stood his own watch.

On another night, the OOD instructed all the guard personnel to be "especially watchful." It seems it was the night of local elections, and the South Vietnamese were famous for lighting fire crackers, exploding cherry bombs, and launching bottle rockets aimlessly into the air.

"Keep your eyes and ears open," he cautioned, "But don't get trigger happy."

That evening as Staff Sergeant Wordsworth was in the barracks area talking to the off-going and on-coming Fire Watches, Catfish let loose with a bottle rocket from a couple of yards behind the Staff NCO.

Wordsworth dove for the dirt as if all hell had broken loose. Screaming "Incoming! Incoming!" he hit the deck and rolled up to the nearest sand-bagged blast wall.

It only took a few moments for Staff Sergeant Wordsworth to realize there were no "incoming", the noise came from inside the barracks area, and there was no imminent attack.

The two lance corporals on Fire Watch stood over the staff sergeant wondering why he had reacted as he did. The surrounding troops began laughing but hushed as soon as they saw the look in his eyes.

Somebody is going to pay for this, he swore under his breath.

The "accident" at the Karate Club was soon put in the past. The karate enthusiasts began enjoying themselves once more. They repeated the various routines set out by Staff Sergeant Wordsworth. They practiced the offensive and defensive moves in short matches against each other.

After daily teasing from the staff sergeant, to everyone's surprise, Lou agreed to join the group. However, his enthusiasm for the sport was lacking and he did little to improve his karate skills. His poor karate performance coupled with the "string" incident, in Wordsworth's world, was simply unacceptable.

One evening Sensei Wordsworth asked for a volunteer to act as an aggressor. Without even considering the raised hands of the other members, Wordsworth selected Lou. The other team members cautioned the "volunteer.".

"Not a good idea, Lou."

"I'd decline the invitation."

"Remember Catfish."

Lou ignored the advice and willingly joined Wordsworth on the mat. Wordsworth ordered Lou to attack him from behind and to grab the sensei by the shoulders. The instructor braced himself for the assault.

The instant Wordsworth felt Lou's hand touch his trapezius muscles, he spun around to deliver a round house kick to Lou's head.

This'll teach that little shit for that "string" gag, Wordsworth grinned to himself.

But Lou wasn't there!

Anticipating the sensei's true intensions, Lou had immediately squatted. The sweeping kick passed over his head. Then, like a compressed spring uncoiling, Lou rebounded with a punishing right upper cut to Wordsworth chin. It was lights out for the staff sergeant. TKO. Game. Set. Match.

Catfish smiled as he commented, "Seems the staff sergeant has a weak stomach AND a glass jaw."

That evening Staff Sergeant Woodworth filed charges against Lance Corporal Archer for assaulting a staff non-commissioned officer. Potentially a court-martial offense.

The following morning, the entire karate class stood before the commanding officer with the same story.

"It was an accident. After all, as Staff Sergeant Wordsworth said himself, 'Accidents will happen.'"

Using the staff sergeant's own words against him had the sergeant major stifling a laugh. The commanding officer was not pleased. He began the pronouncement of the verdict by addressing the assemblage.

"I don't believe any of your stories. I don't believe this was unintentional, and I certainly cannot condone striking a Staff NCO, but the lieutenant colonel rubbed his chin in thoughtful silence as he considered the situation.

He turned towards the staff sergeant and continued, "I do remember informing one staff sergeant that I would hold him personally responsible for any other mishaps or was I not 'crystal clear', Staff Sergeant?"

Wordsworth could see where these proceedings were heading. He reluctantly agreed, "Yes, Sir. You were crystal clear."

The commanding officer stared silently at his desk for several moments reflecting upon the impact his decision would have on unit morale. Finally, with his decision made, the commanding officer spoke in a firm tone.

"I, therefore, find that Lance Corporal Archer is not guilty of all charges. In addition, the karate club is hereby disbanded."

The commanding officer dismissed the junior Marines and waited for them to close the door.

"Sergeant Major, I trust you will find an appropriate assignment where a sports enthusiast, like our staff sergeant here, can prove useful."

The next day, Staff Sergeant Wordsworth could be found in a small room labeled "Special Services" near the soda mess in the H&MS-16 hangar. His singular purpose in life was to issue basketballs and other sports paraphernalia to the off-duty Marines. It would be a long and dull tour of duty for the staff sergeant... unlike the Marines tending to the aircraft.

by James E. Bulman

CHAPTER FOURTEEN

Aircraft Maintenance - February - July 1970

There never seemed to be enough hours in the day to complete all the necessary repairs, take care of your personal business, and do much else other than visit the club for an hour or two.

Jason was sometimes available for deep discussions but there is something different about talking to one of your buddies and talking to a member of the opposite sex.

Lou Archer was quick to learn if you befriended the young lady who managed the soda mess, she might let you know when the next delivery of candy bars or snacks were scheduled to arrive. In addition, she was a friendly voice in an unfriendly environment.

Moreover, the soda mess lady listened to the young Marines when they had nobody else to talk to. The young Vietnamese lady could have hung a shingle on her door like Linus Van Pelt's older sister Lucy in the Peanuts comic strip advertising "Psychiatric Help 5 cents." Dear John letters, money difficulties, marital troubles, and work problems were just a few of the issues she helped the troubled leathernecks struggle through.

She was a pretty lady. Some would say beautiful. Her long raven-black hair made her appear much younger than she was. It was easy to see how some Marines could become infatuated with her.

Throughout the month, you could hear penniless Marines bartering. "I'll fly if you buy!" It soon became clear that Lance Corporal Archer either had an addiction for Coca-Cola or had a massive crush on the young miss who worked the counter.

The smitten Marine would eagerly conduct a "soda mess run" for anyone with an extra twenty-five cents MPC. As the days, weeks and months at Marble Mountain passed increasingly slower, the runs to the soda mess took longer and longer.

A couple of days prior to payday, Jason asked if anyone would make a run to the soda mess.

"I'll buy if you fly," he announced.

The obvious choice would have been Lou, but he was as nowhere to be found.

Dan looked around for any other volunteers. When he saw none, Dan graciously accepted Jason's offer and responded with the appropriate pass phrase, "I'll fly if you buy."

After collecting the requisite MPC paper scrip, Dan casually meandered across the tarred road to the hangar. As he approached the soda mess, he realized the top half of the Dutch-door was open but there didn't appear to be anyone minding the store. Dan glanced here and there. He called out for the operator of the little establishment to no avail. He considered opening the bottom of the Dutch-door and entering the small stock room then immediately reconsidered his decision as he heard a faint moan from within.

Shit! he thought, *there's somebody hurt inside.*

Louder moans.

Dan was torn between entering and running for help.

Deeper moans.

Dan may have been an innocent young boy from a small town in New England, but he easily recognized what was going on within the small store room.

Wait a minute. Dan contemplated for a moment, *it sounds like someone is doing the nasty!*

The moans became more frequent and more guttural.

Holy shit, it's Lou and the soda mess lady, Dan realized.

Dan considered disrupting the tryst but immediately eliminated that option. *Lou would kick my ass from here to Da Nang,* Dan reasoned.

Dan stood there, as indecisive as he could be. That is, until he eyed a pilot making a beeline for the soda mess.

"Oh, shit!" he said aloud.

As the pilot approached, Dan could see the quizzical look on his face.

"Where's the young lady?" the pilot queried.

"Uh... uh... uh..." Dan stammered.

"Well?" the captain asked.

"Well, Sir... You see, Sir... she... er..." Dan was mumbling like an idiot.

"Well?" the captain demanded an answer.

Suddenly, Dan had an epiphany.

"She asked me to mind the store while she took care of business... not actual business... y'know... lady business... y'know..." Dan scrambled for words.

"Spit it out, Lance Corporal," he ordered.

"Yes, Sir... She... Sir... had to take a leak... Sir." Happy with his plausible explanation, Dan smiled like Davy Crocket grinning down a grizzly bear.

Accepting the reasonable story, the captain requested three cans of Coke and handed Dan a $1.00 MPC note.

Minor panic set in. The till was closed and locked. He couldn't make change.

Handing the scrip back to the officer, he informed the customer that there would be no charge for the canned refreshment for the remainder of the day.

More moans!

"What was that, Marine?"

"Rats, Sir. Vermin the size of German shepherds. They're fucking huge. Big! I'm telling you, they're gigantic!" Out of breath, Dan was silent for a moment then added a final "Sir."

The officer shook his head in bewilderment, turned, and walked away.

For the next twenty minutes Dan stood soda mess watch, fending off officers and enlisted men alike with free sodas. Unfortunately, free "anything" draws a crowd. As business became more and more brisk, poor Dan began breaking a sweat as he handed out more and more free sodas which, in turn, encouraged more and more customers.

The moans and groans emanating from the store room made Dan increasingly uncomfortable. Every once-in-a-while, there was a high-pitched squeak added to the deep moans. Dan winced then smiled, wondering which of the two was enjoying the afternoon frolic more, the soda mess lady or Lou.

He also wondered which of the two was the "squeaker" or which one was the "moaner."

The inventory of refreshments was beginning to diminish at an alarming rate. Dan was on the verge of panic when he realized the conjugal visit was nearing its climax... literally. The falsetto of the oft-repeated "Oh, my God. Oh, my God." was replaced by a lengthy shrill "Oh. Oh. Oh!" OOHHHH!" followed by several minutes of silence.

Dan could hear mumbled niceties but couldn't make out exactly what was being said. He guessed it something close to "It was good for me. Was it good for you?"

Anticipating the couple's exit from the store room, Dan considered abandoning his self-assigned post. It certainly would be awkward, but he had to explain the dozens of missing soda cans.

The first to exit was the soda mess lady. Carefully re-buttoning her blouse and pressing the wrinkles from her clothing with her hands. She was somewhat

SWING WITH THE WING

surprised to see Dan. He attempted to explain his presence, but she brushed him off with the wave of her hand.

"No problem, Marine. Thank you. You go back to work now. It's okay."

Dan figured she was embarrassed that she and Lou had been found out. He wanted to explain the inventory crisis, but she was more emphatic a second time.

Totally unbothered, she repeated, "No problem. Thank you. You go back to work now. It's okay. Really."

Her insistence piqued Dan's curiosity.

He turned to witness the second half of the "Dynamic Duo" hiking up his utility trousers as he passed through the store room doorway. Staring in amazement, Dan was struck silent until he heard, "What are you staring at, Lance Corporal?"

Awakened from his trance-like state, Dan immediately responded, "Nothing, Staff Sergeant Wordsworth. Nothing at all."

It appeared that Dan and Lou were the only two enlisted Marines who didn't know the soda mess lady had a side business attending to the sexual needs of her customers.

If this had been a Marine other than Lou, he would be the target of unlimited teasing. Everyone on the air facility knew Lou had a great left jab and a mighty right hook. The jokes were minimal and limited to his closest friends.

Unfortunately, Corporal Blaine in admin became aware of Lou's ignorance and just couldn't let the opportunity pass without some good-natured... okay, mean-spirited ribbing. This became vividly apparent when, at a squadron get together, the admin corporal made a series of rude, crude, and socially unacceptable remarks concerning the soda mess lady.

Remark #1: "Man, you could crack an egg on that ass!" Lou looked up with a who-said-that look on his face.

Remark #2: "I'll betcha she's a screamer." Lou was moving in Corporal Blaine's direction. As were the rest of his buddies.

Remark #3: "I'd drag my balls over three miles of busted beer bottles just to hear her fart over a field phone!"

Lou stepped up to the more senior Marine with a firm, "That's enough!"

Feigning surprise at Lou's reaction the admin corporal remained confident his rank would prevent the junior Marine from committing any grievous act. Knowing the young pugilist's reputation, Corporal Blaine moved back a step while continuing his comic monologue.

"Hey, Lance Corporal Archer, I want to make a soda mess run. I'll fly... if you don't mind sloppy seconds."

"No more comments. None!" Lou fumed.

"What's with you? Just because her legs go all the way up to her ass? She's just another gook with a tight..." Before he could finish his insult, Catfish stepped between the two.

"I'd be careful what you say next, Corporal," he advised.

"Are you threatening me?" the stunned NCO over-acted.

"No, Corporal, just trying to save you from an ass kicking." Catfish responded calmly.

"I'm a non-commissioned officer. He can't threaten me. We'll see what the commanding officer says about this," the admin corporal informed everyone as he turned to walk away.

Lou wasn't about to let Corporal Blaine off the hook quite yet.

"You're nothing but a snitch. A yellow-bellied snitch."

Everyone in the team looked at one another and mouthed the words, *Yellow-bellied?*

Jason quickly interceded to defuse the situation.

"You mean the commanding officer whose wife is 'just another g... er...' Filipino?"

The admin corporal paused and gave some thought to his predicament. He surrendered with, "Just tell your lance corporal to back off."

"No problem," Jason agreed, ending the standoff.

The food was typical military fare. Breakfast consisted of scrambled eggs (instant, of course), grits or hash browns, sausage or bacon, juice, and coffee. Lunch was a light meal. Sandwiches, hot dogs, and hamburgers were continuously rotated. Dinner was a full course meal. Meat and potatoes, vegetables, and dessert.

On paper, it sounded quite appetizing, but in real-life, menus that read as if you were dining at Delmonico's often disguised bland or over-salted, oft-repeated meals.

Each meal was just a break in an otherwise monotonous day, except for one memorable Wednesday.

On that morning, an Air Force C-130 Hercules, fixed-wing, four-engine, turboprop, mid-sized cargo aircraft had made an emergency landing at Marble Mountain.

As noon approached, its enlisted aircrew paraded into the mess hall with all the cockiness of bantam roosters. Espousing their fixed-wing opinions in a building full of rotary-wing helicopter mechanics was probably not the wisest of moves.

"What, the hell, kind of slop do they feed you guys?" shouted one.

"Only a bunch of rotor-heads could eat this shit," added another.

"Where are the real Marines?" a third laughed.

"How do helicopters fly, anyway? They got no wings!" the fourth asked.

The airmen chuckled.

They certainly had everyone's attention. Most of the Marines tried to ignore the rude visitors but Lou Archer's temperature was rising. He was trying his best to keep calm, but it wasn't doing much good.

The quartet ate their lunch with mock disgust. They commented on every bite.

Picking up his slice of roast beef from his open-faced sandwich and holding it high off his plate between his thumb and fore finger, the senior visitor asked, "I think the jockey is still looking for this horse."

The group laughed as he slapped the roast beef back onto his tray.

Lou had finished his meal and was scraping his tray clean into the trash before passing it through a portal into the scullery.

"To hell with this shit. We're outta here!"

The noisy faction left their trays on the tables and headed for the exit.

Unintimidated by the boisterous bunch as they strutted past Lou, he loudly reminded them of their responsibilities.

"You left your trays on the table."

"So, what?"

"You are required to scrape your own tray before handing it off to the scullery."

"Maybe in your rotor-head world shit-for-brains but not in ours... We're air crew."

Another flyboy joined the conversation.

"You must be one of those rotor-heads who can hover."

"Anyone who can hover is queer!" another asserted.

Uncharacteristically, Lou seemed to ignore the insult and walked out of the dining facility.

Surprised at their apparent victory, one fly boy commented, "I told you there were no real Marines here!"

As they exited the chow hall, the group came face to face with one fired-up Lou Archer.

by James E. Bulman

"What are you going to do... take on the four of us?" the senior airman asked in amusement.

"Why?" Lou asked, "Do you think you'll need more help?"

"Screw you, you dumb-ass rotor-head."

"You're about to get your ass whipped by a dumb-ass rotor-head."

One airman lunged at Lou who deftly stepped aside and connected with a right hook to the jaw. The unconscious attacker dropped to the deck without a sound.

The three others surged forward attempting to overwhelm the lone Marine, but Lou was in his boxing mode. Lou remembered his pugil stick training and deftly moved to the trio's flank, so he could face one attacker at a time.

Parrying the next airman's haymaker with his left, Lou countered with his right. Another airman fell to the ground.

Now completely in control, Lou moved forward, maintaining his balance by employing his ring-wise footwork.

He tagged the third flyboy with three quick left jabs to the nose then followed up with an upper cut to the midsection. The airman's eyes bulged as he struggled to catch his breath. Holding his gut with both hands, he collapsed to his knees. He was TKO'd.

The final loudmouth recognized defeat when he saw it and asked for the terms of surrender.

"Look bud, we were just having some fun. Just some fun."

"That's Lance Corporal Bud to you."

"Go clean up your trays!" Lou insisted.

"Yeah. Sure, Lance Corporal," the visitor muttered as he re-entered the dining facility to the jeers, hoots, and hollers of those inside who had rushed to that side of the mess hall to witness the one-sided match through the window screens.

Scrambling to complete his task, the airman piled his team's freshly-scraped trays at the scullery window but was deathly afraid to depart past the sole Marine waiting a few yards from the door.

The airman searched left and right and finally ran back into the mess hall, out a rear exit, never to be seen again.

As the satisfied "defender of helicopters" departed the mess hall area, the Officer of the Day stopped him in his tracks. Having witnessed the brouhaha from inside the mess hall, the OD inquired, "What happened here, Marine?"

At a loss for words, Lou groped for an answer. The only thing that came to mind was the old standby, "They fell down the stairs, Sir."

Looking at the entrance to the mess hall and observing only one step, the OD pondered the situation then asked doubtfully, "All four of them?"

"Yes, Sir. You know how clumsy those fly boys can be," adding a nervous chuckle.

The officer frowned as he saw the onlookers craning their necks from the mess hall windows. Giving it some thought, he instructed the young pugilist, "Next time, tell them to be more careful where they walk."

"Yes, Sir!" Lou responded as rendered a quick salute. He spun around and left the scene of the 'accident'.

"That's how it's done,' Lou commented as the ringside audience erupted in cheers.

by James E. Bulman

CHAPTER FIFTEEN

Assault on the Marble Mountain
Air Facility - July 1970

"Don't get excited," Jason cautioned his Marines. Dan, Jerry, Lou, Catfish, Jason, Ski, and Brian searched the front of the line for anything that looked like an enemy. "There!" Lou yelled, pointing to his left. "Yeah," Catfish agreed. "I saw something move."

Brian was surprisingly silent.

Another Marine on their left yelled, "There!"

A half-dozen Marines responded, "Where?"

Now several Marines to Jason's left entered the chorus, "There!"

The Marines took aim. They each fired a couple of rounds only to witness two black-pajama-clad Viet Cong abandoning their probing action and scrambling back to their starting point.

Holy shit! Dan thought. *This is where they plan to attack.*

Jason had already figured that out. He strained to see but saw nothing unusual.

"Yeah! There!" Catfish chimed in.

Jason rose from his crouch for a better view.

POP!

A half-dozen M-16's returned fire.

Jason murmured, "Cease fire. Cease f..." his voice trailed off.

The Marines nearest Jason instantly knew something was terribly wrong. All heads turned towards their leader. The stunned look on his face matched those of his Marines. Jason crumpled to the ground.

Some yelled, "Corpsman up!" but there was no Navy medical corpsman assigned to this slapped-together unit.

Dan was the first to react. "Jerry! Get Lance Corporal McCoy up here!"

In an instant the doctor's son was alongside Jason. It didn't take a medical degree to diagnose Jason's condition. He had not been wearing his flak jacket. There was now a hole below Jason's right nipple.

Bullet wound to the chest, Jerry observed. He also could see Jason was trying desperately to catch his breath.

"It could be a sucking chest wound," he temporarily diagnosed.

"Seal the wound," Jerry spoke aloud as if reading the Combat First Aid section of the *Guidebook for Marines.*

"Seal the wound," Jerry repeated as he ripped open Jason's uniform shirt and t-shirt. Jerry did not see bubbles emanating from the wound.

His lung may NOT be punctured, a relieved Jerry determined. Either way, he was treating the injured Marine as if he had a punctured lung.

Jason gasped for air.

Snatching his own first aid pouch, Jerry skillfully ripped open one of the pressure dressings from its plastic bag. Setting the dressing aside for the moment, Jerry positioned the empty plastic bag over the wound. Jerry then placed the dressing over the plastic bag.

"Treat for shock," Jerry recited.

Anticipating Jerry's next step, Dan had already removed his flak jacket and utility shirt. He handed the shirt to Jerry who covered Jason's exposed torso to keep the patient warm. Several nearby Marines had done the same and offered their shirts. They quickly re-donned their flak jackets.

They had all been trained in combat-related first aid, but this was more that Jerry could handle. Applying pressure to the wound Jerry could see Jason wincing in pain but his breathing had improved. Jerry had succeeded in sealing the wound.

"Lou," Jerry calmly selected, "I need you to return to the armory and rustle up a corpsman." Jerry turned his face away from Jason, so the injured leader could not see the silent but emphatic, "Now!"

"Will do," Lou replied as he scrambled away.

Dan added, "Inform the Officer of the Day that we have enemy movement on the beach. And we need more troops."

Lou waved his understanding with a "thumbs-up" and scurried to his destination.

Jerry tore into his first aid pouch. He gathered up as much medical gauze as he could find, wadded it up in a ball and applied it to Jason's chest wound.

Jason was staring into infinity.

"Shock. Treat for shock," Jerry recited aloud.

by James E. Bulman

Catfish looked at Dan and asked, "Who's in charge now?"

Lou arrived at the armory and frantically searched for the Officer of the Day. He failed to locate him. Eventually Lou spotted Staff Sergeant Wordsworth rounding the corner of the building. Lou didn't mince any words.

"There are VC coming in from the sea. Corporal Walsh has been wounded. It's bad."

Seemingly ignoring Lou's report, the staff sergeant said, "They are NOT coming in from the sea, Lance Corporal. We've not heard of any enemy activity from that direction from the sentry in the guard tower on the beach."

The senior non-commissioned officer continued, "As for your wounded comrade, you need to transport him to the triage area set up near the armory."

With that said, the senior NCO simply walked away.

Lou stepped in front of the staff sergeant to block his path.

Stopping Wordsworth in his tracks, the lance corporal wasn't to be ignored. "I'm telling you they are coming in from the beach, and I need a corpsman!" Lou demanded.

Brushing off the junior Marine a second time, the staff sergeant replied, "No, they are not and no, you cannot!"

Lou moved closer to the staff sergeant and was prepared for the consequences for what he was about to do.

"Either you find a corpsman or..."

"No, he cannot *what*, Staff Sergeant?" Lieutenant Colonel Reeves interrupted.

"I've got this under control, Sir!" the staff sergeant smiled in a feeble attempt to remove the commanding officer from the conversation.

"I asked you a question, Staff Sergeant!"

"It's nothing, Sir. Just trying to calm down a young lance corporal a bit nervous under fire," Wordsworth lied.

"That's bull shit and you know it!" Lou blurted.

"What's going on, Lance Corporal...," the commanding officer struggled for a moment to remember the young Marine's name then continued, "...Lance Corporal Arbor?"

"Archer, Sir," correcting the lieutenant colonel, "Like I tried to explain to the staff sergeant, there are VC on the beach and Corporal Walsh is badly wounded."

The commanding officer was shocked. He turned to Staff Sergeant Wordsworth in dismay.

"And when were you going to inform me about this, Staff Sergeant?"

"Well, Sir, the sentry in the guard tower hasn't reported..." Wordsworth stammered an explanation.

"Has he reported at all?"

"No, Sir," Staff Sergeant Wordsworth admitted.

"The whole purpose of putting Marines behind the vans facing the sea was to report any enemy activity on the beach."

"Yes, Sir, but..."

"There are no 'buts' Staff Sergeant," the commanding officer continued as his anger increased.

"What is your area of responsibility tonight, Staff Sergeant?"

"None, Sir. I'm not assigned any specific duty tonight."

"Aren't you the Staff Duty NCO for tonight?"

"No, Sir! Staff Sergeant Ortiz and I swapped duty..."

"Oh, yes," the commanding officer paused as remembered, "You're the one who doesn't like to stand his own watches."

Shocked that his duty-swapping had come to the commanding officer's attention, Wordsworth was speechless.

The commanding officer looked at Lou. "How many VC?"

"Thirty... forty," Lou reported.

The commanding officer nodded his head as he contemplated his next move.

"How badly hurt is Corporal Walsh?"

"Bad, Sir. Really, bad. Shot in the chest."

The commanding officer glared at Wordsworth as he issued his orders to Lou in a slow, moderate tone to ensure the lance corporal understood.

"Go to the armory and tell them I want a medical corpsman to move to the beach immediately."

"Yes, Sir!" Lou responded and was gone in a flash.

Seething, the commanding officer moved into Staff Sergeant Wordsworth personal space.

"If that young corporal doesn't make it, I'll have you court-martialed, busted, and sent to Leavenworth where you can hand out basketballs for the rest of your life. Do you understand me, Staff Sergeant?"

"Yes, Sir!"

Calming himself, the commanding officer took a deep breath before addressing the staff sergeant. As he did with Lou, the commanding officer spoke in a slow, moderate tone to ensure the staff sergeant understood.

"You are to locate the Officer of the Day. Tell him I want the Reactionary Platoon to move to the beach."

The staff sergeant dutifully replied, "Yes, Sir!"

The lieutenant colonel looked at the staff sergeant who stood frozen at the position of attention and said, "NOW would be a good time."

Staff Sergeant Wordsworth scurried away.

CHAPTER SIXTEEN

The T-33 - March 1970

By 1970 the overwhelming majority of aircraft in the U.S. Armed Forces' inventory were powered by jet engines, but there were still quite a few propellered aircraft flying reconnaissance missions as well as selective combat sorties.

The two-seated Lockheed T-33B "T-Bird" was designed as a trainer to convert pilots initially qualified to fly propellered aircraft to the new jet-powered aircraft. The T-33 T-Bird (or Thunderbird) was modeled after the United States Air Force's first combat jet fighter, the single-seat F-80 Shooting Star. The Lockheed Aircraft Company produced over 6500 of the versatile "T-birds" between 1948 and 1959. Variants of the T-bird included a carrier-based T-33 Sea Star for the Navy, an all-weather fighter for the Air Force, and RT-33B's to conduct reconnaissance missions for the United States and for multiple friendly countries.

The Republic of (South) Korea was one of those friendly nations who not only purchased aircraft from the United States but supported our efforts in Southeast Asia with military personnel within South Vietnam. The South Korean armed forces loses included over 5,000 service members killed and nearly 11,000 wounded while serving in South Vietnam.

Unfortunately, the South Korean pilot of the RT-33B didn't have many options left.

Eject; try to make it to Da Nang; or try an emergency landing on a short runway at the Marine Corps Air Facility at Marble Mountain just south of Da Nang. Ejecting was out of the question for two reasons. First, he had not heard a sound from his backseat copilot/camera operator since the missile had hit. The pilot hoped it was simply a failure of the intercom system, but in his heart of hearts, he knew the reality of the situation. Second, the reconnaissance photos taken earlier by the RT-33B's nose cameras were of critical importance, or so he had been told. To be honest, he didn't know if the aerial photographic equipment or its film was recoverable considering the amount of damage to which the aircraft has been subjected.

This was supposed to be the final combat sortie for this senior citizen of the sky. Built in the late 40's, the aircraft was scheduled to be rotated out of South Vietnam to an outfit back in South Korea.

Right now, Da Nang wasn't looking so good. The left wing had suffered major damage from a ground-to-air missile. Immediately following the impact, the airman watched as the JP-4 jet fuel poured out of his left inboard fuel tank. The pilot understood the single Allison J33-A-35 turbojet engine burned fuel faster than any aircraft he had ever flown. The pilot had tried unsuccessfully to cut off the fuel flow from that wing to avoid losing all its precious liquid. The result was the fuel gauges for both the left and right inboard tanks were now showing empty.

The pilot tapped the fuel gauges with his bloodied left hand as if tapping it would miraculously cause fuel to reappear. No such luck. Not only were the inboard tanks empty but both the wing tip tanks were leaking badly. His fuel indicators were all at rock bottom.

This Korean War-vintage aircraft was on its last leg... if it had any legs at all.

Bingo, he whispered to himself using the aviation term to indicate he was out of fuel.

As for his arm, the pain wasn't too bad as long as he kept his arm immobilized. Using his right hand, he changed his ultrahigh frequency radio to the emergency UHF "Military Guard" frequency of 243.00 megahertz. The pilot took a deep breath to calm his nerves. With only a hint of an accent, the Korean pilot radioed his status in English to the military air traffic controllers.

"Mayday. Mayday. Mayday. This is South Korean Air Force T-33 Zero-Four-Eight. I'm about to bingo. I need a straight-in approach and a clear runway immediately at Marble Mountain with a medical team."

A gunnery sergeant and a staff sergeant with the Marine Air Traffic Control Squadron were manning the tower when the shit hit the fan for Zero-Four-Eight. Routinely monitoring the Guard channel, this two-man team heard the initial distress call from their Korean ally soon after the aircraft had been hit.

They had anticipated the options available to the pilot and had, on their own initiative, alerted Marble Mountain's crash crew and medical department.

The staff sergeant responded, "Roger, Zero-Four-Eight, we are aware of your situation. You are clear to land at Marble Mountain. Be advised, the runway is only 5,000 feet long."

The pilot was quite aware the "T-Bird" required at least 4650 feet of runway.

Avoiding the "crash" word, the controller tried to reassure the pilot with, "Emergency crews are standing by."

The turbojet engine of this old flyer began to sputter. Fuel was gone. The engine was flaming out.

The pilot could see Marble Mountain's single air strip. He aligned his aircraft with the runway but waited until the last moment to extend his landing gear to minimize the drag on the aircraft. He considered dropping the external fuel tanks attached to his wing tips to reduce the drag a little more but decided that would endanger the residents in the nearby village. It might eliminate a little drag but not enough to matter at this stage of the game. He needed to touchdown as quickly as possible without coming in too short. And, he would need the entire runway.

The engine went silent.

"Sijag haebolkkayo!" he said aloud in Korean more to himself than to his passenger.

"Here we go!" he repeated in English.

He could see the crash crew trucks positioning themselves. One alongside the near-end of the runway. Another at the far end. Mid-runway was the olive-drab ambulance with the white circle and the bold red cross blazoned on every side.

"One if I'm short. One if I'm long. And one if I'm just right."

Luckily, I expended all my munitions during the mission. There shouldn't be any rounds "cooking off" if there is a fire, his inside voice determined.

Initially concerned he was losing too much airspeed, he remembered what his American instructor pilot had told him.

"You lose airspeed, you lose lift. You lose lift, you lose altitude. You lose altitude, you start bumping into things, and that would be very bad in an airplane."

Keeping an eagle eye on his airspeed indicator, he quickly realized he was going too fast. He had to reduce his speed to ensure he didn't overshoot the runway.

He had no trouble reducing his airspeed from 125 mph on final approach to the requisite 110 mph for landing. As he crossed the perimeter fence on the southern end of the base, he set his flaps for landing. Then, in one smooth motion, he extended his landing gear and deployed the speed brake.

The two rectangular braking panels on the belly of the aircraft slammed open, purposely creating a tremendous amount of drag. (Similar to the resistance you experienced when, as a child, you held your hand out the window of your parent's car.)

The speed brake dramatically slowed the T-bird. The reduction in airspeed resulted in a noticeable decrease in his altitude. Instinctively, the pilot kept his left hand on the throttle to nudge the engine power up or down as needed. He laughed at himself.

"That's not going to help today," he chuckled.

by James E. Bulman

As he neared touchdown, he became as focused as a pilot could be. He set the aircraft down with less than fifty feet from the start of the runway. The first crash crew truck was a blur.

He immediately pressed his toes on the top of the foot pedals. The brakes were working but he wasn't slowing down as fast as he wanted. He caught a glimpse of the ambulance as he screeched past the mid-point of the runway.

He pressed the toe pedals harder. Harder! HARDER!! He was standing on his toes.

The members of the second crash crew held their breath as the T-Bird went by.

Watching through field glasses, the air traffic controllers both silently had the same thought. *He ain't gonna make it!*

The pilot played his last card. He pulled his foot off the right pedal and lay both feet onto the left toe-pedal. The aircraft swung to the left, slid off the runway and came to a bouncing stop in the grassy area between the runway and the taxiway.

The staff sergeant in the tower began the old aviation adage, "Any landing you can walk away from..." then quickly hushed himself when he remembered the backseat copilot.

The T-33 landed relatively safely. Nevertheless, it was pretty well shot up, as was the pilot. Thanks to the efforts of the U.S Navy medical team at Marble Mountain, he would pull through albeit with limited use of his left arm and hand.

The backseat co-pilot wasn't as lucky.

Unfortunately for the South Korean Air Force pilot, the repair of the T-33 was not a high priority for the Marine maintenance crews at the Marble Mountain Air Facility. After all, it was a Korean Air Force aircraft. Why should the Marines take the time and trouble to put any effort into its reclamation when they had their own aircraft to maintain? If it had been a United States Air Force plane, well, that would have been... Nah! It still would have been the same low priority.

"If the Koreans wanted it, they would come and get it," the commanding officer repeated more than once when queried.

So, there it sat. Not for weeks but for months.

The truth was the Koreans had attempted to retrieve their aircraft but did not have the tools, equipment, repair parts or technicians qualified in country to make the highly-damaged old bird flyable.

In Korean military logic, the thought process came down to this. You decided to land the aircraft at Marble Mountain. You are responsible for figuring out how to get it out of there.

The hapless Korean pilot would wander the maintenance areas, attempting to befriend any Marine willing to assist an ally. Sad few accepted the polite invitations.

The Korean would stand near the soda mess and strike up conversations with the Marine customers. He would even pay for their soda out of his own pocket. Still no takers... that is, until Dan arrived.

Feeling sorry for the allied aviator, Dan agreed to "take-a-look" at the damaged craft. "Take-a-look" soon became "I can fix a couple things" which turned into, "I'll ask my buddies."

Each of his soon-to-be co-conspirators initially balked at using their off-duty time to work on an aircraft they knew precious little about. But one by one, the ad hoc team came together, and repairs began.

Their biggest problem was the lack of replacement parts. After all, helicopters had few, if any, mechanical similarities to a fixed-wing jet aircraft. Some items like sheet metal, hydraulic and fuel tubing, or aircraft wiring could be fabricated. But for the less than scrupulous young Marine, there are always ways of obtaining parts.

One way was to surreptitiously order the parts along with dozens of everyday items through the normal supply channels using Requisition Form (Single Line Item) DD-1348. Unfortunately, if the supply officer was doing his job properly and checked the Master Parts List for the unit's assigned aircraft, he would see that it was not a part required for his squadron's aircraft. The request would be returned for justification.

Of course, this bit of trickery could be successful if you distracted the supply officer while he was signing a larger-than-normal number of *DD-1348*'s. This ploy only worked a handful of times.

A riskier method was to fly a helicopter to Da Nang. Upon landing, the pilot would inform the Ground Controllers of a problem on their aircraft. This imaginary problem would require an overnight stay. During the layover, a team of Marines would stealthily swap the damaged T-33 parts for identical parts on a similar-type Lockheed-manufactured aircraft.

The U.S. Air Force's F-104 Starfighters were excellent hosts for many of the parts needed for the T-33. The F-104's were slowly being phased-out of combat missions and proved easy pickings for our dauntless repairmen.

The Marine helicopter crew chief and our team would pretend working into the night on the "broken" helo. They would maintain a long-running conversation with the airman walking interior guard duty on the flight line while Dan and his crew swapped defective parts for new.

After all, it wasn't actually stealing. They were just re-directing the parts from a soon-to-be-shipped-home aircraft to a war-fighting aircraft.

The team had a strict code of ethics. They only swapped items that would easily be spotted on pre-flight inspection and would not put the air crew members at in danger.

by James E. Bulman

The riskiest method of obtaining parts was to fly to Kadena AFB on Okinawa and perform the same midnight maneuver. The smooth-talking Jason had connections within the Wing Headquarters Squadron and obtained permission for the team to make the trip to Okinawa in their fixed-wing C-117, the military version of the DC-3 cargo aircraft.

Eventually, time caught up with the Marines.

While the South Korean government was awarding the South Korean Order of Military Merit (First Class) to U.S. Army General William Westmoreland, the senior Korean Air Force commander embarrassed the American General by asking the status of the stranded T-33 that "appears to be ignored by your U.S. Marines," or words to that effect.

As in all military matters... shit rolls downhill.

Four-star General Westmoreland demanded Marine Corps Major General Lewis W. Walt (two-star) provide status by the end of the day. The Army general reminded the Marine Corps general, "We are all part of the same Department of Defense."

The two-star Marine bit his normally sharp tongue and did not respond with his typical reply, "Yeah, but we're the men's department!" Instead, he gave a quick "Yes, Sir."

He, in turn, admonished the one-star brigadier general commanding the 1st Marine Wing who ordered the Marine Air Group-16 commander (colonel) to "Get that damned piece of shit aircraft flying!"

Fuming at the harsh reprimand, the group commander called the H&MS Commanding Officer, Lieutenant Colonel Reeves, onto the carpet and informed the lieutenant colonel, "If you ever expect to see full-bird colonel..." Well, you get the picture.

The squadron commanding officer ordered the major in charge of the maintenance department into his office for a closed-door ass-chewing for dragging his feet concerning the T-33.

Stunned, the maintenance officer wanted desperately to remind the lieutenant colonel of his own words, "If the Koreans wanted it, they'd come and get it." Instead, he returned to the maintenance department and tried to light a fire under the enlisted maintenance chief's (a master gunnery sergeant) rear end for lack of focus on this high priority item.

Having been chewed out by the best, the maintenance chief was unfazed by the change in priorities. Well aware of Dan's covert maintenance team for quite some time, the master gunnery sergeant informed the major that he had already organized a repair team that was just standing by for the official "go-ahead."

Dumbfounded by the master gunny's intuition and initiative, the major simply said, "Okay, Go ahead."

The squadron maintenance chief would never let the major know that the wing maintenance chief, also a master gunnery sergeant, had sent a messenger to H&MS maintenance chief giving him a "heads up" concerning the T-33.

That's the way it's done! The master gunny said to himself.

The maintenance chief gathered together his shop NCOs and informed them of the new priority. Only the best technicians were to be assigned and they were to be given all the assistance necessary (and I quote), "To get that piece-of-shit Korean airplane off my Marine Corps Air Facility."

Several weeks later, after stealing... er... scrounging... er... reprioritizing some repair parts from the U.S. Air Force Base at Kadena, Okinawa, and mainland Japan the RT-33B was ready to fly.

Since there were no Marine Corps or Navy pilots qualified to fly the T-bird, the Marine Corps requested a U.S. Air Force "ferry" pilot be brought in to fly the aircraft to Da Nang. Inwardly, the commanding officer was afraid any malfunction would be reported to the Korean Chief of Staff. The commanding officer refused to allow the Koreans to accept their own aircraft until an American pilot had given the okay.

Several days later the visiting American flyboy arrived in the Maintenance Control office and began perusing the maintenance records of the once derelict fighter.

The four-inch-thick, loose-leaf binder was crammed full of 8.5" x 11" yellow Maintenance Action Forms (MAF's) indicating each repair action performed on the aircraft. Normally, there would be white Naval Aircraft Flight Records about half that size intermingled with the MAF's for every flight. It was apparent to the pilot the absence of white sheets meant the plane had not flown for months yet there were dozens of repair actions.

Those rotten, sons-of-bitching Marines have been cannibalizing parts to keep their helicopters flying while ignoring the Korean airplane. The pilot frowned at the sergeant manning the maintenance control office.

"When was the last time this thing flew?" the pilot asked.

The sergeant behind the counter looked up from his Playboy magazine. "Sir," he began quite seriously, "I ain't never seen that thing fly," adding "and I rotate back to the States next week."

The pilot closed the book, reopened it, and began the reviewing process anew. This time, noting each and every repair action, he intended to verify for himself to ensure the repairs had been completed correctly.

The newly-certified plane captain, one Lance Corporal Dan Keegan, had also done his homework. He had previously reviewed the aircraft log books and had inspected every maintenance action prior to the pilot's arrival. Still, the preflight inspection took nearly two hours.

by James E. Bulman

The day had been anticipated for quite some time. Every Marine in the group was focused on this event. All administrative functions ceased as the office clerks gawked from their windows. All support activities were put on hold as motor-transport mechanics, cooks, military police, and civilian workers peered from the edges of the flight line. All aircraft maintenance came to a halt as repair crews viewed the goings-on around "Zero-Four-Eight."

The Korean RT-33B T-bird that had been derelict for months was about to rise from the ashes and fly once again... they hoped.

Satisfied that the aircraft was intact and capable of aviating, the American Air Force pilot climbed into the front seat. Strapping himself in with the assistance of plane captain Dan Keegan, the pilot drew several deep breaths.

With his notepad strapped to his leg, he methodically flipped through the take-off checklist. All looked well.

The engine started smoothly.

Standing on the sidelines, Ski smiled with satisfaction.

I knew I could get it working, he whispered to himself.

The pilot had observed and congratulated Dan on properly positioning the aircraft to avoid a tailwind blowing into the engine exhaust. This type of aircraft had an inherent problem with unburned fuel blowing back into the engine creating quite a torch. Dan smiled proudly. He had spotted that idiosyncrasy while studying the plane captain's procedures.

This old bird still has some life in her, the pilot decided.

Standing at the front of the aircraft, the newly-designated plane captain went through the checklist which he had memorized.

Nearing the end of the checklist, plane captain Dan marched toward the midsection of the aircraft to the rear of the starboard wing. Climbing onto the back of the wing, he walked across to the external fuel tank at the wingtip and pulled the jettison pin. This was necessary in case of an in-flight emergency and the pilot needed to drop the tip tanks.

Dan jumped off the rear of the starboard wing and rolled under the aircraft to avoid the jet engine exhaust. He climbed onto the port wing and performed the same tip-tank pin-removal maneuver.

After jumping off the port wing Dan marched to the front of the aircraft where he displayed the two pins for the pilot's acknowledgement (two fingers and a thumbs-up). Dan returned to the starboard tip tank, opened a small compartment, placed the pins inside and secured the door with the screwdriver blade of his military-issue TL-29 aviation pocket knife. The aircraft was now ready to taxi.

The entire air facility was filled with anticipation.

The plane captain held his arms straight out from his sides, palms open. Pumping his arms at the elbows, he instructed the pilot to move the aircraft forward.

The engine increased in RPM.

The plane captain continued the arm and hand signals.

The engine increased in RPM.

The plane captain continued the arm and hand signals.

Suddenly, the canopy opened, and the ferry pilot put his palms up and shrugged his shoulders demonstrating the internationally understood hand signal interpreted by all NATO countries as, "Beats me!"

The airplane wasn't moving. The brakes were locked!

The pilot shut down the engine. He quickly exited the T-33 and headed directly to the Officer's Club for some liquid courage.

Dan and the maintenance crews worked throughout the night.

The next morning, the Air Force pilot and our friendly plane captain went through the same ritual.

Again, after pulling and stowing the tip tank pins but with a bit more trepidation, the plane captain motioned the aircraft forward.

As the engine's RPM increased so did the crowd's anxiety. Then, with a great sigh of relief, the aircraft lurched forward a few feet. The pilot braked the aircraft to a stop.

All the onlookers smiled.

The plane captain pointed his right arm to the ground while continuing his elbow-pumping with his left arm. Seeing the left turn instruction, the pilot pressed his left brake pedal and the aircraft turned... towards the right.

Stunned, Dan increased the speed to his hand motions assuming the pilot had simply misunderstood.

After the aircraft turned a full ninety degrees in the wrong direction, the canopy opened. The entire base witnessed the international "Beats me!" signal for a second time.

As the U.S. Air Force pilot climbed out of the aircraft, he looked at the plane captain and announced, "Third time is NOT the charm. I'm not flying this piece of shit!" He stormed off the tarmac and was never seen again at Marble Mountain.

Several days later, after many more hours of repair work by the maintenance crews, a second Air Force pilot arrived. He had been forewarned.

"I want to see it move." he demanded.

A flight line team was ordered to tow the aircraft around the aircraft parking ramp. The tow tractor zigzagged around the tarmac with Dan seated in the cockpit, tapping the brakes, first left, then right, then both.

Everything appeared okay. The new pilot seemed satisfied.

The preflight inspection also went well.

As he did previously, nearing the end of the preflight procedures, Dan pulled the right tip tank pin, rolled under the aircraft, climbed onto the other wing and pulled on the left tip tank pin. But it wouldn't come out. Dan pulled harder. It still would not budge. Now with two hands wrapped around the pin, Dan continued to struggle.

Jason was returning from the hangar along with First Lieutenant Waverly. Jason saw the officer's eyes widen when the he realized Dan's predicament. The first lieutenant yelled at the top of his lungs, "NO!!"

Too distant to hear the officer's warning, plane captain Dan gave the pin one last tug and removed the stubborn pin only to discover that it was the only thing holding the tip tank to the wing.

Again, Dan became living proof of Newton's Third Law: For every action there is an equal and opposite reaction.

In a millisecond, the tank dropped from the wing, smacked the tarmac and cracked open like an Easter egg. Two hundred and thirty gallons of aviation fuel spilled onto the ground.

The loss of the 1500 pounds of fuel from the left tip tank caused the left wing to instantly snap upward. The loss of the left-side counterweight caused the right wing to plunge downward. This sudden movement ruptured the right landing gear. The right tip tank struck the ground with such force that it too split open, adding its 230 gallons to the already volatile mixture.

Knocked to his knees by the violent movement of the aircraft, Dan scrambled his way off the wing and leaped over the accumulating fuel.

Anticipating a full inferno, the ferry pilot initiated the ejection procedures.

The T-33 was capable of "zero-zero" ejection. Meaning, the rocket attached to the ejection seat could remove the pilot from the aircraft at zero altitude and zero forward speed. With his left hand, he pulled the yellow-and-black-striped JETISON CANOPY handle. The canopy left the aircraft.

Then, in a moment of contemplation, the Air Force aviator had second thoughts. His mind pondered factors such as, *Brakes didn't work. Tip tank ejected all by itself. Hasn't flown in months. What else might not work?*

The pilot decided not to trust the ejection seat, the parachute, or any other component on this old bird. In what seemed to be a blur of motion, the pilot shut down the engine, rapidly unstrapped himself, abandoned the cockpit, ran across the wing and bounded over the spill.

Flight line personnel quickly went into action. Marines scurried about, rounding up every available fire extinguisher they could find. Individuals sprayed the ignitable liquid with CO_2, Purple-K Powder (PKP), and any other fire retardant that might help.

Maintenance crews rushed to move nearby aircraft away from the potential conflagration. Some aircraft were hooked to tow tractors and driven clear. Others were physically re-located by hand pushing them as fast and as far as muscle-power would allow. Dan was ordered to notify crash crew.

Dan ran into a maintenance shack, picked up the phone, and dialed crash crew's emergency number. Dan informed the dispatcher in a clear yet somewhat excited tone, "T-33 fuel spill on the H&MS-16 flight line. Hurry, it's big!"

Located on the opposite side of the hangar, the enormous crash response vehicles were on the way within moments.

In a bazaar twist, just as the emergency was playing out on the H&MS flight line, a second Korean T-33 (T-Bird) landed on Marble Mountain's runway and taxied to the transient aircraft line.

It seems the Koreans had heard of the Marine's plan to hand the aircraft over to the U.S. Air Force. Attempting to preempt that move, the Koreans brought along their own pilot to relieve the Marine Corps of the T-Bird.

As the pair of visiting Korean pilots were shutting down their T-33, crash crew was rounding the corner from the far side of the hangar.

Not having seen the Korean T-33 since it had landed several months ago, the crash crew assumed the T-Bird taxiing to the transient aircraft line was the T-33 in distress. After all, Zero-Four-Eight had been in the hangar and out of sight for a long time. Spotting the newly-arrived Korean T-33, crash crew assumed they had arrived at the site of the emergency and were hellbent on dousing the foreign flyer with foam.

Unaware of the happenings on the other side of the hangar, the visiting pilots frantically waved off the yellow emergency vehicles. But crash crew seemed determined to extinguish the non-existent fire where they stood.

Meanwhile, back on the other side of the hangar, flight line personnel had exhausted every fire extinguisher within a mile radius.

Dan was again ordered to notify crash crew.

The dispatcher responded with, "They are on site."

"No, they are not!"

"Yes, they are!" he retorted.

"No, they are not!" Dan repeated.

The dispatcher informed Dan that the crash crew leader was currently talking with the pilot.

"No, he's not!"

"Yes, he is!!"

Frustrated, Dan informed the first lieutenant of the situation. The officer ordered Dan to "Find crash crew!"

Dan ran with all the speed his legs could muster.

When Dan turned the hangar corner, he witnessed the crash crew leader arguing with the Korean pilot: one wanting to spray some foam; the other wanting to protect his aircraft.

by James E. Bulman

Dan interrupted the heated debate and informed the emergency personnel that they were at the wrong T-33. They responded with astonishment.

"There's another?"

He assured them that there was.

Shaking their heads in amazement, they gathered up their firefighting equipment, tossed a sheepish apology over their shoulders toward the relieved allies, and sped to the site of the "other" T-33.

Fortunately, the fuel surrounding the aircraft never ignited.

Unfortunately, "Zero-Four-Eight" was again unable to fly.

The Korean reconnaissance aircraft was towed off the line and parked next to one of the Marine revetments. (Next to... not inside.) It sat there for several weeks while blame and recriminations were passed up and down the chain of command.

After some time passed and tempers cooled, the Koreans organized their own rescue plan to extricate "048" from its Marine captors. No longer trusting Marine Aviation, they called on the U.S. Army to airlift their derelict flying machine out of the hands of the Marine Corps.

Similar in appearance to the medium-lift Marine CH-46 Sea Knight with its tandem rotors, the Army CH-47 Chinook helicopter can lift much heavier loads. The CH-47 can lift up to 10,000 pounds of cargo. Close to twice that of the Marine's CH-46. Since the Korean RT-33B's empty weight was close to 8,400 pounds, the CH-47 seemed to be the Army's logical choice.

The day the Army helo arrived at the Marble Mountain Air Facility, it was greeted with boos, hisses, and raspberries... ya' know, the old Bronx cheer... as well as numerous other profane comments.

Listing to starboard, the T-33 was towed with some difficulty to the compass rose where a team of soldiers attached numerous cargo straps to the leaning legend.

The Army crew chief lay on his belly inside the hovering aircraft, looking out of the "hellhole." He provided directional instructions to the pilot who was unable to view the goings-on beneath his aircraft. The Chinook slowly centered itself over its fixed-wing cargo.

As the helicopter inched its way down, a member of the loading team, standing atop the T-33, raised the eyelet of the loading straps. When the hook from the helicopter seemed close enough, he stretched to slip the eyelet into the locking device when there was a loud CRACK!

The other soldiers rushed to assist the loader as he fell backwards from the T-33. The boos, hisses, and raspberries were silenced. The onlookers instantly realized what had happened.

All aircraft, especially helicopters, generate static electricity while flying. The process is identical to the static created when you walk across a carpet in your home on a dry autumn day and then touch a doorknob. Helicopters, with their high-speed rotating blades slicing through the air, are known to generate up to 200,000 volts of static electricity.

The loader had touched the hook of the hovering helicopter. The built-up static electricity discharged through his body to the T-33 and eventually to the earth. Luckily, his fall was cushioned by his fellow soldiers. The loader was knocked unconscious for a moment but soon came to.

An alternate loader resumed the loading process. This time the new loader used a rudimentary device to rid the helicopter of its static charge prior to hooking on to it. The device was a simple broom stick with an attached length of wire clamped to a grounding rod on the compass rose. A ten-penny nail is attached to the other end. Toss in a pair of electrician's rubber gloves and they were good to go.

As the hovering helo neared the load, the loader simply touched the nail to the hook and "CRACK", the helicopter was safely discharged through the wire to the ground rod.

Once the Marine audience realized that the soldiers were not permanently harmed, the boos, hisses, and raspberries resumed.

The Chinook successfully hooked to the T-33 on the second attempt. It began to creep skyward. The loading straps stretched as the full weight of the T-33 pulled earthward. When all was clear, the Army pilot carefully pulled up on the collective stick and slowly pushed the cyclic stick forward. The CH-47 transitioned from a hover to forward motion with the Korean aircraft dangling below.

The Army Chinook pilots were a bit peeved at the loading crew's performance, and how the Marines seemed to have enjoyed the mistakes made. To satisfy his own ego, the Army copilot looked over at his pilot and commented, "I don't know why those jarheads treated us that way. Heck, they could have used one of their choppers to lift this thing."

The pilot stewed on that for a while then decided to show the Marines what a "real" helicopter can do.

The pilot spun his chopper around and flew back towards the compass rose. Intent on doing a "fly-by" to impress "those jarheads", he quickly increased his forward airspeed to a point where the copilot cautioned his senior aviator, "Take it easy, Steve."

Steve wasn't listening to his copilot as he made a sharp turn, forgetting he was carrying an extremely heavy external load. The centrifugal force of the external T-33 started to pull on the Chinook. Realizing he had exceeded safe operating limits, the pilot over-corrected. The T-33 began to swing wildly. The Army aircrew could feel the load was beginning to endanger the lifting aircraft. The pilot over-corrected again. The tail was now wagging the dog.

The crew chief already had his hand on the HOOK RELEASE handle when the pilot shouted, "Pickle it! Pickle it!!" The crew chief pulled the handle, and the T-bird fell from the helo.

At the loss of the T-33, the helicopter immediately jerked skyward. (Remember Newton?) Unfortunately, the Korean Thunderbird did the opposite. Even though the aircraft had been defueled, it burst into flames as it impacted the ground.

Thankfully, nobody on the ground was hurt. Unfortunately, the Army pilot will hear the boos, hisses, and raspberries for the rest of his life.

CHAPTER SEVENTEEN

Assault on the Marble Mountain Air Facility - July 1970

Lou ran to the armory and located a medical corpsman. He informed the sailor that the commanding officer ordered the Navy man to relocate to the beach where his skills were desperately needed.

Following a quick "Q and A" about Jason's wounds, the corpsman gathered up some medical items then informed Lou he was ready to go. Lou grabbed the medical man by the shirt-sleeve and forcefully half-pulled, half-dragged the man towards the beach.

The two men ran as fast as their legs would carry them toward the beach. As they passed the burning revetments Lou could see the damage that was being inflicted upon the MAG-16 aircraft. With his senses at their peak, Lou spotted a person (more a shadow than a person) lurking about the undamaged CH-46 Sea Knight cargo helicopters. The shadow disappeared through the starboard crew door.

Why would anyone be climbing into a helo when the battle was quite a distance from there? Lou thought the person/shadow might be a Marine shirking his duty. Then again, it might be the bandit Jason and Dan had heard earlier among the Conex containers still deciding where to throw the next satchel charge. Either way, Lou couldn't ignore it. He had to check it out.

He immediately stopped his companion and directed him to take cover. Lou left the corpsman and inched his way to the helicopter.

The rear ramp was down but he was unable to see clearly into the cabin. The only light was that of the flickering fires raging in nearby squadrons.

by James E. Bulman

As Lou cautiously stepped onto the ramp of the aircraft when he heard a rustling noise up forward. There was somebody else in the aircraft... probably in the cockpit or maybe coming up the crew door steps.

As he squinted to improve his focus, Lou had no need to investigate any further to confirm his suspicions. This was the intruder Jason and Dan heard among the Conex containers earlier.

The movement was slight. Lou saw one leg of a pair of the ubiquitous black pajamas surreptitiously attempting to work its way out of the cockpit.

The realization that he was going to have to kill another human being gave Lou pause. Lou's mind raced. He wasn't sure if he had the weapon on SAFE or in the SEMI position.

For only an instant, Lou took his mind off the cockpit and the intruder. He glanced down at his M-16. The SELECT FIRE lever was in the SEMI position. One trigger pull - one shot. He rotated it forward to the AUTO position. One trigger pull - empty the magazine.

Let God sort them out, Lou decided. Whoever was in the cockpit wasn't going to leave this aircraft alive.

Returning his focus on the cockpit, Lou was stunned to see the black-pajama-clad enemy soldier had extricated himself from the pilot's seat and was now staring Lou face-to-face. The sapper was a tiny thing, only a couple of inches over five feet tall, if that. The enemy's face was covered with black camouflage paint.

Beneath the olive drab make-up, Lou could see it wasn't a man at all but an attractive young girl. Lou's mind went into a tailspin. The sapper was the soda mess lady.

She offered her apologies with a weak-hearted, "Sorry, Lou," as she pulled the pin of her satchel charge. She tossed it towards him as she exited the helicopter.

In what seemed to be a single motion, Lou raised his M-16, pulled the trigger, and moved to intercept the explosive device.

Fumbling his rifle, he dove and caught the package. He rolled on the deck of the chopper to reverse his direction (as taught by sensei Staff Sergeant Wordsworth) ow facing the rear of the aircraft, Lou rose and ran for the ramp. The instant he was off the ramp he heaved the lethal charge as far as he could towards the empty neighboring revetment. Lou stumbled off the ramp and fell to the ground. He immediately covered the back of his head with his interlaced fingers and yelled, "Incoming!" Lou heard the explosion an instant before the rush of debris washed over his body. He knew he had been injured but the boxer in him insisted that he get off the canvas. As he struggled to rise, he spotted the female sapper heading for the next row of helicopters.

A feeling of helplessness filled his mind when he realized he was unable to stop her. He had dropped his rifle in the CH-46 when he caught the satchel charge.

He could almost see the self-satisfied grin on her face as she turned towards Lou knowing she had escaped his poorly aimed rifle fire.

Her smile froze on her face.

POP!

POP!

POP!

Lou winced as three 5.56 mm rounds passed just over his shoulder.

He saw the soda mess lady drop to the ground. Lou spun around to see where the deadly accurate rifle fire had initiated. Lance Corporal Dan Keegan slid next to Lou and fired three more runs.

The "Pop. Pop. Pop." was punctuated with Dan informing Lou, "Sight alignment. Sight picture really works."

When Dan saw the look on Lou's face, Dan added his opinion.

"Sorry, Lou. But I never did like that bitch."

"Where did you come from?" Lou asked.

"Jerry sent me to hurry you along. Jason's in bad shape." As they spoke, the corpsman flopped by their sides. His immediate focus was the injuries to Lou's posterior. Lou brushed away the medical man, insisting his services were more needed on the beach.

Dan helped Lou to his feet. Dan grabbed the corpsman's sleeve and lead the pair to the more critically injured Marine behind the van complex.

by James E. Bulman

CHAPTER EIGHTEEN

Okinawa - April 1970

As agreed upon earlier, the newly-arrived Marines rendezvoused at the Park Avenue Club on Gate Two Street, Okinawa City just outside the U.S. Air Force Base at Kadena on the island of Okinawa at, you guessed it, Gate Number Two.

A few days following the T-33 debacle, Dan became aware of a military hop on a C-117 heading to Okinawa. Although it was intended to fly to Okinawa, pick up some supplies, and fly back to Marble Mountain the same day, Dan knew the fix was in. The C-117 Sky Train would contract some mysterious malady that would require the aircraft to remain overnight (RON). Dan and his unofficial T-33 repair team finagled their way onto the hop as a group. It took a lot of begging, pleading, and cajoling but the Group Maintenance Chief appreciated the work they had done. Knowing there would be no reward for their efforts, he pulled a few strings.

The Navy version of the Douglas DC-3, the fixed-wing C-117 twin-engine cargo aircraft was a "tail dragger" leftover from World War II. In the '60s and' 70s, the Sky Train was used mostly for administrative hops to Taiwan, mainland Japan, or Okinawa. It flew to wherever the much-desired mail or much-needed aircraft parts and supplies were located. Sometimes flying hundreds of miles and back for one small package as fast as the propeller-driven warhorse could fly. Other times, it lumbered home filled to the brim with combat supplies jammed into every available crevice.

For less critical missions, it was not unusual for the aircraft to develop an unexplained mechanical malfunction that would require an untold number of hours to repair. The puzzling malady would inexplicably resolve itself after a night of partying in one of Okinawa's many adult entertainment establishments.

The plane touched down at Kadena about 1600.

After landing the aircraft, the pilot immediately informed the tower that they had experienced intermittent engine troubles and needed the crew chief to assess the situation. When hearing of the pilot's "troubles" the two airmen manning the tower looked at each other and rolled their eyes. They would, of course, play along.

"Roger that Sierra Zulu Zero Three. Let's hope your crew can have your problems taken care of by the morning," the senior airman offered with a wry smile. It was obvious to all witnesses that it would require an "unexpected" RON.

Of course, the crew chief would find nothing wrong because there was nothing wrong. It was just an excuse to authorize a night of liberty for all crew and passengers.

Jason and the gang wasted no time taking advantage of the opportunity presented to them by the mysterious aircraft malady.

Not yet evening and still daylight, the first nightspot they chose was as empty as an adult establishment the day before payday... which it was. They looked at each other for guidance but, ever the leader, Jason made up their minds for the them. He walked into the bar as if he owned the place. The team followed.

While their eyes were adjusting to the lack of lighting, they could see they had surprised the bikini-clad hostesses (and I use the term loosely) who worked in this establishment. In a coffee klatch at end of the bar, the startled girls spotted the new customers and scrambled to their posts. One manned the bar. One threw American quarters into the juke box. One mounted the foot-high stage and began rhythmically dancing to The Association's *Cherish*." The remainder of the waitressing squad swarmed the newcomers like bees around honey.

Giggling like school girls, (the Marines, not the hostesses) they protested weakly.

Catfish looked at Brian and informed him, "If this don't get your fire started, your wood's wet!"

Each girl was quite pretty. They were all extremely buxom, especially for typically petite Japanese ladies. They spoke English well enough to encourage the boys to start the night's festivities here and now.

The vote was unanimous...nearly.

Brian was opposed.

"I hate this place!" Brian announced, "C'mon guys. Isn't there a better place than this?"

"Jesus Christ, Brian!" Lou interjected, laying out the obvious. "You just left a war zone, the beers are 75 cents a bottle, you've got beautiful girls crawling all over you, and you're bitching? Jesus Christ!" Lou ended his tirade in frustration.

"But..." Brian tried to explain his position but was quickly interrupted.

by James E. Bulman

"Shut, the hell, up, Brian," Catfish demanded, tossing in one of his southern witticisms. "If you had a ham under each arm, you'd complain that you had no bread!"

In unison, they all repeated, "Yeah! Shut up!"

Brian was overruled by acclamation.

As they were being escorted to their table, Jason had already taken a short leave of absence from the group and had cornered the female club manager. When he rejoined the table, he informed all hands that he had negotiated discount rates on the drinks for the "battle-weary" Marines. Fifty cents a beer was now the going rate.

Adding a fifty-cent tip, Jason slapped four dollars on the table, Jason shouted, "First round is on me!"

They all cheered and proclaimed Jason their hero.

"Here's to Jason!" they shouted.

They chugged the adult beverage in unison.

Jason suddenly announced, "Brian's got the next round."

"I don't even like beer," Brian protested.

The Marines responded with a flurry of negative comments.

"Oh, c'mon, Brian, don't be a skinflint."

"What an old fart."

"Who invited this guy?"

"Okay, Okay, Brian relented. "Next round is on me."

Jason was instantly dethroned. Brian was proclaimed their hero.

Slowly peeling the currency from his wallet, Brian meticulously counted out three one-dollar bills as he placed them neatly on the table. He rummaged around in his pockets and came up with one quarter, two dimes, and five pennies. The tip was noticeably absent.

When the waitress arrived with the seven fresh bottles, she informed the party-goers in broken English, "Happy Hour all over. Beer now dollar each. Dollar each. Seven dollar now." Then she added, "... plus dollar tip."

Eying the meticulously-counted money on the table, she added, "No coin. Just dollar."

Jason smiled in victory.

The partygoers re-elected Jason their hero for pulling one over on Brian.

As he peeled five additional dollars from his wallet, Brian responded with the inevitable, "I don't get it." Brian begrudgingly scooped up the loose change.

Feeling a bit guilty, Jason slid next to Brian in an apparent attempt to apologize but instead Jason inadvertently hip-butted Brian out of his seat. This forced Brian to move to the chair closest to the stage.

Dan thought this was a bit unusual until Jason and he made eye contact. Jason gave Dan a sly wink then quickly scanned the rest of our illustrious team. The fix was in...and Dan was to inform the rest of the guys that something was up.

Dan did as he was silently ordered.

They hooted and hollered as the dancer, who was now topless, slid her way off the stage, and began dancing close to their table. Right next to Brian... More accurately, she was all over Brian.

Brian squirmed uncomfortably. His buddies roared with pleasure at his displeasure.

"C'mon, Brian. Don't be an old fart. Enjoy yourself." Jason chided.

"I don't typically go to places like this," Brian defended himself.

"Well, at least tip the dancer then we'll move out to the veranda," Jason recommended.

Feigning a cashflow problem, Brian tried the old "I-only-have-twenties-in-my-wallet" routine.

Frustrated, Jason relented. "Fine!" he said with mock disgust. "Here's a buck." He handed the one-dollar bill to Brian.

"Slip it into her garter," he instructed.

Whining like a six-year-old being told to brush his teeth, Brian protested, "I hate this kinda stuff. You tip her!" He handed the bill back to Jason.

"Give the girl her goddamn money," Lou interrupted forcefully. His temper was rising.

"She's just trying to make a living," Jerry explained.

That was the clincher. Brian's protestations ended with a reluctant, "Okay."

Catfish added, "Just give the girl her tip."

"Fine. Fine!" Brian relented and hesitantly stuffed the dollar under her garter.

The girl immediately snatched Brian by the wrist. "You next," she instructed Brian matter-of-factly in her accented English.

"What?" Brian tried to pull his arm away as the other hostesses surrounded him.

"You next!" they insisted.

"I'm next what?" His voice cracked like a pubescent high school freshman.

Jason leaned into the crowd of girls and explained, "You're the next dancer, Brian. The first tipper of the day has to perform... in the nude."

Brian's bulging eyes revealed his panic.

Going along with the gag, the team chimed in.

"Oh, c'mon, don't you know?"

"Hell, everybody knows the first tipper of the day has to dance naked."

"Damn, he's such a boot!"

"What a rookie!"

by James E. Bulman

Frantically, Brian struggled for words. He stuttered, stammered, and slurred his objections until he had an epiphany.

"Wait a second. It was Jason's money." Brian argued, "HE should dance!"

Astonished at the logic of his argument, the crowd was stunned into silence.

Catfish whispered in surprise, "Even a blind squirrel stumbles across an acorn every now and then."

But Jason didn't skip a beat, "You know, Brian, you're right."

A shocked Dan spoke for the entire team as he murmured, "He is?"

"How about we flip for it?" Jason offered.

Buoyed by his first-ever victory and after a moment's thought, Brian agreed.

With the deftness of a three-card-monte dealer on Times Square, Jason demonstrated his abilities of legerdemain. He held the quarter between his forefinger and thumb and demonstrated that it was not a two-headed coin. Then, after receiving a nod from Brian, he flipped it into the air and slapped it onto the back of his left hand, covering it with his right.

"Call it!"

Giving it much deliberation, Brian decided, "Heads!"

The pause lasted forever. All eyes were focused on the hidden coin. The drama was excruciating. Jason leaned towards the center of the table. They all leaned closer. Jason looked each one of them in the eyes.

They were as one.

Then, in a single move, Jason shoved his left hand towards the group, raised his right hand less than an inch making it impossible for anyone to actually see the coin.

Dan, Jerry, Lou, Catfish, and Ski cried out in unison, "Tails!"

Jason retracted his hand in a blur, removed the coin, and inserted it back into his pocket.

It happened so fast, all Brian could utter was a weak, "Damn!"

The ladies surrounded him like crazed teeny-boppers besieging Davy Jones of the Monkees. Escorting Brian, they shuffled as a group towards the curtained doorway at the side of the stage. Resisting all the way, Brian continued his protests.

At the curtain, Brian grabbed the doorjamb with both hands (and both feet) stopping the procession in its place.

"Okay, okay! I'll do it. I'll do it! But wait a minute!"

The girls were all smiles.

Hoping his "friends" were out of earshot, Brian whispered for advice while searching for the correct words.

"Y'know, if girls get ...uh ...well, if they get, y'know... 'excited', nothing happens. But if guys get 'excited', we get a... well, we get an... y'know, an... well, excited!"

Now pleading for advice, "What if I get EXCITED?"

They could last no longer. On that question, the girls broke into laughter and released Brian into the custody of his fellow merrymakers. Jason had to explain to Brian that it was all a gag.

Brian had a confused look on his face and finally admitted, "You got me. You got me." Everyone could see Brian replaying the gag in his brain in an attempt to understand what had happened and where he had gone wrong.

Brian immediately began to lobby his cause.

"I knew it was a gag all the time. I was just playing along," he informed each team member, one at a time.

The fun continued into the night with Brian politicking for his cause.

"You won't tell anybody else, will you?" he begged Ski.

"Of course not," Ski assured him.

Tucking a dollar bill into Brian's shirt pocket, Ski added, "Don't get EXCITED!"

The next morning at 0630, the team reluctantly reassembled on the flight line. Ski was, as usual, the last to arrive.

Meeting the crew of the C-117, they soon discovered that the imaginary problem with the number one engine had transformed itself into a real problem. No matter how many tricks the crew chief tried, the number one engine just wouldn't start.

"Don't get excited," Ski cautioned the pilot. "I can have this bird flying again in no time."

"Have you ever worked on a C-117 before?" the crew chief asked skeptically.

"Nope."

"Have you ever worked on Wright R-1820 Cyclone engine before?"

"Nope."

"Then what makes you think you can fix this when I haven't been able to figure it out?" the sergeant continued his interrogation.

Jason stepped in.

"If Ski says he can fix it...he can fix it." He looked at Ski for reassurance, adding, "You CAN fix it, can't you?"

"Piece o' cake."

The pilot cut the argument short.

"Look guys. If I don't get this tail-dragger back to Marble Mountain tonight, my ass is grass." He continued, "The colonel might buy one night's RON but two... never. Plus, the colonel needs to take this baby to Atsugi on mainland Japan for some big conference tomorrow. Give the guy a shot at it," he advised the reluctant crew chief.

Throwing his hands up, the crew chief surrendered, and walked away without a word.

"You CAN fix it, can't you?" the pilot asked again.

Without answering the pilot, Ski shouted to the team, "Get me a check stand."

"I'll get it," Lou volunteered and jogged away in search of the wheeled work platform.

Huffing and puffing, Archer spotted a check stand already attached to a Schramm tractor next to the hangar. He hopped on the tractor and scanned the limited cluster of gauges as he tried to remember how to start the near-antique piece of farm equipment.

After a bit of fumbling, the tow tractor roared to a start. Then, like stink on shit, an Air Force airman positioned himself in front of the large rear tires of the tractor with his arms crossed, blocking Lou's path.

"What?" Lou demanded feigning ignorance.

"This is an Air force base, grunt. You need an Air Force operator's license issued by our base commander to drive one of our tow tractors." His disdain for Marines was quite evident.

"Well, flyboy, I have one right here!" Lou retorted tapping his wallet in his left hip pocket.

"I doubt it."

"Look for yourself."

Lou raised his left cheek of his buttocks to reach his wallet to display his Marine Corps ground support driver's license which he hoped would appease the arrogant airman. The airman approached the right side of the tractor with his hands on his hips.

"Well!" the blue-togged airman demanded impatiently.

As Lou wiggled to remove his wallet, he inadvertently lifted his foot off the clutch pedal. In gear, the tractor lurched forward. The large rear tire hit the airman knocking him down.

Lou felt the vehicle bounce as if going over a speed bump. *Oh, shit!* Lou thought.

Knowing he had just run over the flyboy, Lou quickly thought of the repercussions.

One: *I'm going to be arrested.*

Two: *The entire crew and all the passengers would be placed on a legal hold and prevented from leaving the island.*

Three: *We will never get the C-117 back to Marble Mountain by midnight.*

Four: *The colonel will miss his conference.*

Five: *The pilot's ass is grass.*

Six: *My ass is grass!*

Cutting off his thoughts, Lou heard the nine-cylinder Wright R-1820 engine sputter, as it attempted to start. Suddenly the number one engine spewed smoke, popped, and started as if it had never been a problem.

Making his decision, Lou instantly stomped on the gas while shifting into second gear. He felt two more bumps and, without looking back, realized the check stand had just rolled over the hapless airman. Lou gunned the tractor's engine.

In the far distance, Lou could hear the airman screaming.

"God damn Marines! Asshole Marines! Son's-a-bitching Marines!"

Glancing over his shoulder, Lou could see a small crowd gathering around the injured flyboy.

Arriving at the aircraft, Lou could see Ski smiling like a high school senior on prom night.

"Don't need the check stand now, good buddy." Peering over Lou's shoulder, Ski added, "What's all of the hubbub about?"

Trying to get his message across, Lou answered in rapid fire.

"It's nothing, but we need to get out of here NOW."

"What's the hurry?" Ski asked.

"It's nothing, but we just need to get out of here NOW!"

All the Marines looked towards the ever growing crowd near the ground support equipment area. As a group, the witnesses at the accident scene were pointing directly at the Marine aircraft.

"NOW! Or we'll be stuck here for a month!" Lou yelled as he pulled the yellow wheel chocks from the wheels and threw them to the rear of the aircraft.

In unison, the air crew and passengers realized something was drastically wrong and they had better heed Lou's instructions.

Within two minutes, the pilots entered the cockpit, completed the abbreviated emergency start checklist and were taxiing to the runway. The tower cleared the aircraft for takeoff.

Without hesitation, the C-117 Sky Train turned from the taxiway onto the runway. The pilot increased the RPM of both engines and left Kadena in its rearview mirror.

Minutes later, Kadena Air Traffic Control could be heard over the UHF radio, "Sierra Zulu Zero Three. Be advised, you have a fugitive on board and are directed to return to base."

All eyes swung in Lou's direction.

"Fugitive?" they voiced in harmony.

Sheepishly, Lou whispered, "Sorry, guys."

The pilot thought for a moment then began rubbing his hand-held microphone over his day-old beard creating a rustling noise.

by James E. Bulman

"Please repeat." He requested.

Traffic control repeated the message adding, "Sierra Zulu Zero Three. Be advised, you are broken and garbled. Do you read me?"

Continuing the ploy, the pilot responded with "Roger re-directing to Da Nang as requested."

"Negative, Zero Three. Return to Kadena."

The background noise continued.

"We were never in Futenma."

Frustrated ATC answered, "Not Futenma... Kadena!"

"Well, which is it? Futenma or Kadena?"

Finally understanding what was going on, the controller terminated the conversation, "Roger, Sierra Zulu Zero Three. Understood. We'll notify customs in Da Nang."

Sierra Zulu Zero Three did not respond. Nor did they land in Da Nang. Marble Mountain was their goal.

Those yellow tractors and check stands are classified as ground support equipment (GSE). Referred to as "yellow gear," there are dozens of these brightly-painted items assigned to each air facility. This mobile equipment is necessary to maintain the squadron aircraft.

Some of this GSE are self-propelled; some are towable. There are tow tractors for positioning the aircraft and other equipment on the flight line; mobile work platforms for lifting mechanics to the upper reaches of the aircraft; portable power units to apply electrical or hydraulic power to the aircraft for troubleshooting problems without starting the aircraft engines; lighting units for working through the night; trailers for carrying ordnance; and trailers to move jet engines. Most are generic pieces of equipment and there are some that are specific to one type aircraft. The ground support equipment is generally staged at the edge of the flight line for easy access.

Technically, to use any of this equipment, the U.S. Navy mandates the user must have a valid operator's license for each type of equipment. To obtain a license the candidate must attend a training class on the use, care and safety concerns of the equipment. The student must pass a written test authored by a Marine NCO with no formal test writing training, and whose secret desire is to assess your knowledge of the most insignificant idiosyncrasies of the equipment. The exams were never professionally validated. They often contained questions like "Which is not the best way to start the NC-8 Self-propelled Electrical Power Generator if it is needed immediately?" And, offers distractors like,

        a.) A
        b.) A & B
        c.) Not A & B
        d.) All the above.

Huh?

After successful completion of the written test, the Marine may be required to demonstrate to the ground support NCO how to safely operate the equipment.

Upon successful completion of all these requirements, the Marine is issued form OPNAV4790/102 Aviation Support Equipment Operator's License officially empowering him to operator that one item. Since there are dozens of types of support equipment, the Marine must go through this process dozens of times.

At least, that is the plan. And, as every successful military planner understands, "No plan survives contact with the enemy."

Picture this: The gunny needs a piece of ground support equipment to expedite the repair of an aircraft preparing to launch on a combat mission. You inform the gunny you don't have a license for the item. The gunnery sergeant will most likely reply, "I don't have time for this Navy bullshit. I don't give a rat's ass if you are licensed or not. Get me that piece of GSE NOW!"

You have two choices: 1) Go to the Ground Support Office where you are advised that you lack a valid operator's license. You must register for an operator's class scheduled every Thursday from 0900 to 1000. Unfortunately, today happens to be Friday, or 2) simply climb on the item of interest without officially checking it out, relocate it to the aircraft in question, and use it until the aircraft has been repaired. Then, of course, you return it to the staging area, or 3) since nobody knows you used the item (after all, you never did officially sign for the equipment), leave it where it was last used on the flight line and let the GSE people reclaim it at their leisure.

It is easy to understand that Kadena Air Force Base wasn't the only military facility having issues with unlicensed operators. It was a problem on nearly every Air Force, Army, Navy and Marine Corps air base.

That brings us to the ever-tardy Ski.

Notorious for not following the rules, Ski often used the yellow gear as his own personal form of transportation. Ignoring what may be the pressing needs of the aircraft maintenance department, Ski would drive the powered units to the soda mess to pick up a can of Coca-Cola or to the small PX for some new razor blades, or to another squadron to talk to an old buddy.

Oh, he most certainly intended upon returning the item as quickly as possible but, given Ski's penchant to forgetfulness... well, you get the picture. This lead to a

by James E. Bulman

series of minor incidents culminating in an investigation by the Naval Investigative Service (NIS) (Now known as the Naval Criminal Investigative Service or simply NCIS).

Incident #1: Troubleshooting an engine problem one evening after his normal working hours, Ski needed an external electrical power unit to apply electricity to the helicopter. Instead of officially checking out a unit from the ground support equipment office, he slid into the seat of an old NC-2 staged nearby. He drove it to the aircraft, and following standard procedures, set the emergency brake and placed wheel chocks on both sides of one of the rear tires. He unwound the electrical cable from the spring-loaded reel and plugged the heavy-duty electrical cable into the aircraft receptacle (about as big around as a beer can). He started the mobile generator and applied external electricity to the helicopter to complete his troubleshooting.

After repairing the engine problem, Ski shut down the electrical generator, removed the wheel chocks and jumped back onto the NC-2 intent on driving it back to the staging area before its absence was noticed.

Unfortunately, he only drove about ten feet when the *NC-2*'s forward motion came to a bone-jarring halt. In the darkness, Ski failed to see that the electrical cable was still plugged into the helicopter. To his astonishment, the plug did not separate from the aircraft receptacle. Instead, the entire receptacle separated from the helicopter leaving a gaping hole with double-aught gauge wires dangling where the receptacle had been.

In a moment of panic, Ski pressed his foot on the accelerator and made a beeline for the staging area where he left the mobile power unit, receptacle and all, to be discovered by the Ground Support crew the next morning.

The commanding officer had the maintenance officer investigate the underlying cause of the aircraft damage. Since Ski was working on his off-duty time, never officially logged in as working on the aircraft, and never signed out the power unit, the investigation came to nothing.

Incident #2: As stated earlier, walking guard duty is boring, at best. It is extremely difficult to "walk my post in a military manner keeping always on the alert." It soon becomes a struggle to simply stay awake. To Ski, this was a struggle easily overcome by borrowing a mobile power unit like, let's say, an NC-2 conveniently staged nearby, silently beckoning the young Marine to "Ride me!"

Always up to a challenge, the young Marine heeded the call and decided "to *ride* my post in a military manner keeping always on the alert."

With his rifle awkwardly slung across his left shoulder, Ski discovered the NC-2 could move along swiftly. Although with rear-wheel steering, the self-propelled unit was a bit tricky to maneuver. Ski quickly mastered it... or so he thought. Grossly exceeding the flight line speed limit of five miles per hour, he decided to drive between the helicopters like a downhill skier moving back and forth through the slalom gates. Zigging and zagging, Ski was having a blast. That is, until on one turn He spotted a large wheeled fire extinguisher directly in his path. Reverting to his normal car driving habits, Ski jerked the steering wheel to the left to avoid the pressurized cylinder and immediately realized his mistake. The rear-wheel steering added to the loss of control. The mobile unit was meant to travel at a snail's pace. It was not a Formula One racecar. To make matters worse, the NC-2 has a high center of gravity with the majority of its bulk above the driver's seat.

As Ski yanked the steering wheel to port, the vehicle began to list to starboard. Unable to correct the severe tilt to the right, Ski bailed out to the left. Barely escaping with his life, he rolled onto the Marsden matting as he smacked the back of his head, his right elbow and his knees. His M-16 slammed to the ground, and a single round was fired into a nearby pile of sand. He immediately sat up to witness the NC-2 roll onto its side. The top-heavy unit came to an abrupt stop with a thunderous crash.

How am I going to bullshit my way through this one? he asked himself.

Again, panic set in.

After only a moment's thought, he recovered his M-16. His radio came alive.

Both in the same duty section, Ski knew Jason was the night's Corporal of the Guard.

"Was that a rifle shot?" Jason radioed his sentries, one at a time.

"Post Number One?" he asked.

"Post Number One: Negative."

"Post Number Two?" he asked.

"Post Number Two: Negative."

"Post Number Three?" he asked.

"Post Number Three: Negative."

"Post Number Four?" he asked.

"Post Number Four: Affirmative."

by James E. Bulman

Jason immediately notified the Officer of the Day that shots had been confirmed on Post Number Four.

Following protocol, the OOD put the entire air facility on alert. The air raid sirens at Marble Mountain whirred to life. All outdoor lighting on the air facility was shut down. The Reactionary Platoon was called into action. Group headquarters was put on alert. Wing headquarters in Da Nang was informed. Adjacent allied facilities were notified.

Seeing the reaction to his single rifle shot, Ski could only mutter a whispered, "Oh, shit!"

When the commanding officer arrived on the scene only moments later, he questioned Ski about firing his weapon.

"Well, Sir," Ski began his imaginary tale, "As I walked past the GSE staging area, I heard the NC-2 start up. I swung around and spotted a small person in black pajamas driving off with the unit. Unable to catch up to it, I fired one shot to get him to stop. I think I may have hit him. That's when he lost control and rolled the unit onto its side. I lost sight of the intruder after that."

The CO ordered the reactionary platoon to sweep the area for the intruder.

"Why," the CO wondered aloud, "would an intruder try to steal an old NC-2?"

"Beats me, Sir," Ski speculated, "Maybe trying make a fast getaway?"

The CO, the OOD, and Jason all responded incredulously at the same time.

"On an NC-2?"

"Well," Ski said weakly. "It could be."

Incident #3: Following the last two incidents when Ski had barely escaped getting sentenced to life in Leavenworth, you would think he would avoid the ground support equipment like the plague. Not Ski.

Once again, he needed a mobile electrical generator for troubleshooting.

Did he check one out? Of course not.

Did he have a license? Of course not!

Did he have someone else check one out for him? Of course not!!

Did he "borrow" one without officially checking it out? You guessed it. Of course, he did.

Just as before, Ski jumped into the seat of an NC-2 staged nearby, drove it to the aircraft, unwound the electrical cable from the spring-loaded reel and plugged the heavy-duty, electrical cable into the aircraft receptacle, started the mobile generator and applied electricity to the helicopter to complete his troubleshooting.

While immersed in his technical problem, Ski did not realize he had forgotten to set the emergency brake or position the wheel chocks. The bulky power unit rolled steadily forward until Ski felt the aircraft shudder. Turning to see what had just occurred, Ski watched helplessly as the power unit ripped through the skin of the helicopter.

This time, Ski had a plan of action. He shut down the electrical generator, jumped back onto the NC-2, pressed his foot on the accelerator and made a beeline for the staging area where he left the mobile power unit, with green paint on the left front fender as clear evidence of the collision.

The next day the special agent from NIS was assigned to investigate the possibility of sabotage. He interviewed anyone remotely associated with aircraft maintenance or ground support equipment. Since there was no concrete evidence of sabotage, the final report listed the three incidents as "Human error by person or persons unknown."

Ski was off the hook... again.

by James E. Bulman

CHAPTER NINETEEN

*Assault on the Marble Mountain
Air Facility - July 1970*

"Who's in charge now?"

Perplexed, Dan responded, "I don't know. The six of us were all promoted on the same day. The admin corporal ain't worth a shit so..."

"Should we go alphabetically?" Ski asked.

"By age?" Jerry wondered.

"I get it!" Brian interrupted his buddies with a revelation.

Having never heard those words coming from Brian's mouth, the stunned trio looked at each other then back at Brian and asked, "You get what?"

"Chamberlain," was his cryptic reply.

Confused, Dan and Catfish looked at each other.

"It's Chamberlain," Brian repeated.

"Wilt Chamberlain?" Catfish asked.

Brian's jaw dropped at Catfish's ignorance. "No! It's NOT Wilt Chamberlain," Brian admonished Catfish.

"It's Colonel Joshua Chamberlain!" he prompted, as if everyone on the planet Earth should know who Colonel Joshua Chamberlain was. "Chamberlain at Little Round Top... Maine Regiment... big battle... Civil War... Remember?"

Blank stares from Dan, Jerry, Ski, and Catfish.

Dan knew who he sounded like when he replied, "Now it's my turn. I don't get it. How does all that relate to our situation right now?"

"Didn't any of you study American History in high school?"

"Yeah," Dan answered, "But all the teacher did was prep us for the *SAT*'s."

"Same here," Catfish concurred.

Jerry nodded in agreement with the other two.

Ski commented, "And you see where that got us."

Brian started to present a complete history of the Civil War. His thoughts were racing faster that his voice could repeat. He was talking so fast he began eliminating words from his sentences.

"Okay, Southern soldiers, the Confederates, attacked Fort Sumter, South Carolina, war starts."

Stumbling over his words, Brian realized this was no time for a history lesson. He slowed down and, for once, he cut to the chase. Well, almost.

"You've heard of the Battle of Gettysburg?"

The quartet nodded their heads in unison.

"Colonel Chamberlain was a college professor of rhetoric from Maine. While serving in the Union Army at Gettysburg, his unit was assigned the extreme left of the Union lines on a small hill called Little Round Top."

Dan nodded his head although he had no idea where Brian was going with this history lecture.

Completely stumped, Catfish asked, "What's rhetoric?"

Interrupted by Catfish's irrelevant question, Brian ignored it and continued. "The extreme left. Get it?"

Dan nodded but he really didn't get it. Brian could see it in his eyes.

Catfish repeated his question a bit louder, "What, the hell, is rhetoric?"

"The extreme left," Brian repeated, "The Confederates attempted to get around his unit to out flank the Union Army."

Blank stares.

In frustration, Brian pointed down to their own defensive line.

"They are trying to out flank us. They are trying to get around us on the left and right ends of our defensive lines."

If it was a cartoon, light bulbs would have illuminated over Dan, Catfish, and Ski's heads.

Dan conjured up a tidbit of information from his personal readings. He remembered a key phrase and its implications.

"Refuse the flank," he said as if in a dream state. Dan blurted, "We have to refuse the flank!"

Thrilled he had finally gotten his message across to at least one of his students, Brian shouted, "Exactly!"

"Great!" Catfish agreed, "How do we do that?" Adding in frustration, "And what, the hell, is rhetoric?"

Brian saw no reason to explain any further. Brian didn't care who outranked who, or who was born when, or if H comes before M in the alphabet. He was assuming command. Why? Because he understood the situation, knew what needed to be done, and had a plan to deal with it... sort of.

Ski looked in awe at Brian. Silently whispering to himself, *That's what Marines do... Take charge and kick ass!*

Dan and Catfish had never seen Brian so animated. Brian was in his glory. His arms were flailing about, pointing directions to the Marines on the line. Moving his troops like pawns on a chess board, he was shouting instructions while tossing in a little history.

"Stretch out the line. Double-arm's length. Extend our line as far as possible. Bend the line back like Chamberlain did at Little Round Top. We can't let them outflank us."

"Holy shit!" Catfish exclaimed, "It looks like Brian's in charge."

Brian looked at the stunned faces of his peers.

"Don't get excited, guys," he said matter-of-factly, "I've got this."

Catfish, Jerry, and Dan were silent. Brian smiled at their reaction.

"I need one of you to take charge on the left flank; one on the right flank, and one in the center. Let me know if they are trying the same trick on both sides.

The three were entranced.

Brian stopped smiling and raised the tenor of his question from a request to an order, "NOW would be a good time!"

Catfish, Ski and Dan snapped out of their trances and did as their newly anointed leader ordered. Jerry continued tending to Jason.

CHAPTER TWENTY

The Bronco - May 1970

The ordnance team finished the loading procedure and cautiously moved away from the OV-10A Bronco. One misstep and they could walk into one of the near invisible spinning propellers.

Standing in front of the aircraft, the plane captain, in exaggerated motions, counted the four red-flagged pins he had just removed from the bomb racks attached to the underside of each wing. Holding the four pins in his left hand, he flashed four fingers on his right hand. He gave the pilot a thumbs-up.

Although the twin-engine turboprop, twin-boom aircraft was used primarily for observation and reconnaissance, it was also capable of "light attack" missions.

By flashing his own four fingers followed by a thumbs-up, the front-seated pilot sitting in tandem with the rear-seated observer confirmed that he understood that the pins had been removed, and he could jettison the bomb racks if the situation called for it. Returning the thumbs-up, the pilot was also confirming he understood that his ordnance was now live.

Although the repair of the Korean T-33 had, let us say, a less than positive outcome, as a reward for his hard work and leadership with the maintenance effort, the commanding officer asked Lance Corporal Keegan what he could do for the young, hard-charging Marine.

"I've always wanted to ride in an OV-10," he informed the lieutenant colonel.

"I'll see what I can do," the officer promised.

True to his words, when the OV-10 maintenance department asked for an expert in aircraft communication systems to ride in the back seat to troubleshoot a difficult radio problem, the commanding officer had Dan temporarily assigned to the reconnaissance squadron VMO-2 (Fixed-wing Marine Observation Squadron -2) where he was given a crash course... let me rephrase that... expedited training on the intricacies of the twin-boomed Bronco. That included, of course, how to eject if the need should arise.

Strapped into the rear seat, Dan had barely finished reading the Munitions Checklist aloud for the pilot when the pilot announced, "Ready to rock and roll!"

Without pausing for a reply, the pilot's left hand moved the engine condition levers from NORMAL FLIGHT to the T.O./LAND position while advancing the engine power levers.

The nervous observer tugged on his four-point harness to ensure it was properly hitched, sat back in his seat, and readied himself for take-off.

What have I gotten myself into? Dan whispered to himself.

The twin 715 horsepower Garrett T76-G-4 turboprop engines increased RPMs. The pilot had obviously travelled this path many times, and skillfully steered the Bronco out of the ordnance arming area.

Taxiing over the interlaced Marsden matting, the aircraft received take-off clearance from the young staff sergeant with the Marine Air Traffic Control Squadron manning the portable observation tower on the southwest edge of the runway. Only 24 years old, the staff sergeant was an experienced air traffic controller but a bit gun-shy concerning the *OV-10*'s. He had a few aborted take-offs as well as several hot landings with hung ordnance under his belt. Most were OV-10's.

He glanced over his shoulder at the gunnery sergeant who was reading Mario Puzo's *The Godfather*.

"Keep your fingers crossed, Gunny," the staff sergeant tactfully interrupted the senior Marine.

The gunny looked up, his concentration broken. He dog-eared his page and set the paperback down as he picked up a set of field glasses, stood up and casually focused on the Bronco.

Rolling onto the paved runway, the pilot increased engine revolutions and sped down the airstrip as the aircraft rapidly approached take-off speed.

The senior air traffic controller in the tower zeroed in on the bomb rack dangling from the underside of the starboard wing... dangling!

"Shit!" he shouted. "Abort! Abort! Hung ordnance! Hung ordnance!"

The staff sergeant didn't hesitate.

"Mike Uniform Zero-Two, abort take-off. Abort take-off. You have hung ordnance."

The dislodged bomb rack holding five live 100-lb bombs swayed precariously from its right wing.

From his vantage point the pilot knew there were only a few options for the two man crew. None of them were good.

Option 1: *As gently as possible, abort the take-off, hit the brakes and hope that the rack and its explosive cargo doesn't jostle loose as the aircraft rapidly decelerated and would probably run out of runway.*

Option 2: *Get airborne and circle the base and attempt a landing on the runway he had just left with the rack and the live ammo still attached to the wing, praying the rack doesn't break loose underneath them and blow them both to Kingdom Come.*

Option 3: *Get airborne and attempt a series of severe jarring aerial maneuvers to break the rack free at a safe distance from the base.*

Oh, yeah, Option 4: *Eject!*

In a microsecond, the pilot reviewed his choices.

One: *Too late.*

Two: *Too risky.*

Three: *Probably.*

Four: *Not with this rookie on board.*

Option three it was!

He pulled back on the yoke, pushed the engines for even greater thrust, and retracted his landing gear.

A voice came over the radio, "Mike Uniform Zero-Two, what are your intentions?"

Banking carefully to the east, the pilot looked at the South China Sea. "We're going to try to dump this load in the ocean."

"Roger, Mike Uniform Zero-Two."

The pilot keyed the intercom. "Lance Corporal?"

Dan keyed his microphone, "Yes, Sir!"

"Do you understand our situation?"

"Yes, Sir!"

In a reassuring voice, the pilot calmly explained his plan to his rookie observer.

"I'm going to take this baby over the water. Once there, I will jettison the bomb rack. If that doesn't work, I'll put her through some tough maneuvers that should shake the bomb rack loose."

"Yes, Sir," Dan responded with a quiver in his voice.

"Don't be concerned but just in case, are you prepared to abandon the aircraft?"

Like television beatnik Maynard G. Krebs yelping "WORK?!" Dan responded with a cracked, "EJECT?!"

Attempting to reassure his passenger, the pilot stammered, "No. No. No. That's not the plan. That's just in case."

Forcing himself to calm down, Dan took a deep breath and repeated, "That's not the plan. That's just in case."

"Remember your training. If we need to abandon the aircraft, I will repeat the word 'Eject!' three times so there is no misunderstanding. Understood?"

"Three times. Yes, Sir."

Satisfied that Dan was not going to eject on his own volition, the pilot aimed for the coastline and focused on separating the live ordnance from his wing.

The Bronco quickly reached the water's edge. The pilot scoured the area for any boats that may become unwitting casualties when the bomb rack came loose.

The pilot was extremely concerned about the young Marine passenger sitting nervously behind him. He needed to keep him busy to minimize the chance the lance corporal might eject of his own accord.

"Keep your eyes peeled for any boats in the area."

"Yes, Sir."

The pilot banked the aircraft to see where the five 100-pound bombs would impact.

"You see anything?"

"No, Sir!"

The pilot pulled the yellow T-handle labelled JETTISON STORES. The bomb rack didn't budge.

"Damn!" the pilot and passenger exclaimed together.

"Okay, now I'm going to try to shake that baby loose. Are you buckled in tightly?"

"Yes, Sir."

"Here goes."

Without further conversation, the pilot put the Bronco into a steep climb then nosed the aircraft over into an even steeper dive. Pulling out of the dive with the bomb rack still attached, the pilot zigged and zagged; climbed and descended, rocked the aircraft left and rolled it to the right.

Air traffic control radioed, "No joy, Mike Uniform Zero-Two. What-s next?"

"Let's give it another try." Then, glancing over his shoulder he asked, "You still with me?"

"Yes, Sir."

"Well, here goes nothing."

Again, the pilot tried every maneuver he could think of to no avail.

Dan could tell the pilot was getting frustrated. Dan decided to take a page out of Jason's playbook. Get the pilot talking.

"Did you ever fly with the Blue Angels?" referring to the Navy's Flight Demonstration Team as he complimented the pilot on his aviating skills.

His thoughts interrupted, the pilot smiled at the question, answered, "No..." then as if he had just had a revelation, he repeated, "No... but there is one of their tricks I've always wanted to try."

Almost too afraid to speak, Dan asked, "What might that be?"

"A four-point snap roll. Make sure you are tightened in."

Dan pull the adjustment straps as tight as he could.

The pilot notified air traffic control of his intentions of performing a snap roll to put the aircraft on its left side (90 degrees). After a slight pause, he would snap it to the 180-degree point that would put the aircraft upside down. Following one additional pause, another snap roll to the 270-degree point onto the plane's right side. After only a moment's hesitation, completing the roll, back 360 degrees back to straight and level flight.

In the tower, the staff sergeant's eyes widened, "Mike Uniform Zero Two, be advised, a four-point snap roll is an unauthorized maneuver for that type aircraft."

"I'm aware of that Marble Mountain, but what can they do to me? Shave my head and send me to Vietnam?"

"It's your neck, Sir," The staff sergeant warned.

The pilot commenced his unauthorized maneuver. He snapped the Bronco 90 degrees to the left.

Nothing.

He snapped it 90 more degrees and the bomb rack departed the OV-10.

"Ooh-Rah!" the pilot exclaimed.

Overjoyed with their success, the pilot maintained the Bronco four-point roll at the 180-degree point.

Flying upside down, the two aviators watched as the ordnance hit the South China Sea. The explosions sent geysers of water upward. Finishing the remainder of the "trick" the pilot eventually righted the aircraft.

"Congratulations, Mike Uniform Zero Two, you are clear to land."

Upon landing and taxiing to the flight line, Dan and his pilot exited the aircraft.

"How are you doing, Lance Corporal?" the concerned pilot asked.

His legs were a bit shaky, but Dan looked up at the pilot. Trying to regain his composure, Dan's straight-face soon broadened into a huge grin, "Sir, that was better than an E-ticket at Disneyland!"

by James E. Bulman

CHAPTER TWENTY-ONE

Integrity Check - May 1970

Our team of Marines was becoming more and more proficient at troubleshooting and repairing helicopters every day. In only a few months they became the go-to guys in their respective area of expertise.

Every day damaged or malfunctioning aircraft would return from combat missions. The aircrew trusted that their aircraft would be returned to a Full-Mission-Capable (FMC) status prior to the next day's missions. In other words, they put their lives in the hands of the maintenance crews.

In aviation maintenance there can be no room for errors. There must be a system of checks and balances to ensure each aircraft discrepancy is repaired in accordance with proper maintenance practices. Even during combat.

Here's how it works:

First, the pilot reports any discrepancy concerning his aircraft to the maintenance department. The maintenance department generates paperwork to track the repair and assigns the most appropriate shop (avionics, hydraulics, metal shop, etc.) to repair the problem. Upon completion of the repair, the technician calls for an inspector.

At this point a highly qualified aircraft inspector, who has passed numerous written and hands-on examinations, reviews the completed task and affixes his inspection stamp to the paperwork. The paperwork is returned to the maintenance department for archival purposes.

But there are times when things don't go a planned.

On a Friday afternoon, one of the huge CH-53's returned from a mission with several discrepancies. One involved the Automatic Direction Finder (ADF). In a moment of silliness, the pilot described the problem on the paperwork as "ADF went ape shit!"

Everyone who handled the paperwork took the slightly uncouth write-up with a sense of humor and passed it on to the maintenance department.

The avionics technician assigned to tackle the problem knew the ADF was located on the underside of the aircraft in a sump area where oil and water collected. The tech removed the ADF unit from the aircraft, unscrewed the cover and cleaned the interior of the unit. In addition, he cleaned the space where the ADF unit fit by removing excess lubricant, toweling the accumulated moisture and getting rid of the debris. Once the unit was reinstalled, the tech tested the entire ADF system to ensure it was now fully operational.

The system tested just fine. The technician signed off the paperwork in the same lighthearted manner initiated by the pilot. The maintenance action form now read:

Discrepancy: "ADF went ape shit!"

Corrective Action: "Caught ape. Cleaned up shit."

The tech called for an aircraft inspector to verify his work. The newest aircraft inspector in the squadron was none other than Lance Corporal Dan Keegan.

Dan inspected the re-installation and security of the ADF. He climbed into the cockpit and tested the ADF to confirm it worked in accordance with the appropriate Naval Technical Publication. After accounting for all the technician's tools and hardware, Dan affixed his inspector stamp to the document. He then submitted the paperwork for entry into the aircraft maintenance records.

Later that day the maintenance officer summoned Dan to his office. Dan thought it a bit strange and feared he was in some sort of trouble. Only recently passing his aircraft inspector's tests, Dan feared he had made a grievous error and was about to lose his cherished inspector status.

As Dan entered the maintenance officer's office, he spotted the grinning admin corporal standing behind the seated major.

"Lance Corporal Keegan," the major began firmly, "I am pleased to hear you are now certified by the commanding officer as an aircraft inspector. Congratulations."

"Thank you, Sir," Dan replied as he wondered where this conversation was going. Dan was confident Corporal Blaine had ratted him out on something.

"Unfortunately, the sign-off you completed this morning on the ADF has ruffled a few feathers."

"How so, Sir?" Dan asked as the admin corporal's grin widened.

"You do understand that the maintenance documentation is entered into the aircraft log books and is part of the aircraft's historical record?"

"Of course, Sir" Dan confirmed as he looked at the smirking corporal.

"I've been informed that several members of our squadron were offended by your rather vulgar choice of words detailing the corrective action taken by the repair technician."

You gotta be kidding me, Dan thought to himself. *Marines dropped the "F-bomb" in every sentence spoken aloud and the major is concerned by the word "shit." You gotta be shitting me!*

Regaining his composure, Dan replied, "I could have chosen my words more carefully..."

"I knew you would understand," the major smiled.

"... but I would like to know who I offended," Dan interjected. "I would like to apologize to each one in person."

"That's not necessary, Lance Corporal. Just as long as you understand."

"Yes, Sir!"

The major instructed Corporal Blaine to vacate the office but asked Dan to stay.

The admin corporal was highly disappointed that Dan had gotten off so easily, and he wondered what was going on within the maintenance officer's office.

Waiting for the door to close, the major continued, "Now that that bullshit is out of the way, I need you to sign off my aircraft for me." The major slid a maintenance document in front of Dan and pointed where the inspector stamp needed to be placed.

Curious why this was being done behind closed doors, Dan read the document lying on the desk.

Discrepancy: All Navigation Systems Inoperable.

Corrective Action: Repaired Navigation Systems.

Dan could not interpret the illegible signature of the technician who did the repairs, and he was also troubled by the vague corrective action. Add to that, the aircraft in question was a C-117 on which Dan had little experience.

There's got to be inspectors in the squadron with more experience on the C-117 than me, he thought to himself.

"Sir, I'll go look at the aircraft and if everything is okay, I'll sign it off." Dan informed the maintenance officer.

Slightly irked, the major informed Dan, "I can assure you everything is in order. Just sign off the aircraft."

Dan dug in his heels, "Sir, I have to look at the aircraft."

Now seriously irked, the major's voice rose from a request to an order, "I'm telling you it's good. Sign it off!" adding two well-placed finger taps on the paperwork.

Dan's voice rose in kind, "Sir, I can't put my stamp on it if I don't look at the aircraft!"

"I gave you that stamp!" he reminded Dan.

"No, Sir, you did not," Dan corrected the major, "You recommended me to be an inspector. The commanding officer gave me this stamp," adding, "and I can give it back to him right now."

"Are you threatening me with the commanding officer?"

"No, Sir! But he's just down the hall," Dan informed the officer with finality.

The major took a couple of deep breaths and calmed himself.

"That, Lance Corporal Keegan, is exactly the type of steadfastness I want in my inspectors!" the major continued, "If you don't think it's right then don't let anyone force you to sign off a discrepancy."

Dan realized that he had just passed the maintenance officer's personal inspector initiation test. The major reached across his desk and shook Dan's hand, congratulating him on his integrity.

Dan wondered if other new inspectors went through the same ordeal. He also wondered what would have happened if he had stamped the paper.

Dan's consternation quickly faded, and a broad smile illuminated his face.

He passed the final test.

"That's the way it's done!" he shouted aloud.

by James E. Bulman

CHAPTER TWENTY-TWO

Assault on the Marble Mountain Air Facility - July 1970

Lou, Dan, and the medical corpsman arrived at the beach or what military tacticians would refer to as the FEBA, the forward edge of the battle area. The trio kneeled next to Jerry and the injured Jason. The corpsman did a quick assessment of Jason's wounds and looked at Jerry. The others nervously awaited the results.

"Have you had any medical training?" the corpsman asked Jerry.

"Not really," the unassuming Marine responded.

"Well, you did one hell of a job, Lance Corporal. You saved this Marine's life."

"He'll be okay?" Jerry asked with a quiver in his voice.

"Yep, thanks to you."

Jason dropped from his kneeling position onto his butt. His relief was apparent. He turned his face away from his fellow Marines. After all, Marines don't cry, but within this small group, he wasn't the only one whose face turned away.

"Let's go, ladies!" Brian shouted as soon as he determined Jason would pull through, "No time for chitchatting."

There was no doubt who was in charge. Brian was clearly in his element. Confident. Calm. Focused.

"I need Catfish on the left flank and Dan on the right. Jerry, now that the corpsman is here, you take charge of the center of our line. Stretch the line out. Refuse the flank. Refuse the flank," he repeated.

The trio followed Brian's orders.

Brian's mind was searching for any advantage, any bit of training that might help.

"SMEAC," (pronounced "Smee–ack") he muttered.

The acronym SMEAC stood for Situation, Mission, Execution, Administration and Logistics, Command and Signal.

Brian's Situation: There is an unknown number of enemy troops attempting to out flank his position. They had conventional small arms and satchel charges. He had been informed by Lou that the reactionary platoon was instructed to deploy to the beach. How soon they would arrive was unknown.

Brian's Mission: To prevent the enemy from getting past his position, infiltrating the air facility and wreaking havoc.

Brian's Execution (His plan, that is, how he will execute his plan of action.): He wished he had a plan to execute but truthfully, Brian was still working on it.

Brian's Administrative and Logistics: The four B's. Band-aids, Bad guys, Beans, Bullets. He had one medical corpsman being assisted by Jerry. Brian had no idea as to the number of infiltrators there were. He guessed thirty or forty. Food and ammunition weren't an issue. Each of his Marines should have 200 rounds of ammunition, give or take. He had nothing heavier than M-16's assault rifles. No machine guns. No Light Anti-tank Armor Weapons (LAAWs). No hand grenades.

Brian's Command and Signal: He had no radio or other means of communicating with the rest of the Marines on the air facility. If he needed anything, Brian would have to use the old school method. He needed a runner to get information to the commanding officer, the Officer of the Day or, more immediately to Dan, Catfish, and Jerry. He called Ski to his side.

"You're my runner," he informed the private first class.

Eager to help, Ski replied, "No problem."

The commander of the Viet Cong unit was just as frustrated as Brian. It was taking too long to outflank the Marines. The American's defensive line seemed to be getting longer and longer each time he sent a probe to reconnoiter their position. The probes on either end of the Marine line were rewarded with small arms fire that was highly accurate, forcing the Viet Cong to withdraw before obtaining any worthwhile information. He had been told by his informants working on the airfield that these were aviation Marines who were not as highly skilled in warrior tactics as their infantry brothers. Apparently, his spies were grossly mistaken.

by James E. Bulman

The Viet Cong had already lost a handful of soldiers... some dead, some lying wounded in the no-man's land between the two opposing forces.

The commander realized he had two options. He could either retreat or try a different approach. He knew retreat was out of the question.

He pondered different methods of obtaining his objective to breach the Marine's defensive line. He felt his weaponry was slightly better than his American opponent's M-16s. The American rifle fired 5.56 mm rounds. Whereas, the Soviet manufactured Kalashnikov AK-47 assault rifles fired 7.62 mm rounds. The Americans had a slight advantage in weight. The Russian assault rifles weighed about a pound-and-a-half more than the American's M-16. The VC had no heavy weapons, no crew-served weapons, no hand... *Wait a minute. He might not have hand grenades but each of his soldiers had two or three satchel charges that could be thrown.*

The commander of Viet Cong began to formalize plans for an old-fashioned frontal assault to the center of the Marines' line.

That might just do the trick, he rationalized. *Especially while the Marines are stretched thin to counter our feigning action on the Marines' left flank. Make them think we are attacking their left then hit them hard down the middle.*

He called for his small unit leaders to gather around him. He explained his new plan.

On the opposite side of the firefight, Ski crouched next to Brian. Like his friends, Ski was amazed at Brian's leadership abilities under fire. He could see Brian's eyes searching left and right, trying to keep one step ahead of the VC commander.

"Will they hit us on the left or the right, or both at the same time?" Brian asked rhetorically.

Assuming Brian was talking to him, Ski completed the question, "or in the middle?"

Brian's eyes lit up. Stretching his memory as far back as he could, once again he remembered Colonel Chamberlain. Brian also remembered what he had learned in boot camp and infantry training: Marines don't defend; we attack.

He whispered something to Ski who took off like the wind. Brian smiled to himself anticipating the reaction there would be as he shouted his next order.

"Fix bayonets!"

There was an outcry from his troops.

"Fix what?"

"Is he shitting me?"

"Holy shit!"

"You heard the man!" Catfish hushed the vocal troops, "Fix your goddamn bayonets."

Hearing the clicks of the bayonets being attached to the M-16s let him know the troops were obeying the order.

POP!

A single round came from within the Marine line. There was a murmur of excitement from Catfish's area of responsibility.

"What was that?" he demanded.

A moment passed until the source of the single rifle shot was identified as coming from the admin corporal's M-16.

Catfish was informed by one of his Marines that Corporal Blaine had just shot off his trigger finger while attaching his bayonet to his rifle.

The North Carolinian had a fleeting thought that the admin corporal may have purposely injured himself but was reassured by nearby Marines that it was truly an accident.

The admin corporal was on his way to the medical corpsman.

As he ran towards Dan's section of the line, Ski heard the distinct "POP!"

He fell to the ground. It felt as if someone had just hit him in his left calf with a baseball bat. A quick self-examination of the injured leg showed that he had a through-and-through gunshot wound. He could see bone. He attempted to rise but fell again. The pain was excruciating. Ski knew he had to get to Dan and to Catfish to convey Brian's intentions. He could hear his friends now.

"You should never have counted on Ski."

"He's always late!"

"Why would you pick him?"

"What were you thinking?"

"Pick Dan, Catfish, Jerry, anybody but Ski!"

Ski knew he would remember this moment for the rest of his life. He could also hear the voices of the many Marines who had come before him.

His senior drill instructor repeatedly reminded him, "Losers quit when they feel pain. Marines quit when they accomplish the mission."

by James E. Bulman

He thought of something William Manchester had written during World War II, "Marines do not fight for flag, or country, or corps. They fight for each other."

His mind raced. He knew if he didn't move from this spot his friends would die.

Ignoring the agonizing pain, Ski mustered all the courage he could, as he shouted, "A Marine never lets his buddies down!"

With tears of pain streaming down his cheeks, Ski rose.

A handful of satchel charge-wielding enemy soldiers attacked Brian's left flank. Was it another probe or the full-scale attack? The first rounds from his troops were sporadic. One or two rounds followed by sympathetic fire from nearby Marines.

One enemy soldier threw a satchel charge towards the Marine line. It fell short but the concussion from the explosion got Catfish's attention. He felt a rush of hot air across his face followed immediately by a burning sensation in his eyes. Instinctively, he closed and opened his eyes several times. Catfish held them closed for a few seconds then slowly opened them. The burning sensation was still present.

Closing his eyes again, Catfish fumbled for his canteen and poured its contents over his eyes. The flushing helped. He could see more clearly, but he needed additional water. Nearby Marines unhesitantly offered their canteens to their impromptu leader.

While applying first aid to his eyes, Catfish ordered "If you see any movement, shoot it, but don't waste your ammo! Sight alignment. Sight picture." The small arms fire from the enemy intensified.

Brian figured the enemy was getting desperate. He was confident they would attack one flank or the other. He thought he knew which... the right.

It took Brian only a minute or so to recognize the enemy's next move. He was wrong. They were attacking on the left flank, but Brian's plan was flexible. He could adjust his plan and make it work anyway.

Brian was sure the attack on the left was a ruse. It had to be a distraction for the wholesale frontal assault he anticipated. Brian prayed Ski had time to deliver his message to Dan, Jerry, and Catfish.

The rifle fire from the enemy was basically ineffective. Although inaccurate, it did accomplish one goal. It kept the Marines' heads down and reduced the rate of fire from the Americans.

With an attack on his left and a full-scale assault to his center, Brian yelled at the top of his lunges, "NOW! Shift left! Shift left!"

With five or six Marines anchoring the right end of the defensive line, the remainder of the Marine line rushed to the left to reinforce the left and center of their line. The repositioned troops added much needed firepower to the portion of the line under attack.

The VC commander saw the futility of his plan as soon as he launched it. The satchel charges were too heavy. The small-framed Vietnamese simply didn't have the strength to fling the deadly package more than twenty or thirty feet. He had been told that infantry Marines could hit a bullseye at 500 yards with their M-16 rifles. He doubted that. His spies had advised him that aviation Marines were a lesser breed. Now he realized there was more to these aviation Marines than he had anticipated. For the Marines, cutting down an enemy soldier at twenty or thirty feet was a simple task.

It took only a couple of failed tosses of the weighty satchel charges for the Marines to take advantage of the Viet Cong's folly. As soon as a Marine spotted one of the VC rising as he prepared to hurl his bundle, the Marine would shout and point in the direction of the unwanted delivery. Nearby Marines would turn all their attention to that single attacker.

It was a simple formula: Four or five Marines firing two or three rounds each at a target only thirty feet away was quite sufficient to stop the attacker in his place. Rinse and repeat.

Through his half-opened eyelids, Catfish could see what was occurring. Ever the country boy, Catfish commented, "This is like a game of Whack-A-Mole at the state fair in Raleigh!"

At the center of the firefight, Brian surveyed the situation and made the decision to launch the coup de grace.

Again, as loud as he could, he shouted as he ran to join the men on the left, "Left Flank CHARGE! Left Flank CHARGE!"

The left flank hesitated. The young Marines looked at Catfish for guidance.

by James E. Bulman

Even Catfish was surprised by Brian's command, but the Marine in him overcame any doubts. Brian was in charge. Catfish would unhesitantly obey his orders.

Trying to think of some way to motivate his Marines, Catfish stood up and shouted a phrase first spoken in World War I by two-time Medal of Honor recipient, Sergeant Major Dan Daly, at the Battle of Belleau Wood outside Paris, France.

"You sons-a-bitches want to live forever?" Catfish added, "This is our beach, Goddamn it!"

Repeating Brian's order, Catfish bellowed, "CHARGE!"

With that command, the reinforced left-end of the line moved as one cohesive body from their protective positions into the open. Surprisingly, instead of moving directly forward, Catfish turned their line towards the center as Brian had instructed. Like an open pocket knife, they closed the "blade" of the bayonet-charging Marines towards the stationary center "handle" lead by Jerry. As taught at Parris Island, they yelled, screamed, and cursed while they moved to create an area of interlocking fire between the center of the line and now perpendicular left-end of the line.

The Viet Cong frontal assault stalled.

It stopped completely when the Viet Cong foot soldiers grasped the fact that they were in the beaten zone where the rifle fire from the center and left interlocked. It became apparent they could not break through the Marine defensive positions. Many more VC were falling than had been anticipated. The Vietnamese commander ordered an immediate retreat to the zodiac boats in which they had come ashore.

The Marines were not satisfied with this admission of defeat. They gave chase. They advanced towards the retreating enemy. Firing as they moved forward, the yelling, screaming, and cursing from the Marines continued. They swept their beach of the enemy.

Realizing that any additional shooting was simply a waste of ammunition, Brian ordered, "Cease fire! Cease fire! Safety your weapons."

Marines up and down the beach echoed the order.

As the firing slowed, the realization that they had accomplished their mission took root. These now seasoned warriors looked at one another in amazement. They had done it. They had repulsed the enemy. They had kicked Charlie's ass!

The celebratory high-fives, slaps on the backs, and even a few hugs could be seen up and down the beach.

And immediately the war stories began.

"Did you see me..."

"There I was..."

"... and then I..."

There was no need for embellishment. (That would come later.) They had indeed accomplished their mission. They were indeed true combat veterans.

The celebration tapered off as these devil dogs turned their attention to the dozen or so wounded Marines.

Brian gathered a handful of his men to ensure the dead infiltrators were indeed dead and asked Jerry to set up an aid station for the wounded enemy.

The reactionary platoon soon was clambering around the various objects behind which the Marines had taken cover. The Officer of the Day, First Lieutenant Waverly, jogged to a stop as he surveyed the battle zone.

He was amazed at what he witnessed. He saw a Navy medical corpsman treating several wounded Marines. Another Marine seemed to be conducting triage as he called out the severity of the various injuries he was evaluating. From what he could hear, most of the wounds to the Marines were relatively minor. There were a dozen dead enemy combatants, several wounded, and a few uninjured prisoners of war.

As the OOD worked his way to the corpsman, he asked each of the warriors he passed, "Are you okay? Where's the corporal in change?"

After receiving the same answer over and over, he was again stunned by what he saw as he arrived at the corpsman's makeshift field hospital. The officer could see the wounded Jason and understood how serious his injury was, but he had to ask, "Who was in charge after you were hit?"

With a hint of a smile, Jason mumbled, "Colonel Chamberlain, Sir."

"Who?" the first lieutenant asked.

"I'm the next senior man," the admin corporal informed the first lieutenant.

In a flash, Lou and Catfish both stepped in. Corporal Blaine appeared to be taking the credit for their success.

"Don't even think about it!" Lou warned.

"Don't go there," Catfish added.

Corporal Blaine continued, "... but I was wounded and out of action. I don't know anything about Colonel Chamberlain."

Lou and Catfish stopped in their tracks.

After several erratic breaths, Jason again responded to the first lieutenant with a crooked smile, "Colonel Chamberlain, Sir"

The Marines within earshot all smiled in agreement.

"Yes, Sir! It was Colonel Chamberlain."

"Yep, Colonel Chamberlain saved our asses."

Still squinting, Catfish added, "Yes, Sir. If it weren't for that old Yankee Chamberlain, those VC would be eating mid-rats in our chow hall right now."

Lieutenant Colonel Reeves joined the scene. Confused by the reports he had been receiving, the commanding officer decided he needed to meet this mysterious Colonel Chamberlain.

"Where is this colonel?" the commanding officer inquired.

Nearby Marines smiled knowingly but maintained silence.

by James E. Bulman

More seriously, the lieutenant colonel demanded, "Enough games! I want to see this Colonel Chamberlain, and I want to see him now!"

"I guess that would be me, Sir." Brian nervously approached the commanding officer.

"You would be what, Lance Corporal?" the irritated officer asked.

"I would be Colonel Chamberlain, Sir."

"Lance Corporal, I am not in the mood for jokes. Where is Colonel Chamberlain?"

"Again, Sir, that would be me."

Catfish piped in, "Give him a chance to explain, Sir," he added with a Davy Crocket grin. "You'll love it."

CHAPTER TWENTY-THREE

Personnel to be Recognized ...

August 1970

The squadron adjutant called out the commands in a loud, clear voice, "Attention to Orders."

The squadron sergeant major bellowed, "Squadron, Atten – HUT." Several hundred pairs of heels came together at the same time.

The adjutant paused for a moment to ensure everyone was at the position of Attention.

"Personnel to be recognized, Front and Center..."

Jason had sweet-talked the Navy doctor to obtain permission to participate in today's awards ceremony. He looked at his small band of heroes. Catfish wore an eyepatch. There was concern that he might lose his eyesight in that eye. Ski was not about to miss this event. He was in a wheelchair pushed by Dan. Lou's bandages were out of sight. He took a lot of teasing about the location of his wounds.

Jason, Lou, Catfish, and Ski had received their Purple Heart medals a couple of weeks earlier at a separate ceremony.

Dan, Jerry, and Brian were uninjured during the firefight.

Jason ordered his small band of warriors, "Detail, Forward..."

The adjutant completed the command for Jason's team, "... MARCH!"

With the squadron personnel in formation, Jason lead his fellow heroes to the designated mark in front of Lieutenant Colonel Reeves.

Jason gave the command, "Detail... HALT."

by James E. Bulman

Completing the positioning of his leatherneck brothers, Jason directed, "Right... FACE." They turned in unison towards the lieutenant colonel. Jason immediately ordered, "Hand... SALUTE."

The commanding officer returned the military greeting with a broad smile.

The adjutant continued, "The Secretary of the Navy takes pleasure in presenting the Navy Commendation Medal with Combat "V" to Corporal Jason Walsh for services as set forth in the following citation..."

Earlier, Corporal Blaine had arranged on a folding table the seven red awards folders emblazoned with the Marine Corps emblem in gold. Each folder contained the original citation for the Marine being recognized. The medals were neatly arranged next to each folder.

The admin corporal found this assignment especially irksome. He felt it was adding salt to his wound. He had been informed just that morning that his request for a Purple Heart for his "war wound" had been denied since it was self-inflicted.

The admin corporal handed the lieutenant colonel the award as each citation was read aloud by the adjutant.

The adjutant continued as the commanding officer attached the device to Jason's khaki short sleeve shirt, handed the recipient the folder and shook his hand.

When informed that they were to wear the summer service "C" uniform (khaki shirt and trousers) to the awards ceremony, Jerry thought back to the supply sergeant on Okinawa who instructed the young jarheads to keep one set of khaki dress uniform, "Just in case you get a medal or something."

That supply sergeant could hardly have imagined all seven of them would receive awards today.

Five more times, the adjutant read the citations.

"The Secretary of the Navy takes pleasure in presenting the Navy Commendation Medal with Combat "V" to Lance Corporal Daniel Keegan for services as set forth in the following citation..."

"... Lance Corporal Louis Archer..."

"... Lance Corporal Benjamin Haroldson..."

"... Lance Corporal Jerry McCoy..."

(and newly promoted,) "... Lance Corporal L.N. Baratoski..."

All his co-heroes looked towards Ski and thought the same thought. *L.N.? Why only initials? What, the hell, is his first name, anyway?*

The adjutant paused as the commanding officer affixed the medals to the recipients' shirts.

The adjutant kept his eye on the commanding officer for the prearranged cue.

After pinning the medal on Ski, the lieutenant colonel stepped back for a moment. The pause was intentional. He looked at the adjutant who took a deep breath. His had a case of cotton mouth but he read the final award.

"To all who shall see these presents, greeting: The President of the United States has awarded the Bronze Star Medal to Lance Corporal Brian Walker for heroism under fire from a superior force..."

As the commanding officer pinned America's fourth highest award for heroism on Brian's chest, he leaned closer to the recipient and informed him, "Your application to Officers Candidate School had been submitted. I'm not supposed to let you know but it has been approved by Commanding General, Major General Lewis W. Walt, himself, along with a glowing recommendation which most assuredly guarantees your selection." But, he cautioned, "Keep it to yourself. Get it?"

Brian was stunned, but responded in his now typical fashion, "I get it, Sir."

Upon receiving the awards for their actions on that memorable night, Jason ordered the detail to perform a parting "Hand... SALUTE."

Upon receiving the lieutenant colonel's returned salute Jason commanded "Left... FACE" followed by "Forward ... MARCH."

Returning to their starting point, Jason ordered his men to "Detail...HALT, and a final "Detail... DISMISSED!"

As the heroes turned to congratulate each other, uncharacteristically, Jason shouted, "That's the way it's done!"

The End

by James E. Bulman

FROM THE AUTHOR

I see humor in nearly everything. As you might expect, I was the class clown through both elementary and high school. More than one trip to the principal's office along with numerous threats of suspension did little to suppress my comedic outbursts.

Even in the worst of circumstances, I find myself giggling from some amusing thought. The more serious the occasion, the more humor I seem to find. I guess it's my way of dealing with stressful situations.

All of this leads me to my hitch in the Marine Corps and my tour of duty in Vietnam.

Marine Corps boot camp was easy pickings for a jokester like me. The poster-perfect drill instructors, the extreme physical exertion, and the obedience to every, and any order was manna from heaven for a comic.

Vietnam is another matter.

Please understand my perspective of the Vietnam War. It was mostly from the rear. I repaired helicopters on a relatively secure air field. Although we were the recipients of mortar and rocket attacks, sappers, and sabotage, the average aircraft repairman could not compare his war to the average infantryman's war.

But, as in every war, boredom, booze, bureaucracy, and B.S. lead to some just-plain-silly situations.

I hope the reader has as warped a sense of humor as I have and takes this in-the-rear-with-the-gear look at aviation Marines with a wry smile... and maybe even a chuckle or two.

Please remember this is a novel... fiction... but if any of my Marine Corps aviation friends recognize some of the situations in this tale, I hope I portrayed you as the heroes that you are.

As for my ground-pounding brothers and sisters...

Semper Fi,
James E. Bulman
MSGT, USMC (Retired)
www.swingwiththewing.com
www.jamesebulman.com

THE ELEVEN GENERAL ORDERS

1. To take charge of this post and all government property in view.

2. To walk my post in a military manner, keeping always on the alert and observing everything that takes place within sight or hearing.

3. Report all violations of orders I am instructed to enforce.

4. To repeat all calls from posts more distant from the guardhouse than my own.

5. To quit my post only when properly relieved.

6. To receive, obey, and pass on to the sentry who relieves me, all orders from the Commanding Officer, Officer of the Day, Officers, and Non-Commissioned Officers of the guard only.

7. To talk to no one except in the line of duty.

8. To give the alarm in case of fire or disorder.

9. To call the Corporal of the Guard in any case not covered by instructions.

10. To salute all officers and all colors and standards not cased.

11. To be especially watchful at night and during the time for challenging, to challenge all persons on or near my post, and to allow no one to pass without proper authority.

Made in the USA
Middletown, DE
22 August 2021